Praise for the Laura Bishop Mystery Series

"A promising series debut with pleasing characters, plenty of suspects, and helpful tips on home staging."

– Kirkus Reviews

"A delicious read! Well-researched and authentic to the true life of a home stager, *Staging is Murder* will keep you guessing about whodunit, while taking the mystery out of marketing a home. The fun staging tips in each chapter are worthy of as much investigation as the crime."

– Debbie Boggs,
Co-Founder, Staging Studio

"A first-time home stager, fascinating settings, and meddlesome characters make Grace Topping's *Staging is Murder* an engaging read and delightful series debut."

– Debra H. Goldstein,
Agatha-Nominated Author of One Taste Too Many

"I liked how this mystery was staged from the first chapter, giving me just enough intrigue to whet my appetite for more and the more I read, the more I enjoyed what was going on throughout this tale...Overall, an enjoyable read."

– Dru's Book Musings

"*Staging is Murder* has everything any cozy reader could want in a mystery with a side of humor and so much more."

— Sherry Harris,
Agatha-Nominated Author of All Murders Final!

Staging IS Murder

**The Laura Bishop Mystery Series
by Grace Topping**

STAGING IS MURDER (#1)

Staging IS Murder

A Laura Bishop
MYSTERY

Grace TOPPING

HENERY PRESS

Copyright

STAGING IS MURDER
A Laura Bishop Mystery
Part of the Henery Press Mystery Collection

First Edition | April 2019

Henery Press, LLC
www.henerypress.com

Trade Paperback ISBN-13: 978-1-63511-487-4
Digital epub ISBN-13: 978-1-63511-488-1
Kindle ISBN-13: 978-1-63511-489-8
Hardcover ISBN-13: 978-1-63511-490-4

Printed in the United States of America

*To my mother, Dorothy Marchetti,
who taught me that reading a good book is more important
than dusting. And to Barbara Sicola and Lynn Heverly,
my sisters and biggest cheerleaders.*

ACKNOWLEDGMENTS

My path to publication has been on a long one, filled with numerous potholes and detours. I'm thankful every day that as I traveled that path, I had people walk beside me, pull me out of holes, and point me in the right direction.

My deepest appreciation to everyone who reviewed multiple drafts, gave me guidance, patiently answered questions, and befriended me at conferences. I wouldn't have this book if it weren't for all of you.

Donna Andrews, Linda Barnes, Connie Berry, Janet Bolin, Kait Carson, Jen Danna, Elaine Douts, Ellen Dubin, Diane Davidson, Luce Dudinow, Lin Fischer, Susan Froetschel, Barb Goffman, Debra Goldstein, Nancy Greene, Janet Guinn, Sherry Harris, Lynn Heverly, Martha Huston, Sousan Kunaish, Marilyn Levinson, Kendel Lynn, Susan McNally, Rachel Otto, Terryl Paiste, Neil Pennington, Janelle Peters, Antoinette Pavone, Mai Pham, Sandra Pierce, Shari Randall, Linda Reilly, Paul Rinn, Chris Roerden, Barbara Ross, Barbara Sicola, and Diane Vallere. Thank you to everyone I haven't named. To name everyone who cheered me on would fill this book. Thank you.

My thanks to members of the Sisters in Crime Chesapeake and Guppies Chapters; Steve Alcorn of the Writing Academy; Debbie Boggs and Andress Eichstardt of Staging Studio; my agent, Dawn Dowdle, of the Blue Ridge Literary Agency; and everyone at Henery Press.

And a special thank you to my husband, John, and daughters, Lesley McArthur and Laura Goulet, for their loving support.

Chapter 1

Your home is a stage.

"You work for that woman and you'll end up killing each other. Even your horoscope says so."

I put down my cappuccino, took the newspaper my friend Nita Martino pushed at me, and read the horoscope for Capricorns: *A difficult person will cause you to take rash action.*

I laughed and handed the paper back to her. "Last month it predicted a financial windfall and then foreign travel. Neither came true. I don't think I'll be knocking off my first client—at least not until she pays me."

Nita read our horoscopes the mornings we met at Vocaro's for coffee. Chinese fortune cookies would have been more accurate.

Nita shook the paper. "I've warned you, and now your horoscope is warning you. Why won't you listen?"

"Because if I'm going to build a reputation as a home stager, I need the reference Victoria Denton can give me. She may be difficult, but she knows everyone in town."

"I'll give you a reference. You helped lots of friends stage their homes, including my mother-in-law. Talk about turning ugly ducklings into swans. They'd still be waiting for buyers if you hadn't helped them."

"That was for friends. Now it's business. Turning Victoria's mansion into a showplace will speak volumes, especially since it's such a large undertaking. If it would help, I'd stage a house for Hannibal Lecter."

"Believe me, Hannibal would be easier to work with."

Wanting to change the subject, I rummaged around in my large Land's End canvas bag, pulled out a small box, and proudly handed it to her. "Look at this—my new business cards."

Nita read the card I handed her. "'Staging for You, Laura Bishop, Professional Home Stager.' This is so exciting. Now you can do something you enjoy—and get paid for it."

"The sooner the better. My budget is so slim it's squealing." I didn't mention the crushing debt I incurred because of my mother's illness and funeral expenses. I needed to make a success of my business or it was back to the well-paying IT field that bored me to death but would pay the bills. The staging business would also help me move on from the life I'd left behind.

"Laura, I've told you before I can help—"

"Thank you, but no. With two kids in college, you can't risk your savings on me."

Nita frowned and ducked behind her newspaper. "Uh-oh, there's trouble."

Monica Heller stood at the counter, tapping her foot as she waited for her order. Her linen sheath and sleek, golden, chin-length hair screamed money and sophistication, neither of which Nita nor I possessed in abundance.

"As always, she looks stunning." I sighed, hoping I didn't sound envious.

"If we were from wealthy families, do you think we'd look that good?"

"It's in her genes."

"Genes certainly lacking in my gene pool." Nita took a bite of sticky bun. "Monica may be the best-known designer in town, but

Victoria showed real smarts hiring you instead of her."

"Only because starting out I come cheap. Besides, designers add the owner's personality to a home. Stagers remove it. That way buyers can imagine themselves living there." I took my last sip of cappuccino and sadly eyed my empty cup. My tight budget wouldn't stretch for a second one.

Nita peered over the top of the newspaper again and grimaced. "Drat. She's heading this way. If she bothers to talk to us, she'll have a motive." The heavy scent of Obsession reached us before she did.

"Hello, Laura, dear." Monica gave me a smile that never reached her eyes and barely glanced at Nita.

"I hear you're going to try staging the Denton place. That's quite an undertaking for you. If you find you're in over your head, have Victoria give me a call. I'm sure my assistant could come to your aid." Without waiting for a reply, she glided away like a tarantula that had just injected venom into its prey—me.

I bit hard on my lower lip to keep from saying something I'd regret. She'd made my high school years a misery, and even now, over twenty years later, she still managed to find my weak spots.

Nita ran her fingers through her short, dark curls. "Just seeing Monica makes me feel like I should have my hair done."

Reflexively I smoothed my straight, blondish hair that needed fresh highlights. "I know what you mean. I've decided not to let her get to me like she did when we were at Louiston High."

Nita shook her head and eyed me critically. "All these years later and you're only now deciding that? She might be ticked off because Victoria didn't hire her. Forget about Monica. When do you start?"

"Tyrone and I are going there as soon as he gets off work, which should be any minute." I looked toward the counter to see Tyrone Webster handing a coffee cup to an attractive young woman, who gazed at him adoringly. I couldn't blame her. He was the image of a college-aged Denzel Washington. I waved at him and pointed to my watch. He gave me a thumbs-up and turned back to the cute young thing he was serving.

A few minutes later, Tyrone approached. "Hello, ladies." He slouched into a metal chair and stretched his long legs in front of him. Scanning the room as though what he was about to impart was top secret, he leaned toward me and whispered, "I heard Victoria Denton is in debt up to her eyeballs and the bank is threatening to foreclose."

I slumped back into my chair and thought of the stack of bills lying on my desk. I had a lot riding on this project. If it backfired, Victoria wouldn't be the only one who was broke.

"Do you think Mrs. Denton can sell her house before they foreclose on her?" Tyrone squeezed his basketball player build into my small Corolla. Money had been tight in his family, so he could sympathize with Victoria's plight.

"Tough question. Not many people are in the market for a mansion built before the Civil War. Especially one jammed to the rafters with stuff. We have our work cut out for us."

The drive to the Denton house helped me relax and push aside the thought of Victoria's problems or how I could ensure we'd get paid. It was a pleasant ride with the lovely Allegheny Mountains stretching out in front of us. Opening my car window, I breathed in fresh, warm air. Spring was gradually coming to Pennsylvania, and I was ready for it.

As the small city of Louiston spread out behind us and we approached Lookout Hill and the Denton house, I turned to Tyrone. "Please be careful what you say in front of Victoria. If we're critical of her décor, she'll feel we're being critical of her. No rolling your eyes, even if something strikes you as awful."

"Okay, okay. I guess that means no gagging sounds either?"

"No!"

"Only testing." He gave me a cheeky grin. Tyrone always perked up my spirits. Even while he juggled a number of part-time jobs to help pay for college and help out at home, his spirits remained high, and his zest for life was contagious.

I turned into the Denton driveway, which was lined with giant oaks that would soon create a green canopy over the long approach. At the end of the drive a massive three-storied, limestone building loomed before us. The historic mansion was as old as the town itself. For years the family had opened it for tours each April, and I'd visited it with a school group. When Skip Denton married Victoria and she moved in, she stopped the tours.

Tyrone looked up in amazement. "What a fortress. Does it have a dungeon?"

"No. Only a resident witch."

Tyrone laughed, and I decided I'd better practice what I preached.

"Sorry, I shouldn't have said that. She can be difficult, but she's also having a hard time. The Scottie dog she adored died recently, and she's still mourning the loss. Remember, she's also being forced to sell a place she loves. That has to be awful."

"The place looks haunted. It's not, is it?"

"No. It just needs the right buyer to appreciate it. Our challenge is to make the outside welcoming and transform the inside into something bright, breezy, and beautiful."

Tyrone eyed the gray stone dubiously. "You mean instead of dark, dank, and detestable?"

"You could say that. I'm looking forward to how it will look when we finish."

I parked in front of a garage that had once housed carriage horses. "I've already met with Victoria and made suggestions. If we can pull it off, it'll mean future business for me and more tuition money for you." *If we can't, Monica Heller can say I told you so.* I was determined not to let that happen.

We climbed the steps to the large stone porch. Dried leaves covering the floor and the remains of a dead chrysanthemum standing sentinel next to the front door did little to make a good first impression. We would definitely have to do something to make the entrance more welcoming.

Before we could ring the bell, the door flew open. Victoria Denton stood in front of us, a frown creating deep furrows on her face. She had been attractive once, but years of discontent had drained the liveliness from her manner and etched a permanent scowl on her face.

"You're late." She waved us in with a hand weighed down with four clunky rings and a cigarette. As she led us through the foyer, she paused and ground her half-smoked cigarette into an ashtray atop a mahogany table. I admired the beautiful inlaid wood on the tabletop but cringed at the burn marks surrounding the ashtray. A strong smell of smoke and what might be fried fish hit me. I made a mental note to add air fresheners to my shopping list. People became accustomed to the smell of their own home, which could put off prospective buyers.

We followed Victoria into the living room, where she sank into an overstuffed, flowered sofa that enveloped her petite figure. Ignoring us, she picked up the framed photo of a dog from the nearby table, caressing the photo gently before replacing it.

Tyrone whispered, "Should we sit down?

"If we wait for an invitation, we could be standing here all day," I whispered back and took a seat.

Tyrone struggled to keep a straight face as he gazed at the large collection of Royal Doulton and Hummel figurines and other knickknacks that covered every surface, along with a thick layer of dust. Heavy dark draperies covered the windows and beat back any sunlight trying to get in.

Victoria pointed to Tyrone. "So, who's this, your moving man?"

"This is my assistant, Tyrone Webster."

"That name rings a bell." Victoria eyed Tyrone critically. "How old is he? Nineteen, twenty?" When I nodded, she said, "At his age, how much experience can he have?"

"Enough to help you sell this place." I tried to hide my irritation as she spoke about Tyrone as though he weren't there. "He's studying design at Fischer College and also has experience designing theatre sets for the Louiston Players."

"As I've mentioned before, I'm moving to Florida and want to sell this place. Quickly. It's fine the way it is, but my real estate agent and my ex-husband ganged up on me to *stage the house* as they called it."

I leaned forward. "In this market, staging will—"

"Don't bore me again with all the details." Victoria lit another cigarette. "And don't go over the budget we agreed to." The sudden roar of a lawn mower drowned out Victoria's words. She jumped up, stomped over to the French doors, and flung them open.

"Watch that vine," she shouted. "Carlos, if one of your men ruins my wisteria, I'm going to report your workers to immigration officials." She slammed the French doors and turned to face us. "It took me years to train that wisteria. I'm not going to have a peasant cutting it off at the bottom with a Weed Wacker." She sank back onto the sofa and placed her still-burning cigarette on the lip of the astray.

Tyrone looked stunned. I had experience with Victoria's viper tongue, but he only knew her by reputation.

"Since I can't move out while you do your staging thing, try not to be disruptive."

I watched Tyrone turn away from Victoria and roll his eyes, doing exactly what I'd told him not to do. Young people and their eye rolling. He saw the warning look I gave him and mouthed, "Sorry."

Victoria stood abruptly. "If we're finished here, I'll be in the library upstairs. I'm expecting someone from Hamilton Real Estate soon. Please let him in when he comes." She left the room, leaving her cigarette burning.

I stubbed it out. "No sense letting the house burn down before we can stage it."

Tyrone grimaced. "So much for being sensitive to her feelings."

"Sorry, Tyrone. I need the business, but you shouldn't be subjected to her rudeness." I picked up a stack of magazines Victoria had knocked over. "Try to remember how hard leaving this house will be for her."

If Victoria weren't so unpleasant, I could almost feel sorry for her. Growing up in a less affluent section of town, she took great pride living in the grandest house in Louiston. If the rumors were true, Victoria had married Skip Denton more for the house than the relationship. The marriage had ended, and now she was going to lose the house as well.

"You're right." Tyrone stood in front of a cavernous fireplace and rested a hand on the Carrera marble mantel. "All this and she still wasn't happy. No wonder her husband divorced her."

I sighed. It was a wonder Skip hadn't murdered her.

I gave Tyrone a tour of the house, telling him of changes I'd already discussed with Victoria and noted his suggestions. "This is a grand old house. Look at the coffered ceilings and wainscoting. They're fabulous."

"It reminds me of Hendricks Funeral Home. No one's going to buy it looking like a morgue."

"Wait and see. It's amazing what removing excess furniture, decluttering, and freshening the paint can do. Sometimes moving a piece of artwork to a different location can make a big difference. It's like when you design a stage set."

Old-fashioned door chimes sounded in the distance. I walked

down the long hall and pulled open the heavy oak front door. Before me stood one of the best-looking men I'd ever seen—tall, blond, and with a bearing that spoke of military training. Not since seeing a young Robert Redford in old videos had I seen someone who made me stand and stare.

I disliked him immediately. Good-looking men are trouble, my mother had warned. I learned the hard way she'd been right.

"Is Victoria Denton in?" the Adonis asked. "I'm Doug Hamilton with Hamilton Real Estate."

"Doug, how nice to see you." Behind us, Victoria glided down the long staircase like the female lead in a classic movie, extending both her hands to take his. Charm she hadn't wasted on us now oozed from her.

Doug glanced around the foyer. "I wanted to see how the staging is coming along. Have you made any progress?"

"I keep telling you, my home is fine the way it is. You and Skip are the only ones who think it needs to be *staged* to sell." Victoria's frown clearly expressed how she viewed that. She looked over at Tyrone and me. "Uh, this is Laura Bishop, the stager, and her helper, Tyler."

"It's Tyrone," I said.

Doug nodded at us. "Now, Victoria, if you want to sell this place for a good price, you need to spruce it up. Otherwise, it could sit on the market awhile. In its present condition, you'd be insulted by any offer you received. You wouldn't want that now, would you?" He squeezed Victoria's hand.

Victoria pressed her lips together, forming a thin line. She didn't appear convinced.

"We'll hold an open house in a week and see how it goes," Doug said. "If we don't have any interest then, we'll see what else we can do to attract buyers."

Warmth crept up my neck and face. "A week? We'll need at least two weeks to get this place ready for an open house."

"That's all the time we have." Doug looked into the living room. "If you don't think you can handle it—"

"We'll be ready." How little sleep could I survive on?

"I'll stop back in a couple of days to see how the staging is progressing." As Doug walked with Victoria to the front door and out onto the porch, I heard him say, "You might want to consider my advice to contact Monica Heller. You get what you pay for."

My dislike for him escalated.

Tyrone and I hurried back to the living room.

"Don't let him bother you. He's got as much riding on selling this house as you do," Tyrone said.

"How do you know that?"

"Heard it at Vocaro's. After old man Hamilton had his stroke, he made some serious mistakes at the agency. Doug retired from the Navy and came home to care for his dad. He doesn't know much about selling real estate and is helping out."

I moaned. "My future work as a stager depends on how well we do here. We really need more time."

"Then let's get started." Tyrone turned toward the animal heads mounted on the walls and made a face. "The sooner we're outta this creepy place the better."

Chapter 2

Use mirrors to brighten an area, but only if they reflect something attractive. Mirrors can also make a room look larger.

"Honestly, Nita, if I didn't have so much riding on this job, I'd tell Victoria to call Monica myself." I leaned back in my chair at Vocaro's and sipped the plain coffee I'd ordered instead of the more expensive cappuccino. Fatigue from the previous days' work at the Denton house was catching up with me, and I desperately needed the boost caffeine would give me.

"You must be frustrated." Nita took a large bite of Danish pastry. She viewed pastries as one of the major food groups. "Is Victoria being more than her usual obnoxious self?"

I expelled a long, drawn-out sigh. "Working with her is like pushing a rock up a hill with your head, and when you look up, it rolls back and hits you in the face. Tyrone and I are exhausted. For someone who said she didn't want to be bothered with the details, she's criticized everything we've done so far. When we suggested removing some furniture, she said she liked it exactly the way it is. She doesn't realize how crowded the rooms are, which makes them look smaller. There's never a dull moment there." I pushed away my half-eaten bagel. My appetite had fled hand in hand with my enthusiasm for this project.

"No surprise there. I won't say it, but—"

"I know. You warned me about Victoria, and you were right." I continued leafing through a magazine. "Right now, I need to find a way to break up the massive wall in the front foyer. It's the first thing you see when you walk in and it needs something to make a good first impression."

"Let me go through the magazines at the dental clinic. I recall an article that showed a photo of three mirrors hanging horizontally on a tall wall, one above the other. At the time I thought it was a clever idea. It might work for you." For Nita, one of the joys of working as the receptionist at Dr. Malcolm's dental clinic was having occasional quiet periods when she could enjoy the numerous magazines they put out for patients.

I flipped my magazine closed. "Could you search for it today and fax it to me at Victoria's so I can see how it looks? We're running out of time fast."

"I'll look for it as soon as I get there. We're not very busy at the clinic right now. Do people still use fax? How about if I scan or take a photo of it and text it to you?"

"That would be great, but reception on the hill is really poor. On top of that, my cell phone isn't holding a charge for long and dies out on me. Once I make some money, the first thing I plan to do is get a new phone. In the meantime, Victoria said I could use her fax, so send it to her fax number. That way I can get it today." I wrote the number on the back of one of my new business cards and handed it to her.

"I'll send it this afternoon. If you don't get it today, give me a call. I'm notorious for transposing numbers and sending things off to the wrong place." Nita tapped the card with a rose-colored nail. "This one I should remember. It's close to Dr. M's home fax and my mother-in-law's number. Wouldn't it be funny if I sent it to my mother-in-law?"

"Knowing you and your mother-in-law, you'd enjoy confusing

her."

Nita slipped the card into her purse. "How's Tyrone doing working with Victoria?"

"Like mixing oil and vinegar, Victoria being the vinegar. His usual good humor is fading fast. Maybe if he gets the Quincy Scholarship he applied for, he can give up some of his part-time jobs and avoid difficult people like Victoria. They'll be making a selection soon."

"Tell him to be careful what he says to her. She's on the scholarship selection panel."

"Oh no." A sense of exhaustion swept over me. "I'll have to warn Tyrone."

"Definitely. Victoria isn't someone you'd want as an enemy, and it doesn't take much for her to view you as one."

After arriving at the Denton house, I spent the morning searching the attic for things I could use throughout the house and was delighted to discover a number of colorful rugs, lamps, and some steamer trunks for side tables. They would help make some of the near-empty bedrooms a bit cozier without having to bring in extra items. I worked cautiously in the dim light, careful to avoid the low rafters, and stepped around piles of abandoned household items.

Heavy footsteps sounded on the steps to the attic. I looked up from the stack of linens I'd been going through. Tyrone emerged from the narrow stairwell, ducking so he wouldn't bang his head on the rafters.

"Nita called. She found the magazine article and will be faxing it shortly." Tyrone paused. "I'd have gone to the library to get it, but Victoria hides out there. I didn't want to run into her."

"Can't say I blame you, but I think she went out earlier." I wiped my dusty hands on the back of my jeans. "I'll go get it."

I pushed open the heavy oak door to the library and was

startled to see Victoria sitting at a massive desk with a phone in her hand. I didn't realize she'd returned.

"Don't threaten me. Either you get it to me by tomorrow or I'm going public with this." She slammed the old-fashioned phone down so hard it bounced on the desk.

I hesitated in the doorway, ready to turn away. Victoria caught sight of me and quickly inserted the papers in her hand between the pages of a book and closed it. "What do you want?"

"Sorry. I thought you were out. I came to pick up a fax."

"Well, come get it." Victoria brushed past me in the doorway, grumbling something about having me underfoot all the time.

The fax hadn't arrived yet, so I sank into the chair next to the machine to wait for it. My body ached, and I needed a rest.

A large bookcase filled the wall behind me. I swung my chair around and studied the books on the shelves. Seeing the distinctive purple cover of a Louiston High School yearbook, I pulled it from the shelf, surprised Victoria was sentimental enough to keep it close at hand. The dust covering it tickled my nose.

To kill time waiting for the fax, I leafed through the yearbook, coming across photos of a very young and attractive Victoria. One photo, taken during a high school production of *Nicholas Nickleby*, featured Victoria and classmates Jack Malcolm and Warren Hendricks. That must have been when they developed an interest in the stage and went on to the Louiston Players, a small but vibrant community theater group.

A piece of paper fell from between the pages of the yearbook. Someone had written *Warren Hendricks* in block letters across the top of the page. Below his name appeared a list of dates and dollar amounts. That was strange. Warren was the director of the Hendricks Funeral Home. Was Victoria making payments for someone's funeral? If so, it certainly had been an expensive one. Over the years, Victoria had entered into a number of business ventures, all of them unsuccessful. One of them may have been

been with Warren.

At the sound of the fax machine turning on, I tucked the paper back into the yearbook and returned it to the shelf. I studied the fax pages spewing from the machine. Yes, the perfect solution for the foyer wall.

"Come quick," Tyrone called from the doorway.

In the distance, I could hear shouting. "What's going on?" I'd expected a quiet day but instead was beginning to feel like Dorothy in the eye of a Kansas tornado.

"It's Cora Ridley. She and Victoria are having a shouting match, and it's really heating up. Maybe Cora will deck her." Tyrone didn't sound averse to seeing it happen. "Man, this is so cool."

Cora and Victoria stood at the bottom of the stairs.

"I want my money." Cora waved her clenched fist at Victoria. "I've waited as long as I'm going to wait. Now that you're selling this place, I expect my money."

They had been partners in a catering business. Cora had done the cooking, and Victoria was to use her connections to get them business. Rumor had it that Cora put up most of the money for the venture, which hadn't lasted long. Catering was a service industry, and Victoria wasn't someone who wanted to please people.

"I don't owe you a thing," Victoria said. "Our business went bankrupt. That's the way things go. You don't see me crying over it."

"What do you have to cry about? I put up the money, and you made a mess of it. I never should have trusted you with my money, or my husband."

Victoria reared back. "I don't know what you're talking about."

"You know exactly what I mean. I know all about you and Norman. You may think you fooled me, but you're wrong. For all I care, you can have him, but I want my money. Once I get it, I can leave the creep."

Cora was married to Norman Ridley, a representative to the state legislature, who believed one of the perks of being elected to office was access to any woman he wanted.

"Get out of here." Victoria advanced toward Cora. "My lawyer says I don't owe you a penny."

Cora backed toward the door. "I'll get it one way or another, or you'll be sorry." Turning, she stalked through the front entrance and slammed the door behind her.

Tyrone and I stood there frozen.

Seeing us, Victoria raised her chin and walked up the stairs. "I never should have lowered myself going into business with the likes of her. I won't make a mistake like that again."

When she disappeared down the hall, Tyrone let out his breath. "Do you think Cora will come back?"

"Who can say?" Remembering my reaction on first discovering my late husband Derrick's infidelity, I could well understand Cora's anger. "If she does return, I wouldn't want to be here. After seeing how angry they both can get, it could be deadly."

Later in the day, the Denton house was humming with activity. The window washer and the painters were transforming the place. I was pleased to see how the sparkling clean windows brightened the rooms.

At the sound of breaking glass, my heart sank. Racing toward the direction of the noise, I entered the dining room to see Tyrone staring at his feet. Pieces of wine-colored glass littered the hardwood floor.

"You idiot." Victoria gasped from the doorway. "That was my grandmother's vase."

"I'm really sorry," Tyrone sputtered with embarrassment. "The shelf tipped when I—"

"Sorry doesn't do it." She walked over to Tyrone and poked her finger into his chest, punctuating each word. "How could you be so careless?"

Tyrone backed away from her, rubbing his chest. His face flushed. "I was reaching for that covered jar." He pointed to an Asian-style ceramic jar on an upper shelf.

"It doesn't matter how it happened. You should have been more careful." She leaned over, picked up a piece of the glass, and then straightened. "I shouldn't have let Laura convince me you were experienced enough to work here. In fact, I recently realized why your name sounded familiar. You're one of the applicants for the Quincy Scholarship at Fischer College." She threw the piece of glass onto the floor. "Well, you can forget about it. I could never recommend someone stupid and careless, who presented himself as something he's not." With that, she turned on her heel and stalked from the room.

Tyrone turned to me. "What'd she mean?"

A quiver of regret ran through me. "Victoria's on the Quincy Scholarship panel. I meant to tell you, but with all that has been happening, I forgot."

A shocked look crossed his face and he rushed to follow Victoria. "Look, Mrs. Denton, I'm really sorry. I'll get it repaired or find you another one."

I cringed thinking how expensive it might be to replace the Murano vase. Neither of us had that kind of money.

"Please, Mrs. Denton," he pleaded, but Victoria ignored him and started up the stairs. When she continued to ignore him, Tyrone followed her, his panic visible to the window washer and painters who had come out into the hall.

"Tyrone, wait." I raced after him, grabbing his arm to stop him before he could follow her upstairs. Beads of sweat had formed on his forehead. "I'm sorry. I should have told you about her being on the panel. I meant to. She's not the only one determining the winner."

Tyrone paced up and down the foyer, a worried look flickering in his eyes. "She could say stuff to the other panel members. I need that scholarship, Laura. You understand, don't you? With it, the money I'm making now could help out more at home."

"We'll figure out something. I'll go up to the library and talk to her once she calms down. Maybe my business insurance will cover the cost of the vase."

"It won't matter. She hasn't liked me from the start. Mrs. Denton could really hurt my chances at the scholarship. I need to talk to her."

He took the stairs two at a time, bounded down the corridor toward the library, and then knocked on the door to get Victoria's attention. I stood on the stairs, trying to hear what was happening. I didn't need to try hard. Everyone on the first floor could hear them.

"Mrs. Denton, can I talk to you for a minute?" Tyrone pleaded.

"Go away. You're not going to change my mind."

"Please, I'll do anything."

Victoria swung open the door and stood in the opening. "I said go. In fact, get out now. I don't want you working here any longer. I heard about the trouble you got into. I'll talk to the scholarship panel tomorrow."

"You can't do that." His voice rose. He slowly descended the stairs. His shoulders slumped and his face twitched with anger and fear. "I can't let her do that. Sorry, Laura, but I've gotta get out of here. I'll hitch a ride into town."

Before I could respond, he was gone. Soon after that, the workmen left, and the house became deathly quiet.

The late afternoon light began fading, along with my energy levels. It had been a long day, and I yearned for dinner and a long, hot bath. I also needed to get home to feed my small black cat, Inky. However, I still had some things to take care of, including cleaning up the broken vase.

I stared at the shards of glass lying on the floor. Such a small thing compared to all of the distress it caused. I carefully picked up the pieces, placed them in a paper bag, and took them to a trash can in the kitchen. The painters would be working there in the morning, so I began clearing the countertops of clutter and boxing it for storage in the basement.

From somewhere in the house, a door closed. I stood still, expecting someone to approach, but when no one did, I decided Victoria must have gone out.

Later, with one of the boxes in hand, I switched on the stairwell light and stared into the cavernous unfinished basement. Tyrone wasn't far off the mark when he'd talked about a dungeon in the house.

At the bottom of the stairs, I lugged the box over to the laundry area, where we had stacked other boxes for storage until Victoria moved out. It would have been better if we could have stored them offsite, but Victoria wouldn't agree to that. Turning, I started to leave. The basement gave me the creeps, and I was anxious to escape upstairs.

Suddenly, I heard a loud rumbling noise above me. Looking up, I watched in astonishment and horror as the crumpled body of Victoria Denton fell from the laundry chute and landed at my feet.

Chapter 3

Have your house ready for viewing from the basement to the attic.
Potential buyers will want to inspect it all. Store excess furniture
and packed items elsewhere prior to holding an open house.

Victoria lay motionless on the concrete floor. It took me several seconds to get my wits about me and go to her aid. I knew little about first aid, but I knew enough not to move her in case I caused her more injury.

Victoria was deathly pale. Kneeling beside her, I reached out with a trembling hand and frantically attempted to take her pulse. I couldn't find it. Was I missing the right spot or wasn't there a pulse? I wished I'd paid more attention in first aid class.

Shock. I remembered when someone was injured, they could go into shock and should be kept warm. I looked around the basement for something to cover her with. Nothing was available except stacks of newspapers. Paper had insulating properties. It would have to do.

As I bent over Victoria to cover her, I noticed the strange angle of her head and knew any further aid would more than likely be useless.

I needed to call for help. I stood, but my legs were like rubber, and I could barely hold myself up. My body was refusing to cooperate. I may have been the one in shock.

Gathering as much energy as I could muster, I moved in slow motion to the stairs. It was like being in a nightmare, trying to run and getting nowhere. Making my way up the steps, I slipped several times, skinning both shins. At the top of the stairs, I stumbled across the kitchen and grabbed the wall phone. I had difficulty with the old-fashioned phone and had to dial 911 twice before the call went through.

When the emergency operator answered, I tried to explain what had happened. My tongue seemed thick, as though I'd experienced an allergic reaction to food, and I found myself slurring. All I could think was to give the operator the address, which I had difficulty remembering. "The Denton house on Lookout Hill," I stuttered and then slid to the floor, dropping the phone.

While waiting for the emergency vehicles, I asked myself over and over how Victoria could have fallen through the laundry chute. Surely, during her years of living there, she'd put laundry down it without a problem. The grand old house had oversized dumbwaiters and other large-scale features, so the extra-large laundry chute wasn't out of the ordinary. It had been designed for the days when housemaids used it to deposit large loads of bedding from numerous overnight guests. Only then did it occur to me no laundry had come through the chute with Victoria.

Or stranger yet, had something possessed Victoria to climb into it? Did she view it bizarrely as an escape hatch? But what would she have been escaping from? Would Victoria still be alive if I hadn't moved the large laundry hamper when I tidied up the basement? None of it made sense.

I heard the sirens of the emergency vehicles and gathered up enough strength to raise myself from the kitchen floor and unlock the front door. Looking out, I saw the flashing lights of an ambulance, a fire truck, and a police cruiser. They had come prepared for any kind of emergency.

Two firefighters, weighed down with heavy gear, bounded into the foyer. I pointed to the kitchen. "She's in the basement." My voice quaked. They had to rely more on my finger pointing to the right direction than my words. The next thing I knew, I was sitting in a chair with a blanket wrapped around my shoulders and someone holding out a mug to me.

"It's warm, so take your time," a male voice said. "It will help with the shock."

I looked up and recognized Neil Stanelli, one of Nita's cousins and a Louiston policeman. I tried to straighten and found it hard to grasp the mug. Neil guided it to my lips, and I took a grateful sip of sweet, hot tea. I don't take sugar in my tea, but this time I was grateful for it. After several sips, I let out a sigh and tried to sit up.

"Relax." Neil took the cup from my shaking hands.

"Victoria?"

"I'm afraid she's gone."

I slumped back. I'd strongly suspected Victoria was dead, but having it confirmed made me tremble.

"Do you feel well enough to talk about it? Detective Spangler will be here shortly and will want to question you."

I nodded, feeling embarrassed I'd fallen apart when faced with an emergency. Had I done all the right things? Could I have done more?

Several minutes later, Neil came back. "Laura, this is Detective Spangler."

A tall, dark-haired man loomed over me. From my position, slumped in a chair, he looked seven feet tall. I tried to sit up, but he placed his hand on my shoulder. "Just stay as you are. I need to ask you some questions."

After giving him my full name and address, I explained what happened. I found it difficult recounting the events and my reaction. A chill went through me when I described Victoria's fall from the laundry chute, and I wrapped the blanket around my shoulders more tightly.

"What was your relationship with Mrs. Denton?"

"She hired me to stage her house."

He looked puzzled. "What's that?"

"To make her home as appealing as possible to buyers. She planned to sell it."

He gave me an even more puzzled look.

"Staging can be as simple as organizing and reducing clutter or doing repairs and redecorating. This house required extensive work."

He looked skeptical. "Is that really necessary?"

"It is if a homeowner wants to get a good price and sell quickly." I could see him mulling that over, but he didn't comment.

"Other than staging Mrs. Denton's home, did you have any other connection to her? Did you socialize with her? Were you friends?"

"We only had a business relationship."

"Did it go well? Did you have any disputes or disagreements over the work being done or about anything else?"

How could I explain Victoria hadn't been interested in the staging, that she only took pleasure in finding fault with everything we did? "Victoria was unhappy about selling the house. As a result, she didn't find much satisfaction in anything we were doing."

Much to my relief, Detective Spangler didn't pursue that subject any further.

"What was her frame of mind today? Let me rephrase that. Was she her usual self or did she seem different—upset about anything?"

I waited for a long moment, trying to think how to describe Victoria without sounding mean spirited. "She was the same as she usually was—a bit upset because of a broken vase, but other than that she was the same." I was puzzled at the questions. "If you're asking about Victoria's frame of mind, are you thinking it was suicide?"

"We have to consider all possibilities."

"Victoria would never have done that. She wasn't the type to let things bother her to the point of committing suicide. Certainly not over the loss of a Murano vase." Could the broken vase have pushed her over the edge?

"Was there anyone else in the house?"

"The workmen left earlier." At his request, I gave him their names and what they had been doing. "I wasn't sure if Victoria was here or not."

"You didn't know?"

"It's a big house, and it wasn't unusual for her to come and go while we were working. Before I went down to the basement, I heard a door close and thought she'd either come in or gone out. It didn't matter since I have a key."

"Who else on your work team has a key?

"Tyrone, my assistant, has one. He rides up with the painters so he can let them in. They like to get a really early start, and Victoria didn't want to be disturbed early."

"You don't come in at the same time?" Detective Spangler's pen hovered over his notepad.

"I've been staying here late into the evening, so sometimes I don't start as early as the painters."

"What about the doors? Were they locked while you were here?"

"They're unlocked during the day when the workmen are here. They go back and forth to their trucks for equipment. After everyone left for the day, I locked all the doors, including the doors to the patio. I made sure everything was secure."

"Did you feel a particular need to be so cautious?"

"It was getting dark. Since I was staying late, I didn't want to be in the house with unlocked doors. It was simply common sense."

He should know that. Why was he asking me all these questions? After all, Victoria's death was an unfortunate accident. Wasn't it?

"Do you usually stay late?" His dark brown gaze seemed to burrow into me, which made me squirm.

"On the few days we've been here. We had a stringent deadline to meet, and I needed as much time as possible here to meet the deadline. I stayed late today to have something ready for the workmen tomorrow."

I started to feel defensive. My shins ached, I was tired, and I was becoming impatient. "Look, what is this all about? Why all the questions about locked doors and why I'm here late?"

"It's routine when a death is suspicious."

He continued questioning me, his deadpan expression giving no clue as to what he was thinking. I found it unnerving. He asked me some of the same questions again but in a slightly different way, as though to confirm what I'd said. He made notes in a small notepad, and I wondered what had been important enough to record.

Fatigue began to overtake me, and it became difficult keeping my eyes open.

"That's all for now, Ms. Bishop. If you don't feel up to driving, Officer Stanelli can take you home."

"Thank you. I'd appreciate that." My legs still could barely hold me up, and I wasn't sure how well I could drive. I'd figure out a way to get my car another day.

As the police car pulled away, I looked back at the house and the large dark windows that stared at me. It was the perfect setting for a Gothic novel. I hoped to never see it again.

Chapter 4

The smell of food lingers long after a meal. Use some type of air freshener before an open house to make the house smell less like last night's fish dinner. To eliminate odors from garbage disposals and drains, rinse them with baking soda and vinegar.

At dawn, I gave up trying to sleep. All night, no matter how hard I tried, I couldn't dispel the image of Victoria lying at my feet on the concrete floor. Questions of how Victoria came to fall through the laundry chute plagued me. I sat up in bed and was confused until I remembered I was at Nita's house. Neil had called Nita, and she and her husband, Guido, had met me at my house and insisted Inky and I spend the night with them.

I quickly called Tyrone and told him the news about Victoria and that we wouldn't be going to the house that morning. He was shocked and asked me a lot of questions that I couldn't fully answer. Following that, I cancelled the painters for the day.

Bleary-eyed, I walked into the Martino kitchen and sat down at a large oak table next to Nita, who poured me a cup of coffee. Coffee in the morning was like being hit on the back of the head and told to get moving. This morning, I needed the bitter, strong brew Nita and Guido favored.

Inky followed me into the kitchen. He was a frequent visitor to the Martino home when Nita cared for him any time I was away, so he knew where to find the food she'd put out for him. Guido quickly pulled the stopper out of the kitchen sink so the soapy water could drain. He knew of Inky's penchant for jumping into any pool of water available. Of all the cats at the rescue, I'd picked the one strangely attracted to water. When I filled the basin in the bathroom, I had to stand close to it to prevent Inky from jumping into it. He was an odd cat, but he brought me a lot of comfort.

Concern showed on Nita's face. "How are you feeling? When Neil called us last night and told us what happened, I couldn't believe it."

"That was good of Neil to call you."

"We didn't think you should be alone last night. For once, you didn't put up any resistance." Nita and I became friends in the second grade, and her large Italian-American family had taken me into their fold, treating me like one of the family. After my father left, I escaped from my unhappy home to their boisterous household as often as I could. Here I was in my early forties, and they were still looking after me.

I shivered and tried to warm my fingers on the hot cup cradled in my hands. Leaning over to smell the aroma of the coffee, my long hair hung over both sides of my face like a curtain blocking out the day. It wasn't enough to block the mental images of the evening before. I shivered again and ticked off in my mind the symptoms of shock, wondering if that was what was wrong with me.

"Try to eat something." Nita placed a plate stacked with pancakes in front of me. "You'll feel better." To Italian-Americans, food is love and helps make every situation better. Guido stood at the stove pushing sausages around in a heavy black iron skillet, softly humming off-key.

As much as I appreciated the food, I didn't think it would help. My appetite had fled, and I couldn't bear the thought of eating. Since Nita hovered over me looking worried, I cut pieces of the pancake and took a bite. One bite led to another, and soon the sense of fatigue weighing me down disappeared.

The doorbell rang. Nita went to answer it and returned, followed by Neil, the stubble on his face and his wrinkled uniform a dead giveaway he hadn't been home the previous night.

"Pull up a chair." Guido waved a spatula at him. "You want some breakfast?"

"If you have enough. We just cleared out of the Denton house, and I'm starving."

"When have you ever known Nita not to have enough for an army?" Guido handed him a mug of coffee.

Neil sat down and turned to me. "I came by to see how you're doing. You had quite a shock last night."

I smiled, thankful again for the love and concern Nita's extended family showed me. "I'm a bit shaken up, but I'm okay. Thanks for your help last night."

Nita placed a plate heaped with food in front of Neil. She was happy to have another person to feed, especially now with her son and daughter away at college.

Neil drained his cup and sighed. "I needed that. It was a long night." He then poured maple syrup liberally over the pancakes and dug into them as though he hadn't eaten in days.

After serving everyone else, Nita sat down and brought up the subject everyone else appeared to be avoiding. "What I can't understand is how Victoria fell down the chute. Could she have fallen through when she put laundry in it?"

"I've asked myself the same thing, over and over. I don't know how she could have fallen into it. Victoria lived there for a long time. Surely, she would have known to be careful with the oversized chute. Unless she became dizzy." I looked in surprise at the pancake Nita had put on my plate when I wasn't looking.

"Nothing in those old homes is by code." Guido spoke with knowledge gained from long years working in construction. "Given some of the outdated things in the house, it wouldn't take much to have an accident there."

Neil shrugged and continued eating.

"Come on, Neil," Nita prodded. "Surely you know something. What does Detective Spangler make of all this? Does he usually show up when someone accidentally dies?"

"I'm not supposed to say." Neil poured himself another cup of coffee from the pot on the table. "It's an ongoing investigation."

"They wouldn't tell you anyway." Nita sounded like a teenager again, chiding him.

Old childhood rivalry reared its head, and Neil could never resist trying to be one up on Nita. She was slightly older and had always treated him like a kid. "Detective Spangler is viewing her death as a homicide." His face flushed. Nita had manipulated him into saying something he shouldn't have.

"What?" I was astounded. "He thinks Victoria was murdered?"

Chapter 5

Furnished homes sell faster than empty ones. If you've already moved, consider renting furniture and accessories to stage your home attractively. It will help buyers see how the rooms can be arranged.

Several days later, the sun shone brilliantly over Good Shepherd Cemetery and helped warm the few people gathering in the cold for Victoria's graveside service. Following the previous days' dramatic events, it would have been more fitting if the sky had been covered with dark clouds and sheets of rain were falling. Maybe it was only in movies that it rained heavily at the burial of a murder victim.

"This is such a beautiful spot." I gazed at the green vista in front of us, filled with large trees and a variety of tombstones and small mausoleums.

Nita and I made our way up a steep hill toward Victoria's gravesite.

Stopping to catch my breath, I looked out at the rolling hills surrounding the area. "From here you can actually see the Denton home over on Lookout Hill."

"That's rather ironic," Nita said, still puffing from the climb. "I wonder if Skip had that in mind when he selected the plot."

"Could be. Victoria loved that house, especially considering that awful place she grew up in." We gazed over at the house Victoria thought would bring her happiness and then hadn't.

Reaching the gravesite, Nita and I joined the small group of people standing around the casket.

"I'm surprised more people aren't here," Nita whispered. "I expected a few curiosity seekers would show up."

I pulled the hood of my coat over my head for warmth. "It's this cold snap. It sure doesn't feel like spring."

Near the head of the casket, Skip Denton looked more mournful than I would have expected, considering his stormy relationship with Victoria and their divorce. It might have been easier if they had children to stand next to him. I thought sadly of Macbeth, Victoria's black Scottish Terrier who had died recently and whose framed photo still sat on her bedside table. Photos of him had been all over the house.

When the graveside service was over, Doug Hamilton and his father walked toward their car, Mr. Hamilton limping badly. Spotting me, Doug strode toward me, extending his hand. Surprised, I shook hands with him.

"I'm sorry you had such a terrible experience, finding Victoria the way you did." Doug's bright blue eyes mesmerized me.

I blinked and mumbled something, unable to remember what I said after he walked away.

Warren Hendricks and Dr. Malcolm, Victoria's high school classmates and costars in a number of school and community stage productions, were there to witness Victoria's last scene before her final curtain. There would be no curtain calls this time.

Warren lived in town over the funeral home he had inherited from his father, but he had been a frequent visitor to the Denton home over the years. Dr. Malcolm was Victoria's neighbor on one side, a tall hedge separating their homes. Nita had worked for Dr. M, as everyone called him, for years.

"Would you look at Monica over there," Nita said. "She's

actually wearing a black hat and veil. Leave it to her to look like a grieving widow at her ex-friend's funeral. Who's the man she's learning on?"

"Don't know. I'm more interested in watching Detective Spangler watching us." I pointed to where he stood a short distance away. "I heard the police often attend the funeral of a murder victim to see if anyone acts strangely. Now I know that's true. I didn't see anyone acting suspiciously like a murderer. Did you?"

"No, and before he heads this way, I'm going to the car. If you want to linger, I'll wait for you there."

After everyone else had walked away, Skip Denton remained at the graveside, looking a bit lost. I walked over and gave him a hug. We had worked together on several community improvement projects, and it saddened me to see him standing there alone.

"Thank you for coming, Laura. I appreciate it. Are you going to join us for some refreshments? Luigi Vocaro is putting out a spread for us in the back room of the coffee bar."

"Thank you. I'll be there."

We continued down the hill together, saying little.

At the bottom, Skip stopped. "Victoria wasn't always like she was the last few years. Her disappointment in discovering that marrying me wouldn't turn her into a social success was too great for her to bear, especially considering her upbringing. Even after we divorced, I still cared for her." Skip turned and gazed back at the gravesite. "When Macbeth died, her world nearly fell apart. If she had cared for people half as much as she cared for the house and her dog...."

"Is that why you moved out of your family home and she stayed?"

"My family owned it for generations, but it didn't mean as much to me as it did to her. Now someone else will have it. I couldn't live there again, especially after what happened to Victoria."

My own unhappy childhood helped me empathize with Victoria's desire to escape her circumstances, but marrying into a family with money hadn't brought her happiness.

"What will you do with the house now?"

"I still have to sell it to pay off our debts." He grimaced and a flush suffused his face. "The house is heavily mortgaged, and the bill collectors are knocking at the door."

Tears welled up in my eyes. "I'm so sorry, Skip." I didn't know what else to say.

"It's okay. Victoria was the one who was attached to it. Moving back there would be too much for me to deal with, both financially and emotionally. Besides, I'm happy in my smaller place in town. I need to sell soon, so I'd appreciate it if you'd complete the staging as soon as the police will let us back in the house. From what I've seen, you've made terrific improvements. Would you be willing to go back there, considering everything that happened?"

He had no idea how much I wanted to say no, especially since I'd hoped never to return to the house again. Guido had kindly gone there to retrieve my car for me.

"Of course we'll finish," I said with more determination than I felt. It was against my nature to leave a project incomplete. "But won't the house be held up in probate or something until Victoria's estate is settled?"

"No. Not really. The house belonged to me before we married. I only agreed as part of the divorce settlement that she would get half the proceeds if we ever sold."

With Victoria dead, would all the proceeds now go to him?

After saying goodbye to Skip, I walked down the road that snaked through the cemetery, searching for Nita. I spotted her a short distance away, standing next to her lime green VW bug. Dr. M leaned against it, as though he needed it to prop himself up. He had been Victoria's schoolmate, costar, and neighbor for years, and it appeared he was taking her death hard.

I joined them, throwing my purse onto the backseat of the car. "I didn't mean to keep you waiting." I turned to Dr. M. "I'm sorry about Victoria. I know you were friends for a long time."

Dr. M looked grim and shook his head. "Sad affair, sad affair." With that, he walked away toward his car.

Nita watched Dr. M's retreating figure. "He worries me. Look at his crumpled suit. Yesterday he came into the dental clinic with mud on his trousers. Patients are starting to notice."

"Why do you keep working for him? I stopped going to him years ago when he retied his shoelaces and then put his hands in my mouth."

"I can't quit on him now, especially since he seems to be getting worse. Mrs. M told me that she stopped changing his bath towel three weeks before she left him, and he never noticed. At the rate we're losing patients, I may not have a choice but to look for a new job."

Nita was extremely loyal to her family and friends, one of the things I admired most about her. But as nice as Dr. M was, I felt her loyalty to him was misplaced.

We watched Dr. M pull away, smoke trailing from his aging Mercedes. On the back window, someone had written *Wash Me* in the dirt.

Chapter 6

Display photographs of your home's exterior taken during different seasons to highlight the landscaping features of each season. This will be especially helpful if you are showing your home during the winter.

The day after the funeral, I approached the door to Vocaro's, anxious for some coffee. The tantalizing aroma coming from inside was already helping to revitalize me. Dr. M was leaving and held the door for me.

"You're coming to see me in *Arsenic and Old Lace*, aren't you?" His smile lit up his face. "It's going to be a terrific production."

"I wouldn't miss it." I was surprised by his change in demeanor from yesterday and mentally shrugged.

His thoughts had obviously turned to something happier than Victoria's death and funeral. Not a season went by when Dr. M didn't have a role in a Louiston Players production, and he enjoyed it immensely. He had a real flair for comedy, and audiences loved him.

"Who are you playing this time?"

"Teddy, of course. It's a key role." Dr. M smiled, appearing to be quite pleased with himself. "They need me because of my bugle-playing talent."

I wasn't aware he had any musical talent but nodded anyway. As I recalled, Teddy played one note as he charged up a long staircase, imagining himself to be Teddy Roosevelt charging San Juan Hill. I smiled at the image.

Dr. M's voice trailed away as he left, "I'm selling tickets if you need them."

After getting my coffee, I joined Nita. We sat on a comfortable sofa with our beverages, Nita with her favorite pastry, reading the *Louiston Mirror*. The heat from the gas fireplace warmed us on a cool spring day. Luigi Vocaro, the owner of the coffee bar, provided local newspapers and leather armchairs and sofas where customers could read in comfort. Customers came in, got a newspaper, claimed a comfortable seat, and frequently stayed for hours. It was what Luigi called people's *third place*—that place, following their home and worksite, where they could feel welcome, comfortable, and connected.

Nita was engrossed in the two sections of the paper she read first each day—her horoscope and the obituaries. "Look at this," she held out the paper to me. "How old do you think this woman was?"

I studied the photo in the obituary column, not recognizing the woman. "It's hard to tell. The photo looks dated. I would guess about twenty-five."

"She was eighty-five. Why do you think her family would use a photo of her that is over sixty years old?"

"Maybe that's the photo her family felt she would like." I thought of the photo of Victoria and her obituary in the paper earlier.

"You know what might be interesting?" Nita licked gooey caramel from her finger. "Reading the horoscope for the day a person dies. Having an entry like 'If you were to die on this day...'" She rifled through the newspapers on the coffee table in front of her. "There might be old papers still here. Let's see what it said for

Taurus on the day Victoria died."

"No, let's don't. It would be too depressing." I was feeling a bit down since Victoria's death, but I also noticed Nita hadn't been her usual perky self either. "Nita, with your kids away at college, have you thought about finding some new interests?"

"I know. I really should. After taking all those photography classes, I intended to do more with them but haven't. Not yet."

I worried about my dearest friend who was feeling the pangs of empty-nest syndrome. She needed something to fill her life. I studied the artificial grapes hanging from the ceiling over us, contemplating how I could help Nita. She and her family had always been there for me and I wanted to be there now for her.

Her photography classes. That was it. "Nita, how would you like to put your talent to use and take photographs for me? I need to build a portfolio of my work showing before and after shots of the houses I work on. I could use somebody with your talent."

Nita sat up with more interest than I'd seen her display in some time. "If you call taking several photography classes having talent, I'd love to."

"We'll have to work out payment for the photos."

"No way. Not after all the times you babysat for our kids."

"That was different. If I'm getting paid for using my skills on this job, you should too."

"Well, if you put it like that. Wait until I tell Guido I'm now a professional photographer." A big smile filled Nita's round face. "And to think he didn't take my attending those classes seriously."

It was good seeing her looking more cheerful. In comparison, I cringed at the thought of going back to the Denton house again but picked up my tote bag ready to leave. "I need to get going. I'm a bit anxious to see what condition the Denton house is in since the police have gone over it. I wonder if they found anything during their search that points to who killed Victoria."

"I haven't heard anything new since Neil told us about the

medical examiner's report. Don't tell anyone what he said. I don't want to get him into trouble, especially since I blackmailed him for the information. I know a lot of secrets from his teenage years he wouldn't want to get out."

"I won't say a word. But I have to admit it was a relief to learn Victoria's death had been caused by a blow to her head and not from the fall that broke her neck. I thought I'd contributed to her death when I moved the laundry hamper from beneath the chute. That could have softened her landing."

Nita folded her newspaper. "Lots of people disliked Victoria, but who'd have been angry enough to kill her? Maybe someone hit her accidentally and hadn't meant to kill her. If so, why push her into the laundry chute?"

"That's the million-dollar question. The police may never discover who killed her."

"Look, there's Neil." Nita pointed toward the door. "Coming in with Alex Spangler."

I looked over at Nita's cousin and the tall, dark-haired detective. "He was the one who interviewed me after...Sorry. I still have a hard time talking about that night."

"Don't you remember Alex Spangler from high school? He was a year ahead of us. His wife was the one killed by lightning while jogging."

"I heard about that. What a shock." I was embarrassed at the unintended pun and quickly turned away from the detective.

"Now that's one hunk of a man. He'd be a good catch for you."

"Good-looking men are trouble." I finished my coffee, frowning as the stale remains hit my taste buds. "Now this time I've really got to go."

"You're always saying that, but it isn't always true." Nita started to gather her things and turned toward the door again. "It's strange seeing Neil here. Since he and Luigi got into a fight after a Steelers game, he's been going to Sheetz for coffee. Those guys take football way too seriously."

I watched the two men, one in plain clothes and the other in uniform, standing at the counter, with Tyrone rapidly filling orders. I marveled at the way he could keep the complex orders straight and work the coffee machine at the same time. Even on days when lines of customers wound out the door, he managed to keep up, while still staying friendly and upbeat. People liked him a lot, and he knew more about what was happening in town than the mayor.

Detective Spangler spoke earnestly to Tyrone, and it looked like they were placing a really big order. When Tyrone took off his apron and walked around the counter toward the door with them, I became suspicious and went to follow. I'd known Tyrone since he was a kid and tried to look out for him. After his parents had been killed in a plane crash and he went to live with his grandmother, life hadn't been easy for him.

"Tyrone, what's going on?" I nearly tripped over a chair trying to get to the door. After Victoria's death, the police had questioned Tyrone, the workers who had been at the house that day, and all of Victoria's neighbors, including Dr M, who lived next door to Victoria. They must have been satisfied with everyone's account of where they had been. What earthly reason could they have for questioning Tyrone again?

"Sorry, Laura." Neil headed for the door. "They want to ask Tyrone a few questions down at the station."

Tyrone looked back at me with a bewildered expression. He didn't have a chance to respond before getting into the back of an unmarked police car parked out front. Detective Spangler nodded at me grimly before closing the car door.

I stood in the doorway, frowning as I watched the police car drive away. Nita joined me, carrying the tote bag I had left behind.

"Nita, I have a bad feeling about this. Don't you have a cousin who's an attorney?"

Chapter 7

When going through household items in anticipation of moving,
sort items into those to take along and those to sell or give away.
You'll have less to take with you and reduce the cost of moving
household goods.

That evening, too nervous to read or watch television, I curled up on the sofa in the living room of my bungalow, waiting anxiously for a call from Nita's cousin, Ted Wojdakowski, Tyrone's new attorney.

The craftsman-style bungalow had been my childhood home. I'd moved back in to care for my mother and stayed with her until her death. With my husband dead, I decided to remain there. I totally gutted the house to remove anything that didn't bring a smile to my face. At first it had been hard making changes to the home of my girlhood, but with each paint stroke, I wiped away sad memories of my years there. The cheerful living room, painted soft yellow and white, was now a far cry from the gloomy room it had been when my mother was alive.

One of the items I'd kept was a small red wagon that had been a gift from my father before he left our lives forever. Studying it across the room, where it sat holding two flowering orchids, I smiled, thinking of him. After my parents' divorce, I'd seen him less and less as the years went by, then not at all. I didn't know whether he was alive or dead.

Had my mother ever been happy? She had blamed her unhappiness on my father, citing his unfaithfulness. Which had come first? Her outlook and personality or his unfaithfulness? My father had been friendly and outgoing and made everyone feel special, whether it was a friend or someone hired to paint the house—unlike my mother, who had treated everyone with equal disdain. She had never forgiven my father for his unfaithfulness, blaming his good looks. My late husband, Derrick, had been extremely attractive as well. After he and his female companion were killed in a car crash, I'd sworn off handsome men forever.

It had been Nita's family, the Romanos, who showered me with love and showed me life could be filled with fun and laughter. It had also been Nita who urged me to follow my dreams of becoming a stager. How different my life would have been if Nita and her large Italian-American family hadn't virtually adopted me.

Barely able to keep my eyes open, I pulled an Aran wool afghan over my legs to ward off the chill. As I was about to doze off, Inky jumped into my lap and startled me to full wakefulness. He circled around in my lap until he became comfortable and settled himself. I ran my hands over his sleek black coat, and his soft purring helped relax me a little. My mother had never allowed me to have a pet when I was growing up, and Derrick hadn't wanted pets. Once I had a house to myself, I visited an animal shelter and picked out Inky. Rather, it was Inky who had picked me. My plan had been to get a cat with a light coat, but when a black cat latched on to my pant leg with a look of desperation, I couldn't tell him no.

When the phone rang, I nearly fell off the sofa in my haste to answer it. Inky landed on the floor and glared at me with annoyance.

"Hello, hello." I was holding the phone upside down.

"Laura, this is Ted Wojdakowski. I wanted to let you know I

just left Tyrone."

"How is he?" I was nearly shouting. "And, where is he? I've been so worried about him."

"He's still down at the city jail." There was a long pause. "Look, there's no easy way for me to say this. The police are holding Tyrone on suspicion of murdering Victoria."

"What!" This time I yelled loud enough for my neighbors to hear me. "That's ridiculous. Tyrone couldn't kill anyone. Besides, why would he murder Victoria? I've known Tyrone since he was a child, and there isn't a mean bone in his body."

"All I can tell you is that when the police questioned everyone who was at the Denton house that day, someone said they heard Tyrone threaten her."

"Who told them that? Nita's brother Angelo and his painters wouldn't have viewed Tyrone's comments as a murderous threat. It must have been Ernie Phillips. He washed windows at the Denton house that day."

"I'm not at liberty to say. However, that and Tyrone's previous trouble with the police were enough for them to strongly suspect him."

"What trouble?"

"The time he was arrested for getting into a fight."

"You don't mean the fight two years ago, do you? That was a big misunderstanding. Tyrone shouldn't have been charged in that fight. A college kid came into Vocaro's Coffee Bar drunk, thinking it was a bar where he could get another drink. When Tyrone tried to serve him coffee to sober him up, the kid got belligerent and took a swing at Tyrone. He took a few punches before he knocked the kid out. Unfortunately, they were both taken in for fighting. Still, that shouldn't be enough to accuse Tyrone. What about his grandmother? Won't she confirm he was home?"

"That's another problem. Tyrone didn't go straight home. He said he went for a run to work off his anger and didn't get home until long after the time Victoria was murdered. He doesn't have anyone who can account for where he was the rest of the time."

I sat still, trying to absorb what I was hearing. "I can't believe that's enough to charge Tyrone."

"There's more. A resident of Lookout Hill spotted Tyrone running back down Battlement Drive around dusk."

"I don't care if he was seen coming from the house by the mayor and the whole city council. Tyrone did not kill Victoria. I know him."

"Your faith in him is admirable. He'll need all the support he can get."

"When can we get him out on bail?"

"In cases like this, the bail is pretty high, and Tyrone said his grandmother wouldn't be able to guarantee the bond. I'm afraid he's going to be sitting there for a while."

"Until you can discover who killed Victoria?"

"Look, Laura, I don't want to disappoint you, but you hired Ted Wojdakowski, not Perry Mason."

Early the next morning, I bounded up the steps to the police station, intent on talking to Detective Spangler about Tyrone. Remembering when he had interviewed me I had been in jeans and covered with dust, I dressed in the most businesslike attire I could find in my closet, a Talbot's navy-blue suit from my IT days. I wanted to be taken seriously.

Two uniformed police officers sitting behind the counter didn't even bother to glance up as I approached. I listened to them talk about the Pirates' chances of winning the pennant that year. When it became apparent they were going to continue ignoring me, I rapped on the glass separating them from the lobby.

"Excuse me, where can I find Detective Spangler?" I tried not to look annoyed.

"What do you want him for?" asked one of the officers.

They were both so young I wondered if they were police cadets.

"That's for me to discuss with him."

"He won't see you unless he knows what it's about."

I gritted my teeth. "I'm Laura Bishop. I want to talk to him about the Victoria Denton murder. I'm the one who found her body."

Tweedledee and Tweedledumber eyed me suspiciously. From their vacuous expressions, I wondered if they thought I was there to confess to the murder.

"Wait here." Tweedledumber went through a doorway behind them. Of the two officers, he might have been old enough to shave, but I wouldn't have bet money on it.

About ten minutes later, he returned and pointed to a nearby door. "Come through there and follow me." I trailed after him down a number of gray, dimly lit corridors and past a warren of tiny cubicles that all too vividly reminded me of places I'd worked. It made me wish I'd dropped crumbs so I could find my way out again.

Tweedledumber stopped abruptly and pointed to an office door. "He's in there." With that, he ducked around the corner, looking as though he were afraid I would open the door before he could get away.

This was becoming stranger and stranger. I tapped on the door. It was my first visit to a police station, and it wasn't anything like the ones I'd seen on television.

"Come in." The voice definitely sounded unfriendly. I squared my shoulders, took a deep breath, and pushed open the door.

Detective Spangler stared down at a desk piled high with papers. When he looked up, he seemed surprised to see me, even though Tweedledumber had told him I was there to see him. The scowl on his face was enough to show me I wasn't welcome and made me want to escape. He looked exhausted. His dark hair, graying at the temples, stood in spikes from his head as though he had been running his fingers through it. From the rumpled condition of his clothes and the empty food wrappers and coffee cups around him, I judged he hadn't been home for a while.

I noticed again his dark eyes, which were surrounded by thick lashes any woman would envy. I remembered his eyes from our first meeting. They were mesmerizing, and I could imagine him compelling suspects into confessing simply by staring at them. For half a second, I almost found him appealing. Or I was feeling sorry for him, looking so worn out.

"Ms. Bishop." He nodded to a chair in front of his desk.

I picked up the folders stacked in the seat and looked around for a place to put them. His office looked like a tornado had struck. The bulletin board behind him was plastered with layers of papers, some of them yellowing and curling on the edges as though they had been there for years. It was a wonder he could find anything on it. A cloudy film covered the lone window in the room, making the sunny day outside appear overcast. I eyed the window with distaste. It obviously hadn't been cleaned since smoking in government offices had been banned years ago.

"Here, let me have those." He took the folders from me and dropped them onto the floor next to him. "The caseload keeps mounting, and the paperwork never seems to get done. We're moving to digital records, which you would think would reduce the paper, but it doesn't."

I studied him, wondering how I should start. He didn't seem to be in the mood to meet with anyone this morning.

"Should I come back another time?" I hoped he would agree. When he'd questioned me after Victoria's death, I was glad he stopped when he did. If he had gone on much longer, I would have gladly confessed to anything so I could get some sleep. Thinking more clearly later, I was relieved I hadn't ended up as his number one suspect. Unfortunately, he had cast Tyrone for that role.

"Another time won't be any better," he said before I could make my escape. "This better be important. I don't have time for chitchat."

I gritted my teeth. I wanted to throw the nearby stapler at him but restrained myself for Tyrone's sake. "I want to talk to you about Tyrone Webster." I paused, trying to come up with the right words. "You've got the wrong person."

"What makes you think that?" He slapped the flat side of a letter opener on the palm of his hand at a slow cadence. I could well imagine him playing a terrorist in a movie. He would have been perfect for the role. "And what do you base your assessment on? Your long history of doing police work?"

His condescending manner and sarcasm irritated me. "I've known Tyrone most of his life, and he wouldn't harm anyone. Besides, he didn't have a reason to kill Victoria."

"That's not what we heard." He put down the letter opener and picked up a rubber ball and began squeezing it. Did he do these things routinely to intimidate people? If so, it was working.

"Tyrone was...was upset following the scene about the vase." I realized I was sputtering. "But it wouldn't have been enough for him to want to see her dead."

"He was heard threatening her when she said she would prevent his getting a scholarship."

"That didn't mean he would kill her to stop her interfering with it." This wasn't going well. "There were others on the committee, so he still could have gotten the scholarship. Even if he didn't, Tyrone could survive without it. It would take him longer to get through school only paying for a few classes at a time, but he would be okay."

"There was no evidence of forced entry into the house, and Tyrone had a key. He was also seen running away from the house about the time of the murder. You said yourself you had locked all the doors earlier. Given his history of getting into fights—"

"Tyrone is not violent." I jumped out of my chair. "When the fight occurred at the coffee shop, and it was only one fight, he was trying to calm down a drunken college student."

"Please sit down, Ms. Bishop."

I sank back in my chair, embarrassed at my outburst.

"Tyrone is a friend of yours, so it's natural you'd want to defend him. Besides, we have plenty of reasons to suspect him and nothing pointing to anyone else. Most people arrested for a crime have people in their lives who will say good things about them. Which isn't enough to get them off the hook."

He stood, towering over me, and walked toward the door, effectively ending the discussion. "It's wishful thinking on your part that Tyrone is innocent, but you have to accept we have reason to charge him."

I waited a beat, trying to think of another approach. "Can I visit him?"

"I'm sorry. Only family and his attorney at this time." He leaned over to open the door. He didn't look sorry.

"You've got the wrong man." Those words had been spoken about many a wrongly accused person.

I stood next to the office door Detective Spangler firmly closed behind me. His comment about Tyrone and keys to the house bothered me. Skip Denton might have a key—if Victoria hadn't changed the locks after they separated. Who else could have a key? And had used it?

Chapter 8

Few buyers are looking for a place that reminds them of their grandmother's house. A dated house will look more up to date simply by adding new lighting fixtures and hardware.

The next morning, I attended church and then took a longer route than usual home so I could spend a few minutes in Veterans Park. It was a beautiful sunny morning, and the park's peaceful atmosphere was what I needed. During the night, worries about Tyrone had woken me several times and left me depressed and sleepy. The fragrance from the blossoming lilac bushes in the park had been as effective as an aromatherapy treatment in helping to perk up my spirits.

Visits to the park always brought back memories of the times I'd spent there with my father. A veteran of the Marine Corps, he used to point out the statues and memorials to different veterans groups. A sharp feeling of loss came over me thinking of him. I shook it off and tucked the memories of our times in the park away for another day.

When I reached home, I entered through the back door. Before I could put down my purse, I heard a light knock on the front door, followed by one that was definitely louder. Opening the door, I was surprised to discover Mrs. Mariah Webster, Tyrone's grandmother, standing on the porch, her black vinyl purse clutched firmly against her breast as though anticipating muggers.

Mrs. Webster, who stood about five feet tall and weighed next to nothing, could easily be knocked over in a heavy wind. However, her small stature belied her true nature—a woman of strong character and determination, who had raised Tyrone from the time he was five and molded him into the fine and well-liked young man I'd known for years. When Mrs. Webster chose to smile, which, with her serious manner, wasn't often, you could see where Tyrone got his good nature and good looks. They had the same high cheekbones and beautiful eyes.

Standing there now, Mrs. Webster looked shrunken and tired, and, for the first time since I'd known her, discouraged. Her yellow suit hung on her, and her usually rich, dark mahogany skin looked pale, even next to the bright yellow of her matching large-brimmed hat.

"Mrs. Webster, come in." I opened the storm door for her and led her to a chair, afraid if she didn't sit down, she might collapse on the spot.

"I'm sorry to come without first calling." She spoke softly as though it were an effort to speak. "I came straight from church."

After getting the news about Tyrone, I'd called Mrs. Webster to see if she needed anything. At the time, her sister had been visiting for a few days, so I knew she would be in good hands. But now she was on her own again.

"I'm so sorry about Tyrone. Is he okay at the jail? I heard Ted Wojdakowski got you in to see him yesterday. Since I'm not family, they won't let me in."

"You know Tyrone. He makes the best of everything."

I knew Mrs. Webster was trying to do the same. "I can't believe this is happening." I wanted to comfort her but didn't know how. "Ted is doing everything he can, but right now, he doesn't have much to go on to help clear Tyrone."

"At times like this, it's only the Lord you can truly rely on to help you," Mrs. Webster closed her eyes as if meditating. "But, in His wisdom, He sends us helpers to overcome our difficulties."

Please don't let her say I'm that helper!

"I prayed for my Tyrone, and then I thought of you."

Yikes, she believes I'm that helper. "To do what?" Was Mrs. Webster going to ask me to guarantee Tyrone's bail bond, which, sadly, I wasn't in a position to do?

"Why, to find out who murdered Victoria Denton. You're the only one I can turn to. The police think Tyrone did it, so they won't be searching for anyone else. I don't have the money for a private detective, nor would I trust one even if I could afford it, but I trust you. I'll never forget how you helped Tyrone when that other youngster created a ruckus at the coffee bar."

I hoped panic wasn't showing on my face. Nita always said my facial expressions exposed my feelings. When we were kids, it often got us into trouble.

"All I did was serve as a character witness for him. That's a far cry from trying to find a murderer."

"But you came through for him. Tyrone needs a fighter like you at his side."

"Believe me, Mrs. Webster, I wouldn't know the first thing about how to go about it." I ran my fingers through my hair and paced the room, trying to come up with a response. "Listen, I was a computer specialist and am now a home stager. Nothing in either of those jobs has given me the skills to seek out a murderer."

"You believe Tyrone is innocent, don't you?" Mrs. Webster demanded.

"Absolutely, and if I had a clue how to find out who actually did it, I would help in any way I could." I didn't want to disappoint Tyrone's grandmother, who, for some misguided reason, had such faith in me. I knew my skills, and investigating murder wasn't among them. I'd spent my career trying to find bugs in computer programs, and that had been as close as I'd come to solving a mystery. I also wouldn't do Mrs. Webster the disservice of promising to help and then being able to do little or nothing.

"Please, Laura." Mrs. Webster took my smooth hand into one that had known hard work. "For Tyrone's sake, and mine, please promise me you'll find Victoria's killer. I know you're the one to clear Tyrone's name. The Lord will give you the guidance you need."

Looking into her beseeching face, I remembered Mrs. Webster's comfort and support when she had nursed my mother during her long and final illness. How could she have such faith in me? Feeling myself weakening, and, against my better judgment, I slowly nodded. "But what happens if He doesn't give me enough?"

Chapter 9

*To inexpensively fill empty walls and make a room feel finished,
frame and hang attractive pictures from calendars and
magazines or your children's school artwork.*

"Got time for a mystery?"

I stood in the doorway of a classroom at Holy Spirit School and smiled at the small, gray-haired nun sitting at a large oak desk, nearly hidden by stacks of papers. It was after school hours, but I knew I would find Sister Madeleine still there, preparing for the next day's lessons. On impulse, I decided to talk to her about my promise to Mrs. Webster. It might be unusual to consult a nun about murder, but Sister Madeleine wasn't your typical nun.

Sister Madeleine had been a very young nun when she taught me, and she always had a special fondness for the young girl whose mother had been less than attentive. She had been the one who promoted the friendship between Nita and me, hoping the large and loving Romano family would take me into their hearts. Over the years, Sister Madeleine and I developed a longtime friendship, partly fed by our mutual love of mystery novels.

As a youngster, I'd been shocked to discover Sister Madeleine enjoyed mysteries. A nun reading about murder!

"Do you think we only read religious works?" Sister Madeleine had asked me. "That would leave us awfully lacking in entertainment. What might be shocking is a nun who writes murder mysteries. Maybe I will try my hand at that someday." Over the years, Sister Madeleine had passed along mysteries to me, and I'd become an avid reader.

Now, hearing my question, Sister Madeleine looked up from her desk, a wide smile at the sight of me. "I always have time for a mystery."

I sat down in a miniature desk chair, which was far too small for my tall frame to fit comfortably. "I have to find a murderer."

Sister Madeleine smiled. "Any murderer in particular?"

"The one who killed Victoria Denton."

"Ah. I read about her death in the paper. Tragic affair." She straightened a stack of folders on her desk, took off her wire-framed glasses, and rubbed the bridge of her nose. "And why are you taking on this task? Are the police not investigating it?"

I explained Tyrone's situation and his grandmother's plea for help. "For some reason, Mrs. Webster has faith in my ability to help Tyrone. I promised her I'd do whatever I could, but I don't know where to start. Not that I expect you would…"

"Would what? Know how to expose a murderer? I'm not sure I'd know either. Look, Laura, it's admirable you want to help Tyrone, but getting involved could be risky—and stupid." Sister Madeleine was never one to mince words.

She scrutinized me with an intensity that never failed to intimidate her students. "I also have the feeling I would be wasting my breath trying to talk you out of it."

I sighed and nodded. "You're right, but I have to do something, no matter how little."

Sister Madeleine picked up a stack of folders. "Sorry to cut this short, but I have a meeting with a parent I cannot miss. Walk with me and we'll discuss it on the way."

I followed her down a corridor lined with student drawings.

The building looked very much as it had when I attended school there and still smelled of crayons.

"It may not help, but you could start by asking yourself what Father Brown would do."

I quickened my pace to keep up with the older nun. "Father Brown? I don't remember him. Was he at this parish?"

"No." Sister Madeleine smiled. "Father Brown of the mystery series by G. K. Chesterton."

"*That* Father Brown. It's been a long time since I read that series."

"Great books, even if a bit dated now. Father Brown had a keen understanding of human nature. He was like a clerical Miss Marple and solved crimes by following his intuition. So, for a start, trust your intuition." Sister Madeleine paused at the door leading to the school library. "He also recognized people sometimes become boxed in and kill out of sheer desperation. Look for the person around Victoria Denton who became desperate."

Chapter 10

Remove all evidence of pets. Some buyers won't consider a home with pets. To ensure the comfort and safety of your pet, find a place for Fifi to stay on the day of open house.

The next day seemed unusually warm for spring, and greenery was beginning to pop out all over. As I drove down Battlement Drive, the beauty of the flowering dogwoods and blossoming cherry trees along the road washed over me, easing the tension that had started wearing me down. Their bright blossoms and other signs of spring renewal reminded me there's always hope.

I needed a jolt of hope since my promise to Mrs. Webster weighed on my mind. Awakening before dawn, I'd tried to think of ways I could find Victoria's killer. None of the mystery books I enjoyed for entertainment had prepared me for this.

Find the person who had become desperate. Thinking of Sister Madeleine's advice about Father Brown, I wished now I'd paid more attention to the protagonists' techniques in books by my favorite authors. What would Anne Perry's Hester Latterly do in this situation?

As I approached the turnoff for Lookout Hill, I noticed an older man picking up litter along the roadside. I recognized him as the man I occasionally saw when I drove to the Denton house. It would have been hard to forget him with his low-slung jeans, beat-up cowboy hat, and green plaid jacket that reminded me of the upholstery on my grandfather's Barcalounger. With his weathered face and western-style clothing, he looked like he would have been more at home in Texas than in a small town on the East Coast.

On a whim, I pulled over, turned off the engine, and stepped out onto the gravel shoulder. Might as well get started. I wasn't quite sure what I hoped to accomplish, but I had to start somewhere with my *investigation.* At this point, any information I could gather from anyone remotely near the Denton house might help. Also, this way I could honestly report to Mrs. Webster I'd started making inquiries. Though, knowing Mrs. Webster, I was certain she would expect detailed reports.

"Hello, there." I tiptoed gingerly toward the man, not wanting to slip on the gravel. "Do you have a minute to talk?"

The man stopped what he was doing and watched me approach. He patted the dog beside him, and the dog sat obediently at his feet. I eyed the Brittany Spaniel and wondered whether it was safe to approach. He might smell Inky and jump at me. My childhood experience of being chased by a Boxer had left me wary of all dogs. Fortunately, this dog looked more interested in taking a quick nap than in me.

"Well, sure, sweetheart, I'd be happy to talk with you." The old man had a bit of the Southwest in his voice. He took off his hat politely, revealing grizzled hair and a weathered face with deep lines that spoke of a lifetime working in harsh weather. The way he looked me up and down and the twinkle in his eyes let me know he approved of what he saw.

Oh, dear. I hoped he didn't think I was trying to pick him up. I cringed at the thought. "I'm Laura Bishop. I've been working up at the Denton house on Lookout Hill getting it ready for sale." I pointed to the hilltop.

"Read about the goings on up there." He replaced his dusty hat and extended a rough hand. "Will Parker. I live down the road a bit with my daughter and her pack of kids."

I shook his hand and then wished I hadn't. My fingers ached from his crushing grip.

He leaned down and stroked his dog. "This here is Pinto, named after a pinto horse I once owned, because of the pattern on his fur."

I refrained from petting the dog, even though he looked friendly, or as friendly as he could look, lying stretched out on the grass taking no notice of me. "I've seen you picking up litter on this road." I stretched my fingers behind my back to ease the pain. "That's civic-minded of you. Have you been doing it for long?"

"About a year. Somebody has to do it, or it'll turn into a right mess. Besides, it keeps me busy now I'm retired. My girl, Claire, insisted I come East to live with her, saying I was getting too old to care for myself. A lot she knows. I mainly come out here to get away from the grandkids and to walk Pinto. The kids are too rambunctious, if you know what I mean." He winked at me. "This here stretch of road belongs to me."

"To you?" I was puzzled.

He pointed to the Adopt a Highway sign farther along the road inscribed with "Cowboy Will."

"That's me." His wide grin showed his pleasure. "I was on the rodeo circuit before I came here." At my lack of recognition, he shrugged. "Anyway, this here's my road. I come along most days and gather up whatever trash has landed. Mostly it's plastic bags or newspapers, but I'll occasionally find a few beer cans the Harper boys toss out so as their folks won't find them. If it gets to being more than a few, I'll have a word with them."

"Since you're on this road most days, you must see what's going on around here."

"There's not much I don't see. I've watched you driving through here plenty of times, sometimes alone, sometimes with that kid."

"Did you come along this road last Monday?"

"You mean the day the Denton woman was killed?" When I nodded, he paused, removed his hat, and scratched his head as though searching his memory. "I walked my route that day, but I don't recall seeing anything out of the ordinary, maybe excepting those panel trucks parked up there."

"That would've been the men working on the house. Did you see any cars you don't usually see coming through this area?"

Will shook his head. "Right now, I don't recall any. We don't get much traffic up here. Mostly the local folks and a few motorcycles cutting through to the highway." He looked as though he was about to say more but then changed his mind.

I rummaged in my tote bag for one of my business cards and handed it to him. "Listen, if you think of anything else, would you please call me? It's important."

"Sure, sweetheart." He took the card, put it in the pocket of his plaid jacket, and then patted it. Grinning, he reached down and picked up the Yuengling beer bottle lying near our feet. "I'll definitely call you."

I got back in my car and locked the door, my intuition telling me that giving him my number might have been a big mistake.

Chapter 11

Before an open house, bake something with cinnamon or another fragrant spice. The smell of baking will make your home feel cozy and inviting.

When I arrived at the Denton house, I opened the door and peered inside, reluctant to enter. I didn't know what to expect, but it wasn't the bright area before me. Thanks to Nita's suggestion, the mirrors had transformed the foyer into a welcoming space and would now make a good first impression on buyers. Also, seeing their reflection in the mirror would help them visualize the house as their home.

I lifted my shoulders to steel myself for what I might find, walked in, and carefully locked the door behind me. Knowing the police and Skip had gone over the place from top to bottom helped me relax a bit. As I walked from room to room, I was relieved to find it in fairly good condition after the police crime scene investigation—I'd expected far worse. Black fingerprinting dust around the front door had been the first sign of things out of the ordinary. The police had dusted around the door handles and frames and on other surfaces throughout the house. I was thankful the dust they had liberally applied hadn't been on the freshly painted walls.

Skip had pulled down the yellow crime scene tape earlier. Paper coffee cups and bags from Hibbard's Bakery littered the kitchen table and counters, and furniture had been moved. For the most part, the place was pretty much as I'd left it. I didn't know what condition the basement might be in, and I didn't plan to find out. The memory of Victoria lying on the cold concrete floor still made me shake.

Continuing to walk through the house, I entered the living room. The paint job Nita's brother Angelo and his crew had completed there almost transformed the home. The white wainscoting gave the living room and the dining room a fresh look that would work with both traditional and modern furniture. But even with that, there was still so much to do.

I got to work cleaning off the black fingerprinting dust throughout the house and found it came off with soap and water and a little pressure. I was relieved I wouldn't have to ask Angelo to repaint areas he had already painted. He had enough to do.

As I worked, thoughts about the sale of the house filled my mind. Would having a murder committed in a house be something an owner must disclose to potential buyers? Or, for that matter, would Skip even be able to sell the house? It was turning out to be such a terrific place, and I couldn't bear the thought of someone not having it to enjoy. Being the site of a murder would definitely turn off a lot of buyers. Whoever bought it would need to relocate the washer and dryer upstairs to avoid the basement. I couldn't imagine doing laundry down there now.

I pulled my clipboard and work plan out of my tote bag. I needed to go through the house to determine where we were with the staging. It was then I realized there was no longer a *we* on the project. Now there was only *me* and whomever I could hire to help me. I really missed Tyrone.

If I were going to succeed in this business, I would run into all kinds of problems in the future and would need to develop some contingency plans, like finding back-up help. I couldn't succeed as a one-woman show, at least not with big jobs like this one. Tyrone had helped with a lot of the heavier work, but if I got another commission soon, I would need to have someone fill in until Tyrone was free. Tyrone had a good eye for design, and I missed his contribution to the project and his company. It also helped that he was someone I could rely on.

The thought of Tyrone and my promise to Mrs. Webster depressed me. Taking a break from my work, I sat with my pen poised over a pad of paper, ready to write down ideas for solving the crime. After several minutes, the paper remained blank.

The door chimes sounded, and when I answered it, Nita was standing there holding a paper bag and a cup carrier. My relief at seeing her was so great I reached out and hugged her. Being in the house alone had proved to be as eerie as I'd expected.

"Wow. I haven't received a greeting like that in a while. I guess I was right in thinking you might be feeling a little uneasy being here again, so I've brought lunch." Nita held up the bag and walked inside. "And Vocaro's coffee, although it isn't as good as when Tyrone makes it. Everyone there misses him, especially Luigi. I also thought I'd take photos of your work in progress while I'm here."

"Nita, you're a jewel." I exhaled in relief. "I've been sitting here trying to figure out how I'm going to find Victoria's killer, and I'm dying for a cup of coffee." No sooner had the words left my mouth than I realized what I'd said and to whom.

"You're going to do what?" Nita stared at me as though I'd morphed into another being.

"Find Victoria's killer," I mumbled, knowing that letting Nita in on this would be like opening Pandora's box, only worse. She couldn't keep a secret, no matter how hard she tried. She was like an open book, and what she knew, everybody knew.

"Are you joking? For a start, if the police can't find the guilty person, and we know it isn't Tyrone, how will you be able to?"

"That's the problem. I don't know. I promised Mrs. Webster I would, or at least try. I also need to find the killer before the Quincy Scholarship Committee members make their selection. Tyrone applied for it, but they definitely won't select him if he's still in jail, and they'll be making the decision in the next few weeks. Do you think the library carries a book on how to solve murders?"

"Try the internet. You can find anything there." Nita removed the lid from her coffee cup and spread out the Greek salads and chocolate brownies she'd brought for lunch. Her surprise at my announcement hadn't diminished her appetite.

I sipped my coffee and let out a sigh of contentment. "I needed this." As I reached for the salad Nita brought, I realized how hungry I was.

"Don't put me off." Nita munched on her salad. "If you're really serious, how do you expect to solve this crime?"

At least she hadn't laughed at me. What a friend. "Well," I paused, knowing I was going to sound totally inept. "In mystery novels, the protagonist usually starts by questioning all the people who had any dealings with the victim. So, today I conducted my first interview." I relayed my conversation with Will Parker.

Nita paused with her fork in the air and studied me as though I was that other being again. "Listen, Laura, this isn't Nancy Drew and her pals. With Tyrone in jail, the real killer is out there and doesn't want to be found. This whole thing could endanger you."

"That's what Sister Madeleine said."

Nita's mouth fell open and she gave me a pained look. "You talked to Sister Madeleine, and this is the first time you've mentioned it to me."

"I know. I went in to see her for a chat, and maybe a little guidance. I honestly didn't think I would be able to discover much, so it wasn't worth mentioning to you. I thought if I asked enough questions, I could shake up Victoria's killer enough to make him reveal himself, hopefully to the police and not to me.

"Or herself. This is an equal opportunity crime. Besides, what kind of questions are you going to ask? 'On Wednesday night, did you by any chance bonk Victoria Denton on the head and shove her into a laundry chute?'"

"I didn't think about it being a woman." I closed up my salad container and eyed the brownies. "See what an amateur I am at this. If it were a woman, she would've needed to be awfully strong to pick up Victoria and push her into the laundry chute."

"That's your first clue: must be strong enough to lift body and shove into chute."

"At least we now have one clue. I'm going to need a bunch more to help Tyrone." I bit into a brownie and savored its rich flavor and chewy texture, particularly enjoying the large chunks of walnuts. The brownie tasted so luscious I wasn't surprised the early church fathers, thinking anything so good had to be sinful, had banned chocolate. It would be impossible for women today to survive without chocolate. I certainly couldn't.

Nita and I sat quietly sipping the remains of our coffee. When we finished, Nita deposited the empty containers in the trash can. "Before I head back to work, can you give me the grand tour so I can take some photos?"

As we went through the house, Nita took more shots than I would ever need, but she was enjoying herself so much I didn't have the heart to say anything. When we walked onto the patio, I noticed the decorative coasters I'd placed on a table earlier were no longer there. I looked down to see if they had been knocked off the table, but there was no sign of them. I shrugged and wondered if I'd taken them inside the house.

When we returned to the kitchen, Nita rubbed her arms and shuddered. "This place feels like Victoria's spirit hasn't left yet. It's giving me the creeps."

"I know what you mean. It was uncomfortable coming back here."

Nita stood at the front door, staring back into the house. "Hmm. I may have just the solution for this problem. Let me think about it."

I held up a warning hand. "Nita, I already have enough to deal with." I remembered all too well how Nita's adventurous spirit had gotten us into trouble in the past. I had been Ethel to her Lucy.

"Trust me." She dashed toward her VW parked in the front driveway, got in, and rolled down her window. "Have I ever led you astray?"

"All too many times."

Going back into the house, I closed and locked the front door. Our discussion about the laundry chute prompted me to check it out. Someone had shoved Victoria into it. How difficult would that have been to do? She had been tiny, weighing no more than a hundred pounds, the equivalent of twenty five-pound bags of sugar. Thinking of it that way, I realized it would have taken someone with strength to hoist Victoria into the chute.

That is, if one person had done it, something I hadn't thought of before. What if more than one person had been involved?

Bolstering my courage, I pulled open the door to the chute, carefully leaned over the opening, and forced myself to peer into it. It was dark below, so I was unable to see the basement floor where Victoria had landed. Then it hit me. *I* had been in the house with Victoria's killer. My knees began to feel wobbly. Being so focused on Victoria's death and Tyrone's arrest, I hadn't given much thought to the killer. Could the killer suspect I might have seen him, her, or even them?

My stomach growled. Looking at my watch, I realized it was well after five. No wonder I was hungry. It had been a while since my early lunch with Nita. I started to gather my things to leave when I heard the door chimes sound for the second time that day. Opening the door, I found Nita there again, this time standing next to a small, wizened woman with masses of wild gray curls poking out from a kerchief tied at the back of her neck in an Eastern European fashion. The woman held an old-fashioned broom in her right hand.

"Hey, Laura, this is Madam Zolta. She's going to rid the house of Victoria's spirit and sweep out the negativity." Nita stood there looking quite smug.

A nervous tremor coursed through me. Madam Zolta was a local psychic who had opened her practice years ago and had become an institution in Louiston. From the time I'd been a little girl and had occasion to be near Madam Zolta's small house with its large, orange neon hand above the door, I raced past it, afraid she would come out and snatch me. When I'd been naughty, my mother threatened to have Madam Zolta come get me if I didn't behave. Madam Zolta wasn't one of my favorite people.

Before I could react, Madam Zolta brushed past me in the doorway and headed inside. "Don't you worry, darling. I'll have Victoria's spirit out of here in no time." Hearing her husky voice and thick accent, which could place her origins anywhere from Hungary to Brooklyn, I could almost believe a relative of Zsa Zsa Gabor had just swept in.

"Nita, are you crazy?" I whispered as Madam Zolta walked through the foyer and into the living room. "There are no spirits here, and if there were, I doubt this stuff would work. Besides, what would Sister Madeleine say if she knew we were involved with something like this?"

"We won't tell her," Nita whispered back.

I threw up my hands in exasperation. It wasn't the first time Nita had pulled me into one of her harebrained schemes, and when she did, we both usually ended up in hot water.

Nita followed Madam Zolta into the living room, with me trailing behind her. "Don't you remember the problems Angelo and

Rosie had in the first house they bought? They could never get the kids to sleep there until Madam Zolta swept away the lingering spirits. She's the real thing."

I was far from convinced. "Just how much is this *real thing* going to cost us?"

Madam Zolta popped up behind us. "I never charge anyone for sweeping out negativity. It's something essential I do. Kinda like what you would call a public service."

"See, how can you distrust a person who isn't even going to charge you?" Nita asked.

Anxious to get home, I watched Madam Zolta survey the place and wondered how long this was going to take. "What is she going to do?"

Nita pointed to the broom Madam Zolta had begun swinging from side to side. "That's her besom. She'll use that to sweep the house, pushing out any lingering spirits and all negativity."

"According to tradition, we should be doing this on the night of a full moon," Madam Zolta muttered. "The moon is still waning, so it should work. If not, I'll come back and burn a little sage. That'll do it."

I tried not to roll my eyes, especially after telling Tyrone not to, and wished I were home taking a hot, relaxing bath. Nita was going to drive me to drink, and all I owned was a bottle of Harvey's Bristol Cream Sherry.

"I'm going to start at the back of the house and, going widdershins, I'll sweep each room, moving toward the front door."

"Widdershins?" I asked.

"Widdershins. It means counterclockwise." Madam Zolta demonstrated by making small circles with the besom. "While I'm sweeping, we should all envision the negativity being swept away."

I studied the besom in Madam Zolta's hand. It was beautifully crafted with a slightly bent and highly polished handle and natural bristles. Definitely not a prop she'd picked up at Walmart. As

Madam Zolta swung the besom from side to side, a leather thong at the top of the handle flapped. Always the decorator, I envisioned it hanging decoratively on the kitchen wall and thought of the perfect spot for it.

"Are you envisioning the negativity being swept away?" Madam Zolta demanded, like a teacher pulling her young students' attention back to the lesson. "We all must focus."

Was she reading my mind? I pulled Nita into the hall and whispered, "This is plain silly. Victoria's spirit is not here and—"

"Do you really feel comfortable here?" Nita asked.

I shook my head, having to admit being back in the house following Victoria's death was unnerving. But I didn't think this hocus-pocus was going to help me deal with that. It would take a burly security guard standing at the front door to make me feel comfortable there again.

"Unless you have a better idea, it's worth giving the old methods a try. Grandma Filomena told me the people in Sicily used to put a broom outside their door on Midsummer's Eve to ward off any wickedness that might come knocking."

"Out! Out! Out!" Madam Zolta boomed, her voice filling the room. "Victoria, you must leave! Out! Out! Out!"

When I jumped, Madam Zolta explained more softly, "You must be forceful. Otherwise, she can sense your uncertainty and won't leave. From my dealings with Victoria Denton, gentle prodding isn't going to budge her."

Madam Zolta swept the room. "Come on, dears. Swing your arms to churn up the air and shout, Out! Out! Out! We need to put some force into this."

Nita followed Madam Zolta into the hall. I was tempted to plop into one of the comfortable living room chairs and wait for them, but I didn't want to embarrass or disappoint Nita, who was only trying to help. I followed behind them, feeling very stupid, and tried to get into the spirit of things. I grimaced at the thought. At the same time, I berated myself for being so easily led into things. If I weren't such a people pleaser, I wouldn't be chasing out spirits. I also wouldn't have given into Mrs. Webster's plea for help and now be faced with investigating Victoria's murder.

When Nita and Madam Zolta went down into the basement, I was a coward and stayed in the kitchen. I didn't believe in ghosts or spirits, but with the image of Victoria lying on the floor still fresh in my memory, nothing would compel me to go down there. I also would rather avoid any creepy crawlers we might come into contact with.

When Madam Zolta finished all the rooms and stood near the front door, she paused and let out a loud sigh that sounded as though all the breath and energy had been expelled from her body, and then she slumped. "Victoria's spirit is gone."

"That's a relief." Nita looked at me with a satisfied expression.

Madam Zolta, however, didn't appear happy and stood there frowning. "Something doesn't feel right." She paced up and down the hall, looking bewildered.

"I'm sensing evil lurking here or close by. A male figure, living, not spirit." Abruptly, she thrust the besom at me. "Keep this by the door. I don't usually give these away, but you'll need it to help protect this house from unwanted outside energies."

Oh, great, a broom to protect me. Was that the gimmick? We didn't pay for the sweeping, but the besom cost a fortune? What next, a string of garlic to hang around my neck?

Again, as though reading my thoughts, Madam Zolta said, "No, darling, it's free. From what I'm sensing, you're going to need it. I'm really supposed to burn the besom after a ceremony like this, but since they are so expensive, and in these tough times, I simply give them a quick wash to cleanse them. Where's your bucket?"

"I'll look," Nita offered, quickly going in search of a bucket.

When they finished with the besom cleansing, Madam Zolta looked around one last time. "It might be better if we burned some sage, but I didn't bring any with me. Nita, if you'll bring me back—"

"That's okay. I can manage to burn sage. Thank you anyway." I was anxious to get them out of the house so I could go home. I courteously thanked Madam Zolta for her efforts and waved goodbye as Nita drove them away in her VW bug.

Sweeping away negativity. What next? If this worked, I might consider having Madam Zolta sweep through my house. Despite my efforts to fill my home only with items that made me happy, I often sensed my mother's disgruntled spirit there.

Before closing and locking the front door behind me, I walked around the front foyer and down the hall to the other rooms, wondering about the evil Madam Zolta warned still lurked nearby. What nonsense. But, as I turned to leave, I took a final peek to ensure the besom by the door was in place. No sense taking any chances.

Chapter 12

Clear out excess items from kitchen cupboards and neatly rearrange what remains to make the cupboards look spacious. Slowly deplete pantry supplies to show more space. Crowded cupboards give buyers the impressions your kitchen has limited storage.

When the home phone rang early the next morning, I stared at the display screen, not seeing a number displayed. A lot of good caller ID was when a call displayed Private Name, Private Number. I didn't like answering calls if I couldn't determine who was calling and usually let them go to voicemail, but now that I was in business, it could be a potential customer. It could also be something related to Tyrone, so I answered.

"Hello. Staging for You. How can I help you?"

"Is this Ms. Bishop?" It was a young female with a hesitant voice.

"Yes."

"I have some important information about Tyrone Webster. About where he was the night, uh, Victoria Denton was murdered."

My hopes rose, but I tried to keep them in check. "Who is this?"

"I'm sorry. I don't want to say anything over the phone. Can you meet me so we can talk about it?"

I frowned, my suspicions mounting. "Meet? Can you tell me what this is all about?"

"No. Just please come meet me. It's important." The voice was becoming anxious. "I'll explain everything then."

My first instinct was to say no, but this was about Tyrone. In an instant, I decided to meet the young women, but with caution. "All right. I'll meet you, but at the place I select."

"Terrific."

"I'll meet you inside the entrance of Turner's Grocery at noon. Can you meet then?"

"Absolutely."

I could almost hear the relief in the young woman's voice. "How will I know you?" I asked.

"Don't worry, I'll find you." With that, the young woman hung up.

I didn't feel comfortable with the meeting, but there would be lots of people around, and if the meeting came to nothing, at least I could find something for dinner and stock up on pantry supplies, especially cat food for Inky. He wouldn't eat just anything. While I'd been focusing on my work at the Denton house and my investigation, the cupboard had become bare. M. C. Beaton's Agatha Raisin frequently had this problem and lived mostly on microwave dinners. I didn't want to reach that point.

I arrived at the store early so I could reconnoiter before the meeting time. Once inside, I strode up and down the store aisles, looking for anyone who appeared suspicious. When I was satisfied the elderly couple picking through the display of frozen vegetables and the teenaged boy studying the selection of acne medication weren't a threat to me, I positioned myself near the entrance of the store. Each time the doors swung open, I looked up hopeful it was the young woman I was to meet. I was anxious to hear what she had to say about Tyrone and hoped it would be something that would help him and not make things worse.

When the time for our meeting came and went, I found myself tapping my foot in annoyance, wondering if someone was playing a practical joke on me. I hoped it wasn't a ploy by someone who was now emptying my house of all my possessions. If the young woman truly had something to tell me about Tyrone, why hadn't she shown up? Thinking my long wait might be viewed as suspicious, I picked up a can of Campbell's soup on display and pretended to read the label.

"Ms. Bishop?"

I looked up. A young woman stood next to me, a timid expression on her face as though she wasn't sure she should approach me.

"Yes?" I didn't recognize her, although she seemed familiar.

"I'm Kayla, Tyrone's girlfriend. I'm the one who called you."

My relief at having the girl arrive at last was palpable. If she had information about Tyrone, I was anxious to talk to her.

"Kayla. Of course. I've been in such a daze, I didn't recognize you." I hoped my excuse for not recognizing her sounded believable. Tyrone had dated a number of young women, and I'd stopped trying to keep them straight. Recently, though, he had been talking about Kayla more than any of the other young women who came into Vocaro's, more to see Tyrone than for coffee. Tyrone, with his handsome looks and friendly banter, was certainly good for business, if the steady stream of coeds from nearby Fischer College was any indication.

"I was wondering if you've heard how Tyrone is doing. I went down to the jail to see him, but they wouldn't let me in."

Was that the reason for all this secrecy? To find out how Tyrone was doing? I hoped disappointment didn't show on my face.

"I thought of going to see his grandmother, but I didn't want to bother her."

If I were a young woman interested in Tyrone, I wouldn't have the courage to approach Mariah Webster either. She was very protective of Tyrone and suspicious of any young woman who could interfere with his education.

"I haven't been able to get in to see him either, but I'm working on it." I stood with my arms crossed and waited for Kayla to continue.

"I'm sorry for asking you to meet like this. My mom would hassle me if she knew I was inquiring about Tyrone. She told me to stay away from him, that he's a killer. I know he didn't kill Mrs. Denton." Her eyes filled up with tears. "Tyrone is so gentle..."

I put my hand on Kayla's arm to comfort her. "I'm glad you believe in Tyrone. He needs loyal friends."

"It's more than that. He couldn't have done it because, well...he was with me." She raised her head defiantly.

My hopes rose again. This was what Tyrone needed. An alibi for the evening Victoria was murdered. That would mean Tyrone would be freed, and, best of all, I wouldn't have to continue investigating the murder.

"Have you reported this to the police? You should tell Detective Spangler."

"Ah, no. I was kinda hoping you'd tell him for me."

"Me?" I shouldn't have been surprised the young girl didn't want to see Detective Spangler. I didn't want to see him again myself.

"You've always looked out for Tyrone, and he says nice things about you."

As I studied Kayla's face, I became suspicious. "Where were you with Tyrone that evening?"

"He was at my house. Yes, that's where he was."

"With your mother there?" I studied Kayla's startled look for a long moment and then asked her gently, "He wasn't there though, was he?

Kayla looked down and studied her Tory Burch ballet flats as though they were the most important things in the world. She eventually looked up again and sighed. "No, he wasn't. Since I know he couldn't have done it, what could it hurt if you told the police he was with me?"

"For a start, it would be a lie, and if you lied under oath, they could charge you for perjury. Then you'd both be in trouble. Tyrone wouldn't want you to go to jail trying to help him. Knowing you believe in him will help him more."

"I didn't think about that. I guess I shouldn't have suggested it, but I'm so worried about him." Kayla scrunched her shoulders like a turtle pulling its head into its protective shell. "Do you think he did it?" she whispered, as though seeking confirmation of what she believed.

"Absolutely not." I spoke with more force than I intended—to dispel any doubts Kayla might have. I gathered Kayla was having a hard time holding out against her mother's belief that Tyrone was guilty. I couldn't blame her for wanting to protect Kayla by keeping her away from an accused murderer.

"I knew you'd say that." Kayla looked relieved. "Do you think if I wrote him a letter, they'd give it to him? I tried texting him, but I get no response."

"They more than likely took his phone away. If you write, they may open it to make sure you haven't sent something he shouldn't get, so be careful what you say."

Kayla blushed. It made me so glad I wasn't her age anymore.

"I'll try again to see him somehow. When I do, I'll tell him you're anxious for him to be released."

"Would you?" A smile appeared on Kayla's face for the first time. "That'd be terrific."

I walked away disappointed Kayla's information had come to nothing, but pleased Tyrone's friends weren't deserting him. Now all I had to do was find a way to get into the jail.

Chapter 13

If you paint the walls, be careful with the colors you select. Colors can affect mood. Pick colors that are neutral and not taste specific. Blues and grays can make a room feel restful. Yellows and warm colors will make a room energizing.

I put my arm around Mrs. Webster's narrow shoulders and whispered, "Now, remember, lean heavily on me and act like your legs would buckle if I let go."

We were walking into the city jail so I could see Tyrone. Upon applying to visit him, I'd been told firmly again that only family or a legal representative could gain admittance. I decided they made up the rules based on the prisoner or visitor. Obviously, I didn't have much sway in the community.

Mrs. Webster had visited Tyrone before, and I hoped a different officer would be on the desk this time. I also hoped Detective Spangler wasn't around today.

As we approached the front desk, I nearly fell sideways as Mrs. Webster sagged in my arms and gave me her full weight. I could barely hold her up. She was being too good an actress.

"I'm here to visit my grandson, Tyrone Webster. This here's my niece." She gave the officer a firm look, daring him to challenge the relationship. As many an individual in Louiston had learned over the years, Mrs. Webster was a force to be reckoned with. Although Officer Nguyen looked startled seeing Mrs. Webster's mahogany complexion and my pale skin, he was wise enough to recognize that force.

I was surprised by the declaration. It hadn't been in our plan, and I barely managed to keep a straight face.

Mrs. Webster continued, "My niece was kind enough to bring me here. I can't manage to walk without her."

Grabbing his keys, Officer Nguyen quickly led us to the visitors' room and told us to wait there. He kept looking over his shoulder as he scurried away.

If we hadn't already been depressed about Tyrone's situation, the waiting area would have depressed us. It reflected the misery of the people coming there. The dismal green walls looked as though they had been painted with split pea soup and the furniture designed for torture. The designer in me imagined how much more cheerful yellow or any other color would be, both for the prisoners and for the families who came to visit them.

After a few minutes, Officer Nguyen escorted Tyrone into a small booth on the other side of a partition separating the two areas. Tyrone looked tired and uncomfortable in his orange prison uniform. His shoulders slumped so much as to make him look much shorter than usual. However, his broad smile showed how pleased he was to see us.

Anxiety about how I could help him built within me, and my stomach churned. I could only imagine how Mrs. Webster must be feeling.

"Hello, Gran. Hey, Laura. Thanks a lot for coming. You feeling okay, Gran?" Tyrone looked concerned.

"Don't worry about me, young man, I'm doing fine. We're here to see about you. You're looking a bit thin. Are they feeding you enough?"

I knew Mrs. Webster was hiding her feelings well. Food was a safe enough subject and a good icebreaker.

"Yes, ma'am, they are. Though, the cooking isn't anywhere near as good as yours."

Mrs. Webster sniffed. "I wouldn't think so. I'd bring you some of my peach cobbler, but they won't let me bring in anything."

"I sure would enjoy it. The cooks here could sure use some lessons from you."

Mrs. Webster removed the hat she was never without and placed it in her lap. "Let's focus on getting you out of here."

"Yes, ma'am." He turned to me. "How's the staging going? I'm sorry to let you down—"

"You haven't let me down. This is all a horrendous mistake, but we're doing everything we can to get you cleared and released. Just think of this as an opportunity to do research. If you ever need to design a theater set with a prison scene, you'll know how to make it appear authentic."

"Then you believe I didn't kill Victoria?" He looked at me anxiously.

"I never doubted you for a second. Kayla believes you're innocent as well."

"You talked to her?" Tyrone's smile lit up his face, and, for the first time, he looked cheerful.

I nodded.

Mrs. Webster's eyes narrowed. "Who's Kayla?"

"A friend from Vocaro's," I said quickly. "All Tyrone's friends are asking about him. Also, Warren's anxious for Tyrone to get back to work on the stage sets."

"That's good to know." Mrs. Webster seemed to be mollified.

"What I don't understand is what were you doing on Battlement Drive that evening?" I asked Tyrone. "I thought you'd gone home."

"I know. It was really stupid. After I left you, I got a ride home. I couldn't face Gran in a bad mood, so I decided to go for a run. I slipped into the house, changed clothes, and got out before she could notice me. As I ran, I started wondering if I talked to Mrs. Denton again, maybe I could make it good with her somehow. It was only when I got close to the house that I lost my nerve and turned back down Battlement Drive. Gran had already gone to bed when I got home."

"I learned a long time ago not to wait up for him. I wish now I had." Regret was obvious in Mrs. Webster's voice.

I reached over and took Mrs. Webster's hand to comfort her. "It wouldn't have changed anything. With someone seeing him near Victoria's house close to the time of the murder, and him admitting he was there, you hearing him come in later wouldn't have given him an alibi."

"Do you think Mr. Wojdakowski can get me out of here soon?" Tyrone rocked back and forth in his seat, giving away that he was more anxious than he let on.

"I wish I could promise—"

"Laura's going to find the murderer," Mrs. Webster declared. "I prayed on it."

"You are?" Tyrone gazed at me in surprise. "If anyone can do it, you can."

What faith those two had. I could understand their belief in heavenly guidance, but their confidence in me was humbling. I worried about disappointing them.

"Tyrone, I don't want you to get your hopes up. I promised your grandmother I would do what I could, but there's no guarantee I'll have any luck. I also have to figure out how to even go about this. I don't have any experience solving crimes."

My comments didn't seem to diminish Tyrone's confidence. "You helped me once before. I know you can do it again. How can I help?"

"Think, Tyrone. When you were nearing Victoria's house, did you see anyone coming or going. Did anything strike you as unusual for that area?"

Tyrone sat there quietly for a long moment as though searching his memory for anything unusual that evening. "I don't think so. An occasional car drove by, but nothing else. At the time, there was no reason for me to pay any attention. I wish I had."

"You couldn't have known. If the killer was someone unconnected to Victoria who got into the house searching for valuables, I don't know if the person could ever be found."

"Do you think it could have been a burglar?"

"While I was in the kitchen and then down in the basement, Victoria might have discovered an intruder and challenged him. But who would know what's missing? Victoria can't tell us, and if it was something Victoria obtained after Skip Denton moved out, he wouldn't know either."

"Visiting time is over," a crackling voice announced over a speaker.

As we said our goodbyes, I held back when Mrs. Webster walked away. The brave smile on Tyrone's face faded, replaced by a look of fear he'd hidden from his grandmother.

"Listen, Laura, do you think you'll be able to help me? I've got to get out of here—back to school before the scholarship panel makes its decision. You know how much I need that scholarship."

I studied his face and sighed inwardly. How like a young person to be focused on his education, while I was worried about him going to prison for life.

"I'm going to do everything I can, but you've got to realize I'm only an amateur."

"I appreciate anything you can do for me, but please be careful. I don't want you to put yourself in danger. Whoever the killer is could come after you if he feels threatened."

"I plan to stay out of danger." I shuddered and fervently hoped I could avoid it.

The thought I could have been the victim of the intruder

instead of Victoria shook me again. It made it harder to face going back to the house each day. I'd made a promise to Skip to complete the work, and I planned to keep it. My promises were dragging me deeper and deeper into trouble. This was my first job in a new business, and my future success depended on my completing it, danger or no danger. I also wanted the satisfaction of proving Doug Hamilton wrong.

Chapter 14

You only get one chance to make a good first impression. Brighten the outside of your home by power-washing sidewalks, driveways, decks, and patios. Also add plants to flowerbeds and dark mulch to provide a crisp, rich contrast.

I took advantage of the warm day and opened all the windows in the Denton house to remove the smell of paint and the stale air that had accumulated over the winter. I also decided to do some work outside, hoping the fresh air and activity would clear my mind. The meeting the day before with Tyrone had caused me to have another restless night as I tried to develop an approach to conducting a murder investigation. Maybe I should search Google for a plan. *How to trap a murderer? Suspects you may not have considered. Questions to ask suspects.* Surely there was something online that could help me.

The thought of Tyrone sitting in jail bothered me. Also, trying to find the time to help him while meeting my staging deadline was creating havoc with my stress level. I needed physical activity. Either that or lots of chocolate.

I adjusted the brown wicker lounge chairs I'd arranged on the patio. The thick blue-and-taupe striped cushions I'd selected for the furniture and the extra-large blue market umbrella helped tie it all together. Skip had added money to the staging budget, and, with the additional time to complete the work, I was able to make more improvements to the house. If I'd had enough time and money, I would have hired a carpenter to erect a pergola. Its overhead wood beams would provide prospective buyers with the illusion of additional living space. Still, I was pleased with the overall effect.

Taking a moment to catch my breath, I sank into a lounge chair, enjoying the comfort of the soft cushions, and thought again about what steps I should take next. The mystery books I read always seemed to focus on motive, means, and opportunity. At least the means or method used to kill Victoria was evident. She had been hit on the head with a blunt instrument and then pushed into the laundry chute.

Who had a motive to murder Victoria or the opportunity? Considering the numerous people she had crossed over the years, it would take months to whittle the number down to a manageable few. Who had been angry or desperate enough about something to kill Victoria?

What about the people Victoria had come into contact with recently? Victoria had crossed her former business partner, Cora Ridley. I remembered the argument between Cora and Victoria at the Denton house Tyrone and I witnessed. Cora had looked angry enough with Victoria to commit murder. Surely Cora would have cooled down after the argument. Besides, she wouldn't be able to get her money with Victoria dead. Maybe jealousy was a stronger motive. After all, Cora had accused Victoria of being involved with her husband. With her violent temper, could Cora have been driven to murder?

I plumped the pillow behind me and tried to get more comfortable. Follow the money. That had been the theme of another mystery I'd read. Skip would get half the proceeds from the house with Victoria alive. With her dead, he might get it all. Would there be enough profit after the sale to warrant him killing her?

Was there a life insurance policy on Victoria that Skip could collect? I liked Skip, but lots of killers had been likeable.

Who else had a financial connection to her? There was the list of dates and dollar amounts with Warren Hendricks' name on it I'd found in the library. Could he have fought with Victoria about the money she owed him and hadn't paid back? The thought of the mild-mannered funeral director getting angry enough to murder Victoria made me smile. Warren was much better at dealing with people who were already dead.

But if I followed the money trail further, who else might have been connected to Victoria financially? Doug Hamilton and his father of Hamilton Real Estate might enter into it. They would earn a commission if the house sold, but that certainly didn't sound like a motive for murder. What about the bad business decisions the senior Hamilton had made following his stroke? Could Victoria have been involved with any of those or discovered something about the Hamiltons? Or had she agreed to list her house with the struggling agency to keep Doug quiet about what he had discovered about her? That might have accounted for his smarmy manner the time he visited Victoria. I decided to talk to Connie Stockdale, who used to work for Mr. Hamilton. She might be able to shed some light on Mr. Hamilton's problems.

If I stretched hard to find suspects, there was always the interior designer, Monica Heller. Had she been angry enough with Victoria for choosing me to stage the house instead of her that she carried a grudge? Or could Victoria have had a reason not to choose her and Monica didn't want it to get out?

I laughed, knowing I was grasping at anything that would help Tyrone.

I also had to think about opportunity and alibis. Weren't people always trying to find someone to give them an alibi? At least they were in the books I read. My head was beginning to ache, thinking about it. All of this confirmed how complex trying to solve a murder could be. I didn't envy Detective Spangler his job.

I forced my mind to move away from thoughts of murder. Across the patio, a profusion of purple wisteria blossoms hung like clusters of grapes along a low fence that spanned the length of the garden. I breathed in the sweet fragrance from the blossoms and pleasure filled me. I wished Victoria could see how beautifully her prized plant was doing. And with no sign of Weed Wacker damage.

At the sound of a lawn mower starting, I jerked awake, realizing I'd dozed off in the warmth of the sun. Carlos was pushing a power mower along the sloping hill behind the patio. He managed the work crew that maintained the grounds. Could Carlos have taken Victoria's threat to report him to immigration officials for hiring illegal workers seriously and gotten into a fight with her over it? The fight might have gone from verbal to physical before he realized what was happening. For the life of me, I couldn't imagine Carlos or any of his workers having the temerity to approach Victoria, but then I wondered how well we actually know people and how they would react if they felt threatened.

Seizing the opportunity to talk to him, I walked over to the hill and waved at him. He waved back and turned off the mower.

"Hello, Miz Bishop" He took off his hat and fanned himself.

I liked Carlos. The few times I'd seen him, he'd always been pleasant. He worked hard, and the area surrounding the house reflected his efforts. It was obvious he took great pride in his work.

"Please, call me Laura. You don't have any helpers today?"

"Uh, no. My cousins, they had to go away, visit other relatives."

"I understand." I did. Victoria's threats scared them off.

"Carlos, I know the police questioned you after Mrs. Denton's death. Would you mind answering a few questions for me?"

Carlos looked alarmed and stepped back warily. "What kinda questions?"

"I'm trying to prove Tyrone Webster didn't murder Mrs. Denton, and I am hoping to find a clue as to what could have happened."

Carlos seemed to relax a little. "That evening Mrs. Denton was killed, I was at the hospital with my little Maria. She fell at the school playground—broke her arm—so I have what you call an alibi."

"Please don't misunderstand me, Carlos. I don't suspect you of anything. I'm trying to find out if you saw anything unusual while you were here, anything that might help me clear Tyrone. Did anything unusual happen on the day Mrs. Denton...died, or even before that?

Carlos didn't respond, and I wondered whether he was searching his memory or didn't want to say anything.

Much to my relief, he responded.

"Only one thing...the night before Mrs. Denton died. The UPS man delivered a package to the entrance out back...the one closest to the driveway. It was getting late and starting to rain. I worried Mrs. Denton might not notice the package outside and there's no porch or cover there. I knocked on the kitchen door, and when no one answered, I pushed the door, it was slightly open, and slid the package inside. I didn't go into the house, honest. Mrs. Denton was on the phone there."

"What was strange about that?" I wasn't sure where this was going.

"She was really angry."

"Do you think it was because you startled her?"

"No, she was angry before she looked up and saw me. Then she was angry at me too."

I remembered the time I overheard her on the phone with someone. She had been annoyed that time as well. In fact, she had slammed down the phone. Could she have been upset that Carlos had overheard her conversation?

"Did you hear anything she said on the phone while you were at the door?"

Carlos twisted the brim of his hat back and forth and his breathing quickened.

"Please believe me, Carlos. Anything you heard might be helpful."

"Let me think. The police, they didn't ask me about the package. At the time, I was upset because she was angry with me for opening the door. I didn't mean to scare her. When no one answered, I only wanted to push the package inside."

"What was her mood on the phone? Did she sound casual, like she was talking to a friend, or did she sound like she was doing business?"

"Like I said, she sounded angry—at the person she was talking to. Something about her getting the money." He paused again. "I believe she also said something about *tomorrow*. Si, that's what it was. *I want the money tomorrow or else*. Si, that's what she said, *or else*."

"*Or else?* Did it sound like a threat to you?"

"It did. That's why I pushed the package in quickly and left. I didn't want to wait around. Was that important?"

"Si, Carlos. It was. Thank you very much. By the way, I hope Maria is doing better and your cousins come back after visiting their other relatives."

I walked back to the patio seating area to collect the shopping bags and wrappings that had covered candles and colorful mats I'd placed on the table. The mats were there, but the candles were gone. I searched the area, but there was still no sign of them. Thinking about it, I realized I'd noticed a number of small items missing. At the time, I'd blamed myself for misplacing them. Now I wasn't so sure.

Chapter 15

Light colored or white fabrics perk up a drab room. Inexpensive remnants are an affordable way to make window or shower curtains and recover throw pillows.

I drove toward home deep in thought. As I sat at an interminably long traffic light, I again mulled over the list of people who had surrounded Victoria before her death. Tapping my fingers on the steering wheel, I couldn't decide whether my growing impatience was because of Tyrone's situation, my frustration, or my increasing hunger pangs. I'd skipped lunch, so all of them.

When the light changed, I spotted Monica Heller's tall figure going into a fabric store nearby. Without making a conscious decision, I turned into the lot, parked quickly, and followed her into the store. No time like the present to question her.

As casually as I could, I roamed the store aisles looking for Monica. When I spotted her nearby, I turned slightly away, trying to decide how best to approach her, and, once I did, what I should say. I was determined to tamp down the discomfort I usually experienced being around Monica. I had no way of confirming it, but I always suspected there had been something between her and my late husband Derrick.

I examined the fabric in front of me. If nothing else, while there, I could get the fabric I needed to recover throw pillows I'd found throughout the Denton home. Although still good, the dark pillows would no longer match the color schemes Tyrone and I'd selected for various rooms. It wouldn't take much effort, time, or money to give them new life, and the payoff would be well worth it.

Hearing my plans, Mrs. Webster had insisted she would cover the pillows for me, saying she wanted to use her sewing skills to show her appreciation for all I was doing to help Tyrone. I took her up on the offer, with a plan to find a way to pay her, knowing money must be tight for her with the loss of Tyrone's income.

"My, you must be going upscale with the Denton staging," a voice drawled behind me.

Turning, I found Monica Heller standing nearby. Well, that solved the problem of how best to approach her.

As always, Monica was impeccably groomed and looked remarkably like the pictures I'd seen of Grace Kelly, her blonde hair swept up in a French twist and wearing a dress that could have been designed by Edith Head or, at the very least, Alexander McQueen. Standing next to her was like being back in high school wearing my cousin's hand-me-downs.

"You do realize, don't you, those fabrics are fifty-five dollars a yard?"

"Nothing but the best for this project." I picked up a bolt of silk as though ready to purchase it. No matter how many years we had known each other, and my new attitude about dealing with her, Monica's condescending manner still managed to raise my hackles.

"How is the staging coming along?" Monica stroked some of the silk. "Skip is a dear and should be easier to please than Victoria would have been. You lucked out."

I had to admit there was a certain amount of truth to her tasteless statement. As long as I kept within the budget Skip and I'd agreed to, I'd have a free hand to stage the rooms as I saw fit. But the new budget definitely wouldn't cover the cost of silk pillow covers.

Monica started to move away, but I stepped forward to delay her. I didn't know if Monica could contribute anything to my investigation, but I had nothing to lose by questioning her. Well, maybe a little face, but it would be worth it if it helped Tyrone.

"Monica, how well did you know Victoria?" I hoisted the bolt of silk over my shoulder, wishing I had gotten a cart. For good measure, I added a second one.

"Why do you ask?" Monica's expression became suspicious.

"I'm curious. I found her to be quite sad, and I was wondering what might have been going on in her life before she died." *Died* was definitely a euphemism for *murdered*, but I still had a hard time using the *m* word.

Monica shrugged, as though she didn't have anything more pressing at the moment and might deign to respond. "I met her about fifteen years ago. We belonged to the same women's league, so we met socially from time to time. Why she was sad? She was divorced, broke, and going to lose her home. Isn't that enough to make anyone sad?"

"I still can't get over the cause of her death. Do you know anyone who would have wanted to harm Victoria?"

"Oh, my dear, I don't think we have enough time before this store closes to cover the number of people who had something against Victoria. I know it isn't nice to talk unkindly about the dead, but Victoria found it much easier to make enemies than friends."

"In which category did you fall?" I asked, with more gumption than I knew I possessed. I couldn't come right out and ask Monica if she had been upset when Victoria had hired me to stage her home instead of her—or angry enough to kill her for another reason.

Monica's brow furrowed, and her eyes flashed. "What are you insinuating?" Her tone was so cold I almost saw icicles hanging from each word.

"Uh, nothing." I lifted the bolts of silk a little higher. "I was wondering if the two of you were close enough for her to have confided in you about problems she might have been having with anyone. After all, someone caused her death."

"Are you now playing detective as well as stager? Where *do* your talents end?"

Embarrassed, I sputtered, "Since I was there at the time of her death, it's natural I'd wonder who did it."

"Well, I can clear your mind of one thing—it wasn't I." Monica gave me a withering look and brushed past me, knocking several bolts of silk to the floor.

That certainly went well.

Chapter 16

*Brighten rooms by removing heavy curtains and removing or
cleaning dusty blinds. Clean windows will make your house
sparkle. Pay particular attention to carpets and floors.*

Slipping quietly into Franklin Auditorium through an open back
door, I took a seat in the back row. Except for the few spotlights
shining onto the stage, the auditorium lighting was dim, and it took
a few seconds for my eyes to adjust to the dark. The Louiston
Players' rehearsals were usually closed to the public, but since I
wanted to talk to Warren Hendricks there rather than at the funeral
home he owned, I didn't want anyone asking me to leave. Tyrone
had volunteered with the Players, and, with Warren's link to
Tyrone and his long friendship with Victoria, I hoped he might be
able to give me some information. Anything was worth a try.

The musty smell in the auditorium reminded me of the many
plays I'd seen there, sometimes with my father, who had loved the
theater, and later with friends, since Derrick hadn't been interested
in going. The place was also a reminder of my dismal performance
when I'd auditioned for a part in *The Merry Widow*. Unfortunately,
my enthusiasm and desire to be a part of the play hadn't been
matched by any acting or singing talent on my part.

Sinking low into my seat, I became aware of my shoes sticking to the floor from years of accumulated spilled soda and smashed candy bars and moved to another seat. I loved this old theater, even if it could use a good cleaning.

Warren stood in the front row, waving directions to the actors on stage. I smiled, recognizing the set for *Arsenic and Old Lace*, one of my favorite plays. I'd seen it a number of times, and it still made me laugh.

Warren slapped a script on a seatback, punctuating each word with another slap. "Not so fast." He plopped back into his seat. "You have to wait until Mortimer opens the lid of the window seat and sees the body before you change positions. Try it again."

Watching him, I marveled at how fitting it was that Warren, a funeral director, was directing a production chock full of dead bodies—twelve, if I remembered correctly.

The actors changed positions. Of the four onstage, I recognized Dr. M playing Teddy, an amiable lunatic who thought he was Teddy Roosevelt, a perfect role for him, and the local florist, who was playing Dr. Einstein. With his wiry frame, thinning hair, and glasses, he looked almost like Peter Lorre, who starred in the film. I didn't recognize the other two actors on the stage.

Cora Ridley and another woman stood in the wings. They were playing the main character's dotty aunts. Cora was looking toward me, so I waved at her. She didn't wave back, maybe too embarrassed about the scene she had created at the Denton house I'd witnessed.

As the rehearsal progressed, Warren's exasperation became more evident. "Enough. We'll regroup tomorrow night. And, for Pete's sake, Nick, either learn your lines or we'll get someone else to take over the role. We don't want to look like fools on opening night." As he picked up his script, he muttered, "Why do I do this to myself each season?"

"Because you love it, frustrations and all." I walked up behind him. "And, if they got another director, you'd be upset."

Warren turned. "Why, Laura, what a nice surprise. You're right, but don't tell anybody. I have my reputation as a cranky old director to uphold."

"Your secret is safe with me." I sat next to him. "How many times have you directed this play over the years?"

"I've lost track. People enjoy it, so we can't go wrong. Are you here looking for a role? I may need someone to fill in for one of our actors if she moves to Texas with her husband."

"Not on your life. One humiliation on stage was enough for one lifetime. Don't you remember how awful I was when I auditioned for *The Merry Widow*? Actually, what I came to talk to you about is Tyrone."

"I can't believe they've arrested him. Anybody who knows him would tell you he couldn't hurt a fly. Why, if he finds a spider in this old barn, he takes it outside and lets it go."

"We all know that, but convincing the police is another thing."

"Is there anything we can do to help him? Tyrone is my set person, and I need him back—now. We don't have time for the police to come to their senses."

Tyrone had been volunteering with the Louiston Players since high school, hoping to gain more experience in the theater. His work with them had piqued his interest in set design. He impressed everyone with how he could establish the right mood with so little to work with.

"I wish I knew what we could do. We all know Tyrone couldn't have killed Victoria, but how does one go about proving it?" It wouldn't hurt finding out how others might go about it.

"I wouldn't know. I only *direct* plays about murder. Have you talked to Tyrone since they arrested him?"

"Only briefly. Getting into the jail to see him wasn't easy. I used the excuse that Tyrone's grandmother is feeble and needs assistance when she visits him."

"The police officer on duty must not have known her."

"Mrs. Webster is a spry old thing. She did such a convincing job of acting, you might consider her for a future production. She'd be good enough to earn a Helen Hayes Award."

"Are you kidding? She'd end up directing me." Warren stroked his graying beard with both hands. I noticed the black turtleneck shirt and fawn-colored trousers he wore were a far cry from his usual funeral home garb.

Warren became more serious. "How was Tyrone when you saw him?"

"Pretty upbeat, but his good spirits are waning. Having his grandmother visit him in jail cheers him up, but it also embarrasses him. I tried to bolster his spirits by telling him he'll know how to design a set for a prison scene."

"Knowing Tyrone, he laughed. It would take a lot for him to lose his sense of humor."

I twisted the shoulder strap of my handbag and decided to jump right in with my questioning. "Warren, you knew Victoria well. Did you know what was going on in her life? Did she ever say anything that would lead you to think she was feeling threatened by anyone?"

"No, but then I hadn't seen her much recently. You might talk to Cora. She was the closest thing Victoria had to a friend. They were business partners for a while."

I remembered the argument I'd witnessed between Cora and Victoria. I would hardly use the term *friend* to describe their relationship.

"Weren't you in business with her, too?" I tried to sound casually interested.

"Wherever did you hear that?" Warren's tone was sharper than I expected.

Startled by his reaction, I wished I hadn't raised the issue. "When I was in Victoria's library, I came across her yearbook and was looking at pictures of all of you. I found a paper tucked inside it with your name on it. Since it listed dates and dollar amounts, I assumed she either owed you money or the two of you had a business arrangement of some type. Sorry. I didn't mean to pry." Not much.

He sat there quietly as though struggling with his thoughts. "I hadn't planned to say anything about this to anyone, but, since she's dead, it won't matter. For the past couple of years, Victoria had been in a bad way financially. Out of friendship, I loaned her money from time to time—never expecting she'd pay it back. It's interesting she kept a record of it."

"That was kind of you, Warren." I wondered if he was revealing the full story.

Aware that rehearsals were over and Warren must be anxious to get home, I picked up my purse and stood, ready to leave. "If I see Tyrone, I'll tell him you're looking forward to him coming back to work. Since he's been in jail, he's concerned no one will want to employ him when he gets out."

"Tell him I want him back here. And good luck staging Skip's place. Give me a call if you need some help. I've been known to lift a hammer occasionally to make repairs."

"Thanks, Warren. I appreciate that."

I walked up the aisle toward the exit, wondering about Warren's reaction to my question about being in business with Victoria. It had surprised me. Looking back at Warren, I wished I'd been brave enough to ask him where he had been on the night Victoria had been murdered.

Chapter 17

*Place a receptacle near the front entrance for wet umbrellas if it
rains on the day of open house. To protect new carpets or floors,
leave disposable shoe covers for buyers to use.*

Coming out of Franklin Auditorium, I walked toward the parking
lot nearby and noticed, with dismay, it had started to rain heavily.
On dark nights with heavy rainfall, I found it difficult to see the
road clearly, especially with car lights coming toward me. Reaching
into my oversized tote bag, I pulled out my compact Burberry plaid
umbrella and opened it. I'd been thrilled when I found it at an
estate sale, knowing I could never have afforded a new one. When I
reached my car, I quickly jumped inside and locked the door. It had
been a long day, and I was anxious to get home.

After I pulled out onto College Avenue, I noticed, with
annoyance, the high beams of the car behind me. The extra glare
and the heavy rain made it harder than ever for me to see the road.

I slowed down nearly to a crawl, hoping the driver would grow
impatient and pass me. With little oncoming traffic, the car could
have easily gotten around me but didn't. In my rearview mirror, I
noticed how close the car was to mine. Was he trying to push me
along or out of the way?

Concerned, I sped up to get away. With the road slick from the rain and spring pollen, I didn't want the car sliding into me. I turned left then right onto a parallel street, hoping to lose the car. With exasperation, I looked back only to see the car still close behind me.

No matter how fast or slow I went, the car continued to tail my bumper. My annoyance turned to fear. It began to rain harder, and I turned my wipers on as fast as they could go. Suddenly, I jerked backward and was stunned to realize the car had actually rammed into me. I pressed hard on the accelerator, hoping another car wouldn't come from the other direction and blind me with its lights. Under other circumstances, I would have pulled over to see if there was any damage to my car and get information from the other driver. This time, my only goal was to escape.

Feeling desperate to get away, I turned down Tenth Street, my hands shaking so badly I could barely steer, and aimed my car toward the police station. When I reached the station, I planned to jump out and run inside to escape the maniac following me. Abruptly, the other car turned right onto a side street and disappeared.

Thoroughly shaken, I pulled into an empty space in the Burger King parking lot under a streetlight and sat there, trying to control myself. What had happened? Had a college kid gotten bored and decided to annoy one of the local residents? Or had I accidentally cut off an enraged drunk driver who had decided to take revenge on me? If so, whoever it was had succeeded in terrorizing me.

I considered reporting the incident to the police but knew it wouldn't do any good. The heavy rain and bright lights from behind had prevented me from seeing the driver or the make of the car. Without the information, the police couldn't do anything. I would decide in the morning whether to make a report or not. Tonight, I couldn't handle it.

My hands still shook and my heart was pounding as though I'd stepped off a roller coaster. After resting there for a few more minutes, I became calm enough to drive home. Driving sheets of rain continued to pound against my windshield like waves hitting the shore, and I drove slowly, the route taking twice as long as usual. When I reached home and parked in the driveway, I rested my head on the steering wheel, still trying to calm myself. Getting out of the car, I checked the back of it for damage, but the bumper of the old Corolla I had inherited from my mother already had so many dents it was hard to tell if any of them were new. I thought longingly of the Volvo I had sold to help finance my start-up staging business.

Letting myself into the house, I leaned against the locked door, wishing I'd installed an alarm system, or at least a half dozen deadbolts. After dropping my purse and tote bag, I dashed from window to window to ensure they were locked and pulled down the shades. Could someone have followed me home? I peeked between the curtains of the front window and saw no strange cars on the street. Only then did I start to relax.

I let out a deep breath, kicked off my shoes, and shrugged out of my jacket. The radiator was hot to the touch, but I still shivered with cold. I wrapped a wool afghan around myself and collapsed into a deep lounge chair. Even with Inky cuddled up next to me purring, I failed to get warm.

When I continued to shake, I got up and walked over to the cabinet where I stored bottles of spirits. There was only one—a bottle of cream sherry I kept on hand to use in a special chicken dish and to serve an elderly aunt at Christmas time. Oh well, it would have to do. It would at least help warm me. I poured myself a small serving and slowly sipped the sweet drink, letting it warm my body and relieve my shakes. I didn't usually turn to alcohol, but tonight's experience had left me needing something to calm my frazzled nerves. Hot chocolate or tea wouldn't do it.

Inky's meowing reminded me I still needed to take care of him. As much as I didn't want to move, I dragged myself to the kitchen and put out food and fresh water for him. The sound of scraping outside startled me and caused my heart to pound. When the sound continued, I realized it was only tree limbs hitting the house since the wind and rain were still in a fury.

Exhaustion overcame me. Without thinking, I crawled into bed, fully clothed. It had been that kind of night.

Chapter 18

Consider slipcovers to camouflage old or worn upholstered furniture. Attractive throws or afghans can also help.

Inky's paws stroking my face woke me the next morning. It took me a while to get my eyes open and focused since I was feeling disoriented. When I swung my feet over the side of the bed, my neck ached and I rubbed it, trying to relieve the discomfort. Not finding my bathrobe at the end of the bed, I looked down and saw, in surprise, I was still fully dressed. The memory of the previous night's experience came flooding back.

In the light of day, I wondered whether the experience had been as bad as I thought at the time. After all, it had been a dark and rainy night. Could I have overreacted? But, with memories of being flung backward and then forward when the car rammed into my bumper, I knew I hadn't overreacted. It was no wonder my neck and back ached. Weighed down by my worries about Tyrone and all the things I needed to do that day, I pushed aside memories of the incident.

The clock on my bedside table showed it was after ten. I couldn't believe I'd slept through my alarm, if I even remembered to set it. Thankfully, Inky had woken me. Otherwise, I might have slept until much later.

Maybe it was the cream sherry. It sounded innocuous enough, but the sweet, potent drink, much favored by little old ladies in Regency romance novels, could sneak up on an unwary drinker. The little I sipped had been on an empty stomach, as my growling stomach reminded me.

After feeding Inky, I showered quickly and rummaged through my closet for something appropriate to wear for my lunch with Connie Stockdale. Connie had worked at Hamilton Real Estate Agency for years. Nita and I had arranged to meet her at the Orangery so we could ask her about the Hamiltons.

The spicy scent of cedar met me when I opened my closet door. I pulled my favorite jeans from the crammed closet and then immediately put them back with disappointment. The Orangery wasn't the type of place to wear jeans.

Settling on an apple green cowl neck sweater and a black pencil skirt, I quickly dressed and began gathering the things I would need later at the Denton house, including work clothes to change into when I got there.

As I walked into the living room for my purse, I noticed the light blinking on the answering machine and pressed *Play*.

"Hello, sweetheart, this is Will Parker from up on Lookout Hill. I thought about what you asked me. I need to talk to you about something that keeps nagging at me. Come see me along Battlement Drive tomorrow afternoon and I'll tell you about it."

Remembering his flirtatious *sweetheart* endearment and wicked smile when I met him, I wondered if he was just using this as an excuse for a chat. What a character.

Because of my plans to meet Connie, I knew I might not make it to Lookout Hill while he was still there. Since Connie traveled frequently, I didn't want to reschedule our meeting. My watch told me I had just enough time to drop off Inky for his scheduled vet appointment, pick up Nita from the dental clinic, and get to the restaurant on time. My conversation with Will would have to wait.

I raced into the dental clinic, trying to catch my breath. I definitely needed to get more exercise. The waiting room, with its numerous mismatched upholstered chairs, was empty.

"Hi, there," Nita called from behind the reception desk. She studied me critically when I came closer. "What have you been doing? You look like you've been run over by a Mack truck that backed up to finish you off. Are you okay?"

"Thanks. You certainly know how to make a girl feel great." I studied myself in a mirror behind the reception desk and frowned at my reflection. "I'll tell you about it on the way. Are you ready?"

"I have to wait for Dr. M's last patient for today to come out. Tell me now."

I recounted the previous evening's events, trying not to make them sound melodramatic.

"I can't believe anyone in this town would do that. That's awful. Did you report it to the police?"

"I couldn't see a thing and wouldn't be able to give them any information to act on." The memory of the previous evening's events still sent shivers down my spine.

I looked in the mirror again and patted down my flyaway hair. "By the way, I may have to rush through our lunch with Connie. I need to get up to Battlement Drive this afternoon to meet Will Parker."

"Will Parker? Who's he again?" Nita asked.

"The man who picks up trash along Battlement Drive. I talked to Will after Victoria was murdered and asked him if he had seen anything that evening. He left a message on my answering machine saying he recalled something and wants to tell me about it. He could be using it as an excuse for a little chat, but you never know."

"If you wouldn't mind, Nita," said a voice from behind us.

Nita and I turned to find Dr. M and Doug Hamilton standing there waiting for Nita to take Doug's chart and handle his bill. I jumped in surprise at seeing Doug and inadvertently stepped on his foot. When I stumbled trying to move away, Doug grabbed my arm to steady me. Our gazes met momentarily, and heat spread up my neck and face.

"Hello, ladies." He smiled, releasing my arm.

His white teeth were gleaming even more brightly than before, if it were possible. Why did he have to look like a movie star?

"Are you next to see Dr. Malcolm, Laura?" Doug asked.

"No. I'm here to pick up Nita. We're meeting a friend for lunch. I'll get the car. Sorry, Doug. We're running late." Abruptly, I turned and raced from the building toward my car, thankful he had to settle his bill and wouldn't be following right behind me. Why did he make me so nervous? It was that handsome man syndrome.

I backed out of my parking place and pulled over to the curb near the dental clinic entrance, hoping Doug wouldn't walk in our direction.

Nita got in and fastened her seatbelt. "What's with you and Doug Hamilton? You ran off like a scared rabbit."

"I don't know. It's stupid, but you know how good-looking men make me uncomfortable. It started in high school when I fell in front of the three best-looking guys in the freshman class and they laughed at me. Then there was Derrick and his unfaithfulness. Plus, my mother always believed if my dad hadn't been so attractive, she wouldn't have had so many problems. It seems any time I've had a difficult time in life, a good-looking man was always involved."

"Maybe you've been surrounded by too many men with good looks. If you were an ugly duckling, I could understand it. You make half the men you come across feel awkward with your looks— nice figure, green eyes, blonde highlighted hair—"

"To conceal some gray that's creeping in."

"Nevertheless, I see men watching you, and it definitely isn't because they feel sorry for you. Stop judging men by their appearance. Women usually accuse men of doing that."

"I'm not." I frowned again. It was becoming a habit.

"That's exactly what you're doing. Not all men with good looks are like your dead husband, your dad, or the kids in high school. Some are real creeps, but there are also good ones out there. Look at my Guido. He's a good-looker."

"You're right. It's a hang-up I have." I clutched the steering wheel harder.

"Promise me you'll work on it."

"I promise." I crossed my fingers. "But Doug Hamilton is still a suspect, and not because he's handsome."

Nita threw up her hands. "I give up."

Chapter 19

Evaluate the artwork hanging in each room to ensure it enhances the look of the room. Artwork too big or too small for a space, or hung too high or too low, can detract from a room's charm or appeal.

I pulled into the parking lot of the Orangery. At one time the building had housed a German restaurant but was now a quaint English-style teashop that had opened on the outskirts of town a few months earlier. Its whitewashed walls, exposed beams, and open fireplace provided the perfect atmosphere for a teashop. I loved the place, but I itched to rearrange the English cottage prints on the wall hung too high.

The teashop had been slow to attract patrons since most area residents were used to fast-food restaurants or local ethnic eateries and didn't understand the allure of having tea with little sandwiches, scones, and cookies. I frequented it as often as I could to help them stay in business until word got out what a charming place it was. But now with my tight budget, I couldn't go as often as I would like. The atmosphere was gentle and relaxing and a reminder of a bygone era when presentation was every bit as important as what was being served.

Nita and I spotted Connie Stockdale waiting for us at a round table in the corner, one bordered by rows of racks holding ornate Victorian-style hats patrons were welcome to wear to get into the spirit of the place. The Orangery was a favorite gathering place for members of the Red Hat Society, providing them with an ideal setting for their luncheons.

I judged Connie to be well over seventy, but she had the energy of a woman far younger. She'd worked for Phillip Hamilton for a number of years and had recently retired so she and her sister could travel more. They had just returned from visiting Machu Picchu in Peru, and I could only marvel at how they had been able to tour the rugged mountain terrain at their age. Their example again piqued my interest in traveling.

I'd always wanted to travel but had been married first to Derrick, who didn't like to travel, and then to my career in IT, which had kept me extremely busy. I once planned a long trip through Europe and had even gotten a passport. About the same time, I met Derrick, who swept me off my feet, promising that if I cancelled my trip and married him, he would take me to Europe in style one day—when we became more established. Foolishly, because I couldn't bear to be separated from him, I'd gone along with his plan. Of course, we had never become established enough to satisfy Derrick. Later, as he had become more occupied with golf, work, and other women—in that order—my passport had expired without a stamp in it.

After we caught up on Connie's recent trip and studied the menu, we placed our order for a full English cream tea. Soon afterward, a waitress clad in a black Victorian bombazine dress and voile apron returned, balancing a tray laden with pots of fragrant tea and a three-tiered tray heaped with sandwiches, scones with thick cream, and pastries almost too pretty to eat. Pieces of chopped egg, delicately coated with mayonnaise and bits of watercress, spilled from between tiny, diamond-shaped slices of bread. We stared at the selection, not knowing where to start—

everything looked delicious.

The waitress hovered close by in case we ran out of food or tea soon, which wasn't likely to happen.

Nita selected one of the sandwiches trimmed of its crust. "Okay, Connie, we want the dirt on Mr. Hamilton."

"Nita." I looked up startled, shaking my head at my friend's lack of finesse.

"What? Okay. You handle it." Nita appeared oblivious to my discomfort and continued to munch on her sandwich of sharp Cheddar cheese.

"Connie, we don't mean to be nosy, but we need to know something about what happened to Mr. Hamilton's business after he had his stroke," I explained. "I'm trying to determine if Victoria Denton was involved in any way."

"Why would you think Mr. Hamilton was involved with Victoria Denton?" Connie asked with some surprise.

"She may not have been." I paused. "How can I put this delicately—"

"She wants to see if Mr. Hamilton or Doug had a motive for murdering Victoria," Nita interrupted again.

Connie choked on her tea and coughed several times. She caught her breath and wiped her eyes. "You think they murdered Victoria Denton?" She looked at us, making me squirm in my seat. "Okay, Lucy and Ethel, have you two been sniffing laughing gas at the dental clinic?"

"I know it sounds crazy." I was embarrassed at how bizarre it sounded. "But I'm trying to do whatever I can to prove Tyrone Webster didn't murder Victoria. To do so, I've got to find out who did. Or raise enough questions that might steer the police toward another suspect."

"But why suspect the Hamiltons?" The expression on Connie's face could have been total disbelief or amusement. It was hard to tell.

"Yes, why the Hamiltons?" echoed Nita, reaching for a scone, which she liberally spread with thick cream and jam.

"I don't suspect them *per se*." How could I explain without sounding like a total idiot? "I'm looking at everyone who had any connection to Victoria recently. When I heard Doug was helping at the agency because of bad decisions his father made, I wondered whether Victoria could have been involved with any of them. If so, whether she could have promised to list her house with them on the condition Doug remained quiet about what he may have discovered about her."

Nita stared at the flower arrangement on the table, as though imagining herself elsewhere, while I continued fidgeting in my chair uncomfortably. I decided to make it easy on Connie, even if I still strongly suspected Doug. "I would like to be able to eliminate them as suspects."

Connie had a gentle nature and was too polite to tell us we were idiots. She reached over and patted my hand. "What you're trying to do is admirable, but you're misguided suspecting the Hamiltons. I worked for Mr. Hamilton for a good number of years and you couldn't find a more honorable man."

"But honorable men often do foolish things and then compound it by doing something equally foolish to cover it up. Could that have happened to him after his stroke? Could he have had any business dealings with Victoria besides listing her house? Please, Connie, I know you're being loyal and don't want to reveal his business affairs, but I need to see if they could have any relevance to the murder. I'm trying to help Tyrone." This was going worse than I had expected.

Connie poured herself another cup of Earl Grey tea and paused for a long moment studying us. "Okay, I'll give you a bit of information, which may have absolutely nothing to do with anything, but you can't tell a soul where you heard it." The older woman slowly sipped her tea, in no rush to divulge the information.

Nita and I leaned forward, anxious to hear what she had to say.

"Mr. Hamilton invested heavily in property on Winston Lake where a group planned to build lakeside condos. Interested investors were taken to the site by boat so they could admire the position of the property on the lake. I heard later there weren't any access roads to the site because it was surrounded by land owned by the state. Boat owners could still get to the property, but it would be really hard and expensive getting heavy construction equipment to the site.

"Making the property worthless for development," I added. That sounded promising. "And, of course, the investors didn't learn this until they put up their money?"

Connie nodded. "They might eventually get access rights, but it could be held up in bureaucratic red tape for years. Now whether Victoria was involved with it, I couldn't say."

"How heavily invested was he?" Nita asked.

"I don't know, and that's all I'm going to say about the matter. If you have further questions, talk to Norman Ridley. He was the developer. But be careful—he's so slick he could bite off your arm and you wouldn't notice it was missing until later."

Chapter 20

Placing fresh-cut flowers throughout your house before showing it is like adding jewelry to complement an outfit. It will give your home an extra little touch. Even a few flowers in a baby food jar can add charm.

After dropping Nita back at the office to get her car, I picked up Inky from the vet and took him home. It was already mid-afternoon, and I knew I wouldn't get much done that day at the Denton house, but the trip there might give me the chance to see Will Parker along the way. I hoped I hadn't missed him.

As I turned onto Battlement Drive, I spotted flashing blue lights from a police car blocking the road. Somebody was going to get a ticket. The police officer waved me over. I hoped it wasn't going to be me. The thought of having to pay a fine with my meager savings worried me. I'd already sacrificed my daily cappuccino; now even regular coffee might be beyond my reach.

"Sorry, ma'am, you won't be able to get through here right now. There's been an accident." Farther up the road, I saw a number of emergency vehicles and Detective Spangler getting out of his car.

"Can you tell me what's happened?" I asked. "I was supposed to meet someone along this road."

"A man was hit by a car, and they're getting ready to take him to St. John's Hospital."

"Oh, no." I tried to absorb the news, envisioning Will and his cheeky smile. "Was he an older man in western-style clothing?" I hoped I was wrong.

"I believe so, ma'am. Was he the man you were to meet?"

I nodded sadly. If I'd gotten there sooner or called to say I would be delayed, he might not have been hit. Would it have made a difference? I would never know.

In addition to my concern for Will, I worried about what the shock of this would do to his daughter and grandchildren. "Do you know how he is?"

"He was in pretty bad shape when we got here." The officer held up his hand to wave another car to the side.

"What about his dog? He would have had Pinto with him. Is he okay?"

"The dog is fine. He stayed right by the gentleman."

"I'd like to find out where he lives so I can go by and talk to his family. Would you be able to tell me? I'd like to offer them my help."

"Sorry, ma'am. I don't know. The other officers up there will be looking for identification on him and will be notifying the family."

"If he doesn't have any identification, you might let them know his name is Will Parker. He said he lives with his daughter on this road, but I don't know which house. Is there any way I can find out about his family?"

"If you call the station later, they might be able to give you more details. Tonight's TV news or tomorrow's paper may also have information. Reporters desperate for news usually follow up on calls we get like this."

"What will happen to his dog? His name is Pinto."

"We'll check the houses up here. If we can't find anyone at home, we'll call in Animal Control. They'll check his tags."

"Oh, no." I knew Will would be worried about Pinto. If Inky were taken to an Animal Control center, even if for a short time, I would be upset.

"Don't worry. We know he isn't a stray. They'll keep him until we can notify the man's family and they can come get him. We can't leave him here."

I didn't think there was anything more I could contribute. "How long will it be before I can get through?"

"It may take a while. After the ambulance leaves, we'll be here searching for clues."

I looked up. The ambulance turned onto Battlement Drive, its lights flashing and the siren beginning to wail. "Clues for what?"

"For the identity of the car that hit the old gentleman. It was a hit and run."

I sat there for several seconds still shaken and my heart racing. How could anyone hit Will and leave him there?

Turning my car around, I headed back toward town. What had Will wanted to talk to me about? Something he said kept nagging at him. Had he seen someone coming or going near Victoria's home the night of the murder and remembered it? Or suspected something?

Feeling depressed about what had happened to Will, I wasn't in the mood to go directly home. I wished I knew where his daughter lived. I didn't know if there was anything I could do to help, but I'd at least like to offer.

As I drew closer to town, I decided to visit Mrs. Webster. She would be getting anxious to hear news about my investigation, no matter how trivial. On my way, I stopped at the Magnolia Blossom, a florist on Tyler Avenue, where I picked up a basket of spring flowers. I hoped they would help cheer Mrs. Webster and soften the blow that I still hadn't found the killer. I also picked up a basket of flowers for Will, if I could get into the hospital to see him. If not, I could leave them at the front desk for him.

The Webster house was nestled in a grove of evergreen trees, near the edge of the college grounds. A split rail fence covered with fragrant honeysuckle surrounded the small brick bungalow, and a wide variety of roses filled a well-tended flower garden for which Mrs. Webster was famous. The roses, starting to bud, would soon be in full glory. The smell of damp, rich earth reminded me of the times I'd helped tend the Romano vegetable garden and how beautiful Louiston was this time of year as it came alive again.

When I knocked on the door, Mrs. Webster pulled back the curtain and peered out the front window. I appreciated that she didn't automatically open the door but first checked to see who was there. I had no reason to suspect Mrs. Webster was in any danger, but she couldn't be too careful.

"Girl, come on in here." Mrs. Webster broad smile showed how happy she was to see me. "It's so good of you to stop by."

I handed her the basket filled with tulips, daffodils, and other spring flowers. "These are for you. They might help cheer you up."

"That was thoughtful of you." She placed the basket on the coffee table. "Thank you, but you shouldn't have spent your money on me."

I smiled. That was so like Mrs. Webster—always doing for others but never feeling comfortable accepting anything for herself.

"Have you eaten yet?" Mrs. Webster picked up a pair of oven mitts. "There's meatloaf in the oven. Will you join me for supper?"

Each time I had visited the Webster home, Mrs. Webster always offered me food. Feeding people was one of her greatest pleasures. I wondered how Tyrone stayed so slim all these years. Must be the running he did.

"If I'm not imposing, I would love to join you." I was unexpectedly hungry, even after the sandwiches and cakes I'd consumed for lunch, which seemed like days ago. They'd been delicious at the time, but the dainty morsels hadn't stayed with me for long.

"Then go wash your hands and I'll set another plate."

"Yes, ma'am." I got up to obey. When I returned, I viewed the changes to the kitchen with surprise. "I love what you did in here."

"The cream paint on the cupboards was your suggestion. I can't do anything to help Tyrone, so painting the cupboards kept me busy, and my stress level under control. If he's in jail much longer, every board in this house will end up with a fresh coat of paint. After that, I may start making new curtains for every window."

"How was Tyrone when you last saw him?"

"Anxious about missing school and the play production. But, most of all, he wants to be working on the Denton house with you. He appreciated your confidence in him but feels he's left you in a bind."

"Everyone misses having Tyrone around. Luigi Vocaro said business has been down with Tyrone away." Tyrone had worked for Luigi during high school and people liked him, particularly the older folks who frequently came in searching for someone to talk to. Tyrone asked them about their families and their lives. He knew their woes and their war stories, and he never corrected them when the stories changed from one telling to the next. "Luigi is lucky to have him, and he knows it."

"That's kind of you to say, Laura. Tyrone is a good young man. It's terrible having him in jail. He's worked so hard and stayed out of trouble all these years. How could this happen?"

"It's only a matter of time before he's released." I wished I could say that with more conviction.

Mrs. Webster put a large plate in front of me, overflowing with meatloaf, mashed potatoes, green beans, and corn bread. I stared at the plate, wondering how I was going to eat it all. I took a bite of the mashed potatoes smothered in rich brown gravy and sliced mushrooms and closed my eyes as pleasure filled me. I hadn't eaten anything that delicious since I began working on the Denton house, and even some time before that.

We ate in companionable silence. I admired Mrs. Webster's restraint in waiting to ask about the investigation and marveled at her ability to stay centered and calm, just as she had when she nursed my dying mother.

When we finished, Mrs. Webster scooped up a slice of pecan pie for each of us, my eyes widening at the size of the pieces. It would be useless to protest. If I ate her food every day, I would have to buy a whole new wardrobe.

"What have you been able to discover?" Mrs. Webster eventually asked.

"I'm sorry to say, not too much. It's going slowly." As we ate our pie, I filled Mrs. Webster in on the people I'd talked to so far.

"No one saw anything unusual the day of the murder?"

I decided not to mention Will Parker's accident. It was senseless letting her think Will might have seen something.

"I found out Carlos, the gardener, has an alibi, so we can mark him off our list of possible suspects." I wished I could tell her more. I set down my coffee cup more forcefully than I'd intended. "This is so frustrating. TV detectives make it look much easier."

"I'm grateful you're delving into this for Tyrone." Mrs. Webster put her hands up to her brow as though to wipe away some of the stress and fatigue showing on her face. "The police are satisfied Tyrone did it, so they won't be investigating this further."

"I did get one piece of information, for what it's worth. Mr. Hamilton invested heavily in a property development project set up by Norman Ridley. I overheard Cora Ridley accuse Victoria of having an affair with Norman. There may be no connection, but it's worth investigating."

"Norman Ridley is a real sleaze ball. I nursed his mother at his home, and the goings on there would have appalled anyone who hadn't already seen the things in life I've seen. How he ever got elected to the state legislature, I'll never know."

"Sometimes people get the officials they deserve, especially if they were stupid enough to vote for him."

"I'll tell you this," Mrs. Webster waved her fork in front of her as though for emphasis. "If Victoria was involved with Norman, they were up to no good. And I don't mean the hanky-panky type of no good."

I got up to help clear the table. "What about Victoria's supposed affair with Norman? Could that have driven Cora to murder? She's been putting up with his affairs for years, so why now?"

"I don't know why Cora and Victoria would want to fight over a tomcat like Norman, but some women are stupid. Cora has a violent temper. I was on the receiving end of it enough times to know. It wouldn't surprise me if she murdered Victoria in a fit of rage. When do you plan to question her?"

Mrs. Webster's piercing gaze pinned me to the chair, and I found myself unable to answer. Her words were less a question and more a directive. If Cora's temper was as bad as people said, I wasn't sure I wanted to ask her whether she had murdered Victoria, no matter how vaguely I worded the question.

"Why don't we both go see her?" I hoped Mrs. Webster would agree. "Since you know her well, she may react better to being questioned if you're there?"

Mrs. Webster snorted. "Like I said, I was witness to too many of her shenanigans when I worked in her home. She'd see me as nebbing into her business. Besides, with Tyrone being a suspect, if I were there, her defenses would go up."

I sighed and gave in. "I'll figure out a way to run into her." I didn't look forward to being on the receiving end of one of Cora's eruptions. Did her outbreaks ever turn physical?

Chapter 21

For open house, leave the driveway and front of your house free of cars or other vehicles. You want to give potential buyers a clear view of your house.

It was nearly dawn, and the din of chirping birds was becoming annoying. I wrapped my jacket more tightly around me, wishing I could turn on my car heater. However, even with my limited experience, I knew enough not to have my car running while on stakeout. It was bound to draw attention, and someone in a nearby house might come out and question me, or worse, call the police.

I was parked on a tree-lined road close to the Ridley home to be in position to trail Cora when she pulled out of her garage, whenever that might be. I wanted to question her on neutral territory and hoped this wasn't a day when Cora decided to sleep until noon. Mrs. Webster said Cora stopped for breakfast on her way to work at Millennium Bank most mornings. Unfortunately, she didn't go to the same place each day.

I sat waiting in hopes Cora would come out soon and drive to a place that was warm and had hot coffee. Until then, I shivered in my seat and sipped a cold Pepsi, hoping its caffeine would help keep me awake.

Through the budding trees, I had a clear view of the Ridley

house. Another week of warmer weather and the sprouted leaves would have blocked my view and I could have missed seeing Cora drive away. A small thing, but, at this point, I was grateful for any break that helped with my investigation.

I studied the Ridleys' two-story colonial with its ugly mustard paint. I shook my head in disbelief. What were they thinking when they selected such an awful color?

It didn't take long for me to become bored. Other than slouching down even further in my seat when an occasional car drove by, I had nothing to do or to keep my thoughts occupied. I wished I'd downloaded an audible book on my phone. I could have listened to Robert P. Parker's character Spencer and learned from him how to trail someone without being seen. He was a pro and wasn't afraid to approach a suspect who might become violently angry. How would Spencer deal with Cora?

Fictional detectives gave the impression stakeouts were more interesting than what I was experiencing. I was cold, cramped, and convinced I was wasting my time. However, I needed to question Cora, and hopefully soon so I could go on to work at the Denton house. Conducting a stakeout would be a lot easier if I didn't have a job and work to do. Once I talked to Cora I could report back to Mrs. Webster and have it off my mind.

Just when I was beginning to give up hope Cora was going to work anytime soon, the garage door went up and Cora's gold Cadillac backed out. I sat up abruptly, nearly spilling my Pepsi, and fumbled with my keys to start my car. After my long, uncomfortable wait, I didn't want to lose her.

Cora drove toward the center of Louiston, and, after multiple turns, ended up in the vicinity of Vocaro's. Could she be going there? My hopes rose, but then the Cadillac coasted past the coffee shop. Drat. Why couldn't Cora go to Vocaro's like almost everyone else in town so I could casually bump into her there?

When a traffic light turned red, I braked abruptly, thankful another car wasn't behind me. I hit the steering wheel with the palm of my hand in frustration. No matter how much I wanted to keep up with Cora, I wasn't going to run a red light.

I tried to keep the Cadillac in sight, but when it disappeared from view and the red light became the longest I'd experienced in my life, a word I never used came out of my mouth. Now I could understand why detective fiction contained so many curse words. A detective's frustration level must be overwhelming.

With no traffic in sight, as soon as the light turned green, I accelerated with as much force as a NASCAR driver. I wouldn't run a red light, but I didn't mind a little speed. Circling several of the mid-city blocks and still not seeing Cora's car, I was ready to give up when I spotted a gold Cadillac parked in the lot next to Hibbard's Bakery. It might not be Cora's, but it was worth checking inside to see if Cora was there. I hadn't gotten close enough to her to see her license number. If she wasn't inside, my only other option was to drive to the Millennium Bank and hopefully intercept her in the parking lot. Since I didn't bank there, it would be obvious to Cora what I was up to.

When I opened the bakery door, the aroma of freshly fried donuts hit me. My stomach growled, and I realized how hungry I was. After the huge meal Mrs. Webster had served me the evening before, I didn't think I would ever be able to eat again. One whiff and I was ready to give into the temptation the array of donuts presented. First, I needed to look for Cora. Later, I would come back to the counter and select donuts for the painters at the Denton house. At least then my stop at the bakery wouldn't have been a waste of time.

I scanned the seating area the bakery provided for customers who wanted to eat on the premises. My relief at seeing Cora seated in a booth toward the back of the crowded shop was almost palpable. I quickly ordered a cup of coffee and a croissant at the counter and sauntered over to where Cora was sitting, trying to act as casual as possible.

"Hey, Cora. Mind if I join you? Seating is a bit limited here."

Cora glanced up. She frowned and didn't look happy at the prospect, but good manners won out and she motioned for me to take a seat.

I slid into the cracked vinyl booth and placed my coffee and croissant on the table. Now that I was there, I wished I'd thought more about this part of the stakeout before I got there. I didn't know how to begin.

Cora continued to stare at me, which I found unnerving. To give myself time to think, I reached for two packets of sugar, which I never used in coffee, and stirred them into my cup. I then made a big production of dropping my napkin on the floor and reaching down to retrieve it. *Think. Think.*

"So, how are the rehearsals for *Arsenic and Old Lace* coming along?" I popped up from under the table. I was sounding a bit too chipper. "I heard you have the part of Aunt Abby."

"It's going well. We open tomorrow night. You going?" Her expression was so blank I couldn't imagine her performing on stage, especially in a comedy. If she had a flair for comedy, she hid it well.

"I wouldn't miss it. I love that old show."

Cora took another bite of her chocolate glazed donut. Starting her day with so little nutrition accounted for her grumpy attitude.

I took a sip of coffee and grimaced when my taste buds detected the sugar. *Quit stalling and jump right in.* "That was so sad about Victoria Denton. I understand you two were partners at one time."

"Partners?" Cora gasped, and bits of chocolate donut flew across the table. "That woman robbed me."

I'd hit a nerve. "What?"

"She convinced me to go into business with her, catering for people in their homes. You know, the type of people who give elite dinner parties or do expensive business entertaining."

I didn't know. I hadn't done any expensive entertaining recently.

Cora needed no prompting. "I'm a gourmet cook. Our agreement was for me to do all the cooking and Victoria would use her social connections to get us business and help out. Fool that I was, I put up the money with the agreement she would pay me back from her portion of the earnings. There were no earnings." She shouted the last sentence, causing heads to turn in our direction.

"It was a disaster from the beginning. You have to deal with all kinds of people and want to please them. Victoria didn't care about pleasing people and we flopped."

I wasn't convinced Cora was into pleasing people either, but I didn't interrupt. Cora wanted to vent, and it was to my advantage to let her.

"When I last confronted her about it, she had the nerve to say our business went bankrupt and that I didn't see her crying over it. What did she have to cry over? I put up the money. Money I couldn't afford to lose. I never should have trusted her with my money or my hus—" Realizing what she was about to say, she stopped.

Cora wadded up her napkin and threw it onto the table. "Anyway, I'm *glad* she's dead."

I recalled all too vividly the argument between Cora and Victoria I'd overheard. Especially when Cora had said, "I'll get it one way or another, or you'll be sorry."

I gulped and channeled Mrs. Webster. "Enough to have exacted revenge?"

That's when I found myself covered with the remains of Cora's coffee. It could have been worse. At least it wasn't hot.

Cora fled, and as I reached for napkins to blot at my jacket, I heard a familiar voice and winced.

"You certainly know how to win friends and influence people."

Detective Spangler strolled by, looking straight ahead, a paper cup and a Hibbard's bag in his hands.

Police officers and their donuts. I watched his receding back, wishing I had given him a good comeback. Why was it I could never think of one until well after an event? Something about that man annoyed me, but, at the same time, I found him a bit intriguing. Shaking my head, I gave myself a stern reminder about the hazards of dealing with handsome men.

Chapter 22

Antique shops and secondhand stores are good sources for inexpensive items needed to stage a room attractively. The staging is temporary and need not be expensive.

Work that day had been exhausting, and I left the Denton house earlier than usual. Mental stress and lack of sleep the night before had left me feeling drained, and I longed for the comfort and solitude of my home. Earlier I'd called Mrs. Webster and recounted my meeting with Cora. Mrs. Webster was disappointed nothing more had come out of the encounter. I thought sadly about my ruined jacket.

I also tried to get into the hospital to see Will Parker. When they said he was in ICU and only family could visit, I left flowers at the front desk for him.

On the way home, I decided to stop at Antiques and Other Stuff, one of my favorite shops in town. A visit with Josh Sheridan, who owned the place, would help perk up my spirits. Josh had converted two old factory buildings into storehouses that had more *other stuff* than real antiques. However, it was one of those places where I could browse for inexpensive but tasteful accessories to help homeowners finish staging their homes.

I also liked to browse yard sales for items I could use, but, more often than not, I would find the right item at Josh's to finish a room. Other times, I came away with only the pleasure gained from spending a few enjoyable minutes with Josh, who was interesting, well-read, and a lot of fun.

Getting out of my car, I looked up to see a short, dark-haired man exit the shop and get into a pickup truck. There was something vaguely familiar about the man, but I was unable to place him. I shrugged and walked toward the shop.

An old-fashioned bell jangled as I pushed open the door. When I entered, a musty odor greeted me. If someone blindfolded me and led me into an antique shop, I would instantly know where I was. They all have a similar, musty odor. I stood in the doorway, waiting for my eyes to adjust to the dim light inside.

A tall stack of rolled carpets concealed a small office area, where Josh spent a lot of his time. He was available to help anyone who came in, but when alone, he read to his heart's content, selecting reading material from the massive supply of secondhand books he stocked. He was a happy businessman.

"Hi, Josh," I called out.

"Hey, Laura," a voice drawled from behind the carpets. Though it had been many years since he'd migrated north from Georgia, Josh still retained the sound of his southern roots.

When he came out from behind the carpets, he towered over me, his lanky frame carrying little flesh. In fact, if the Louiston Players ever needed someone to play Ichabod Crane, he'd be their man.

"I sure was sorry to hear about Victoria," Josh said. "That must've been a shock for you, findin' her that way."

"The whole thing has been dreadful. You heard about Tyrone?"

"Sure. Couldn't believe it when I read about his arrest." Josh placed the book he was carrying onto the top of a glass display case—the opened pages of a Harry Potter book facing down to save his place.

Josh spun around once and stood there for several seconds. When I studied him quizzically, he nodded twice, looking down at himself. He had draped a lightweight dark wool blanket loosely around his shoulders. Josh, a real movie and clothing buff, took great delight in dressing like his favorite characters.

Since I shared his interest in old books and movies, guessing who he was dressed as had become a game we enjoyed each time I came into the shop.

"Oh, I beg your pardon. Let me take a better look and then guess." I studied the blanket again, which reached nearly to his shoes.

"Hmm. I'm going to guess Harry Potter. The blanket looks like the school cape or the invisibility cloak he wore at Hogwarts." Actually, when I first saw Josh, I thought he wore it to ward off the chill from the damp day.

He looked disappointed. "How did you guess so quickly?"

I smiled and pointed to his book. "The Harry Potter book you put down was a dead giveaway." I felt guilty taking advantage of the book clue, but most times I couldn't guess correctly with the one guess he allowed me, so I decided to use the clue.

"If you aren't in a hurry, let me show you a piece I got in today." He walked over to a display case and picked up what looked like a wooden chalice. "A few minutes before you arrived, a fellow brought this in, said it was pre-Columbian. He gave me a sob story about how he needed to sell his collection to pay his debts. I certainly can't authenticate it, but since it's a nice-lookin' piece and he wasn't askin' much for it, I bought it. When I have time, I'll do some research to see how fake it is."

"You could be holding a real find." I laughed, feeling some of the stress I was carrying ease away. I needed a few good laughs.

"I very much doubt it's genuine, but then you never know." Josh placed the chalice back on the display case. "With Victoria gone, what's gonna happen to the stagin' you were doing up there?"

"I promised Skip I'd complete the job. So, technically I'm working for him now. In fact, I came in to see if you still have the small oak church pew I looked at last week. It would fit perfectly in a hallway at the house."

"Sorry, Laura. Monica bought it two days ago. I'd have held it for you if I'd known you were interested in it."

"Oh, drat." I was annoyed Monica had been the one to get it. "It was my fault. I should have bought it when I first saw it. I'll look around for something else."

"Go right ahead and have a good look. If I can help you with anything, give me a holler. Oh, and Laura, if you hear Skip is gonna get rid of anything up at the house, I'd sure appreciate you lettin' me know."

"You'll be the first person I tell. I promise. In fact, I'll mention it to Skip."

I wandered through the building, stopping to look at the jumble of furniture, lamps, and collectibles, most of which were displayed haphazardly. I wondered if there was a market for most of the things there, but I was also aware that piles of worthless-looking items could often contain a real find.

I thought again about the man who left the shop as I came in. It bothered me I couldn't remember who he was. Where had I seen him before? I'd have to ask Josh if he knew the man.

After wandering up and down rows of furniture piled so high it was a wonder they didn't topple over, I spotted a double-seated Windsor settee. It wouldn't be as perfect as the church pew, but it would do nicely. It was an excellent piece to add to the inventory of items I could use in staging homes without sufficient or appropriate furniture. Previously, when I'd staged homes for friends, I used their possessions. Sometimes I needed to supplement what they had. Renting furniture was also an option.

I found Josh and negotiated a price we both were satisfied with. As I stood there writing a check for the settee, the bell over the door jangled, announcing another customer. Josh and I turned to see Warren Hendricks saunter in.

"Hello, folks," Warren greeted us.

Josh supplied the Louiston Players with many of their props, so Warren was no stranger.

"Laura, I was heading over to Franklin Auditorium for our dress rehearsal tonight when I noticed your car out front and wanted to talk to you. You know our show opens tomorrow night?"

I smiled. "Sure do. Nita and I have tickets, and we're looking forward to it."

"I wanted to let you know I was serious about my offer to help you at Skip's house. We don't have any guests at the funeral home at the moment, so I have free time during the day."

"Warren, that's kind of you to offer. Right now, I've got a pretty good handle on things, but if I find myself in a bind, I'll let you know."

"You do that. I've done a lot of set design, so I could be of some value." He tried to appear modest but didn't succeed.

When he left, I stood there, baffled. How had Warren recognized my car?

Chapter 23

Remove camping or sports vehicles and boats from your property and store them off-site. An RV or trailer in your driveway could make your home look smaller and less attractive to buyers.

"Nita, this is crazy." The next morning Nita drove us down a gravel road into the Green Acres Campground. The road wouldn't be a problem for heavy vehicles towing an RV, but Nita's little VW bug hit every pothole.

Mrs. Webster, who sat in the backseat, was being jostled from side to side. "Take it easy, girl. My kidneys are fragile, and, at my age, nobody's going to donate me a new one."

Nita had called me at home early that morning, saying she'd be by shortly to pick me up so we could investigate something. She would explain when she got there. It was Saturday morning, and I wanted nothing more than to sleep longer. The evening before, I'd been so exhausted that if my eyeballs had fallen out of my head and rolled across the floor, I'd have been too tired to pick them up. Since Nita had sounded so insistent, I pulled myself out of bed and got ready.

I gritted my teeth as we bounced along, patiently waiting for Nita to explain but afraid to learn what she was up to now. I still regretted telling her about my promise to Mrs. Webster—a promise

I was regretting more with each passing hour. My efforts to help Tyrone had turned into *our* investigation, and Nita and Mrs. Webster were acting like assistants to my Adrian Monk.

"Remember I scheduled an appointment last evening at Curl Up and Dye? What I heard there got me thinking. You know, it's truly amazing what people will confide in their hairdressers. Mine should hang a 'Counselor In' shingle and raise his prices. I told him to point his customers to their horoscopes—"

"Nita." I winced as we hit another rut in the road.

"Okay, okay. Anyway, my hairdresser said one of his customers who lives over near Lookout Hill had been complaining about the noise from a motorcycle gang staying at Green Acres about the time Victoria was murdered. I heard it's a pretty big gang. They may still be there."

"What's that got to do with Victoria's death?"

"You said Victoria might have been attacked by an intruder intent on stealing her stuff. Since the campground is so close to Lookout Hill, we should check it out."

"Those bikers aren't locals and might not be staying around for long," Mrs. Webster said. "We can't delay."

I believed Mrs. Webster was grasping at anything possible, so I couldn't blame the older woman for being eager. If it were my son or grandson, I would be grasping at anything I could as well.

"When I passed Mrs. Webster walking along Eleventh Avenue, I stopped to give her a ride. When I told her about my theory, she insisted on coming along." Nita turned to look at Mrs. Webster in the backseat.

I screeched as we headed toward a tree close to the road.

Mrs. Webster righted the hat that had fallen over her forehead. "Right you are. If I can help ferret out information that might help Tyrone, I'm up to staring down a member of Hell's Angels."

I couldn't believe my ears. "Just because they ride motorcycles doesn't mean they should automatically be suspected of a crime. If you're thinking it could have been somebody from the campground, it could have been anyone there, not just a person riding a motorcycle."

Nita frowned. "Do you have any better ideas?"

"You aren't afraid of a few cyclists, are you?" Mrs. Webster asked.

I was willing to consider anything, but a motorcycle gang was way beyond my experience. "Do you think they're still here?" Please say no. I couldn't imagine going up to a bruiser with tattoos up and down his arms and asking if he had broken into a local home and murdered the owner.

"We'll soon find out." Nita sounded excited, and I realized how much she was enjoying this. What happened to the quiet, sane life I used to have?

Green Acres was a year-round campground not far from Lookout Hill. It had once been a farm owned by the Dexter family, who had turned it into a campground when farming had become too hard for them. Its spacious pull-through lots appealed to RV owners, especially retired full-timers, who had sold their homes and now traveled around the country, setting up home wherever they wanted. Many of them parked there so they could audit classes at the college for free or attend programs at the Fischer College Center for the Performing Arts at a discount. During summer, the place was overrun with families with children enjoying the outdoor activities. The campground had been a smart business investment for the Dexters.

Nita swerved again, this time to avoid a large pothole. "Angelo, Nicco, and my other brothers have done work out here for the Dexters, so I know them. They won't mind answering some questions."

I bit my lip. Or they'll think we're nuts and never do business with the Romano brothers again. Nita was showing more energy than she had since her kids had gone away to college, so this line of questioning might be worth momentary embarrassment or getting our knuckles crushed by a belligerent gang member if it perked her up. As we pulled in next to the reception building, I could see a number of motorcycles in the distance.

Great, they're still here. I eyed the cycles glumly. I wasn't in the mood to stand nose to nose with someone who would rather arm-wrestle me to the ground than say hello—and that was only the females.

Pushing open the entrance door, we were greeted by the smell of smoke from the wood fireplace and the fragrance of spiced apple cider. The spring day had turned cooler, and the heat from the fireplace wrapped around us like a cashmere blanket.

An older woman with curly gray hair and cheeks made rosy by the warm fireplace stood up to greet us. If possible, her bright smile got even brighter when she recognized Nita.

"Nita Romano, what a nice surprise." Mrs. Dexter came forward with outstretched arms. "It's been years since I last saw you tagging behind your brothers when they came out here to work."

"Hi, Mrs. Dexter." Nita returned the hug that encompassed her. "Actually, I'm a Martino now. Remember, I married Guido Martino." When she stepped away from the warm hug, she looked behind her and pulled Mrs. Webster and me forward. "These are my friends, Mrs. Mariah Webster and Laura Bishop. Ladies, this is Mrs. Susan Dexter, one of the best cooks in the county. You should taste her chocolate pie. It won first prize at the county fair."

"Actually, only second prize, but you're sweet to remember. It's great to see you, but what brings you out here to Green Acres? Looking for a campsite?"

"Laura here has some questions for you." Nita turned and pointed to me.

I gritted my teeth. Rat poison. That's what I'd put in any chocolate pie I served Nita.

"Go ahead," Nita urged. "You're always telling me to let you ask the questions."

Before I could say anything, Mrs. Webster spouted, "We're here looking for the member of Hell's Angels who may have murdered Victoria Denton and let my grandson take the blame." Mariah Webster had more gumption than Nita and I put together.

Mrs. Dexter looked bemused, and, for a moment, appeared not to know what to say.

"Let me explain." I tried not to sound like the idiot Mrs. Dexter now thought I was.

Mrs. Webster would now get a piece of the same pie.

"Why don't you ladies take a seat around the fireplace? Mrs. Dexter motioned to the Adirondack chairs nearby. "We'll have a cup of cider and get to the bottom of this." She then casually walked over to the door and turned the *Closed* sign outward.

Chapter 24

Look to magazines and model homes for decorating and staging ideas.

"How was I to know the podiatrists coming in for their annual conference would be riding motorcycles?" Nita wailed as we walked around the campground.

After we told her our story, Mrs. Dexter had described the conference being held at the college. "If the truth be known, the conference is a good excuse for the motorcycle-riding podiatrists to attend a mini-bike rally."

Mrs. Dexter would have made the perfect minister's wife. I was thankful she hadn't laughed and shown us the door.

"Nowadays, those fancy motorcycles are so expensive to buy and maintain, it's usually the doctors, lawyers, and other businessmen and their wives you see riding them," Mrs. Dexter had explained. "We even have a number of women coming on their own bikes. The ones that don't have RVs stay in our cabins or at local hotels. If they're driving from a long distance, many will tow their Harleys and ride them about town after they get here. It's not such a big group as to disrupt the town, but they've been doing it for years, and they enjoy it."

"How about the ones staying here?" I hoped my relief at not

having to question a member of the Hell's Angels wasn't obvious.

"They've been coming for years, and I know most of them by name. Believe me, there isn't a single member of Hell's Angels among them."

Mrs. Webster was harder to convince. "You wouldn't believe what some of those doctors are willing to get up to. During my years of nursing, I've known a few who thought they were a law unto themselves."

Nita and I mollified Mrs. Webster when we agreed to walk around the campground to see what we could discover. A few simple campers in a variety of styles were scattered throughout the grounds, but the conference had attracted a number of long RVs, bigger than many of the homes in Louiston. They looked quite luxurious, with bumped out sides to make them bigger when they were off the road. A few had satellite dishes attached. Occasionally, when a door opened, we got a glimpse inside. These people had brought with them all the comforts of home and then some.

Mrs. Webster stared hard at one large vehicle. "These folks have more money than sense—selling up a perfectly good home on solid ground for one with wheels."

I looked longingly at a sleek RV with an awning-covered outside seating area. "But think how enjoyable it would be to pick up and move whenever and wherever you want. One day you could be in Rhode Island seeing the ocean from your window and a few days later enjoying the mountaintops of Colorado." Again, the yearning to travel came over me.

"Sounds like gypsies to me." Mrs. Webster gave a loud sniff and adjusted her hat.

As we wandered around the campground, we hadn't seen anyone suspicious enough to question about Victoria's death, but I wondered what a murderer would look like.

The day was starting to get colder, and I silently signaled to Nita we should leave. I could see Mrs. Webster was tired, more than likely from disappointment than fatigue. We needed to get her home so she could rest. With her usual vitality, it was easy to forget her age.

As we turned to leave, two men came out of a decrepit old camper. A rusty screen door slammed behind them. They saw me looking at them and stared back at me with a startled look. I watched them as they quickly jumped into a beat-up Ford pickup, wondering why they'd given me such a strange look.

As the driver backed the truck out of the parking space in front of me, I looked through the vehicle's dusty window and found myself gazing directly at Carlos' helpers, the ones who had gone away to stay with other relatives. I was certain who they were, and I was equally certain they'd recognized me. One of them also looked remarkably like the man I'd seen leaving Josh's antique shop.

Chapter 25

Soft music playing in the background during an open house will make a house sound less hollow.

That evening, Nita and I arrived at the Franklin Auditorium early for the performance of *Arsenic and Old Lace*. The Louiston Players always drew a large crowd, and tonight was no different. I could have used a few more hours to catch up with things at home, things I had been neglecting while working at the Denton house, but exhaustion convinced me I needed a break and some laughs. Besides, I didn't want to disappoint Nita by not going along with her as we had planned.

We made our way down the aisle to our seats, still smarting from our embarrassment at the campground earlier. What about Carlos' helpers? Why were they in the campground? Had they recently returned to the area, or had they never left? And had one of them really been coming out of Josh's shop? I was becoming suspicious of everyone.

I was also concerned about Will Parker's condition. That afternoon I'd phoned the hospital again, hoping someone would give me information about his condition. No matter how I pleaded, they would tell me nothing. Privacy was one thing, but this was ridiculous.

When we were seated, I spotted Doug Hamilton with Monica Heller a short distance in front of us. Great. I got to sit there and watch Mr. Charm with Ms. Charmless. Had they become a couple?

Nita jumped up. "I'm going for a Coke. Do you want one?"

"No, you go ahead. I want to read the program before the play starts."

I flipped through the booklet in my lap, trying not to glance up at Doug and Monica. I skipped over the advertisements and the names of contributors until I found the list of cast members. I recognized many of the names on the list, including Dr. M and Cora Ridley.

That was strange. There was no listing for Nick. I remembered the rehearsal I sat through when Warren had threatened to replace him if he didn't learn his lines. Since his name wasn't in the program, I guessed Warren had carried through with his threat to get another actor if he didn't improve. I was disappointed for Nick, whoever he was.

Tyrone had been given full credit for the set design. I was pleased his contributions to the production had been acknowledged, even if he hadn't been around to complete the sets. I wished Tyrone could have been with us to see his work.

"Here, I brought you a Snickers—the staff of life." Nita handed me the candy bar as she plopped back into her seat. "I wish Guido had come with us. It's getting harder and harder for me to get him out of the house for the things *I'm* interested in. Let one of his buddies wave two tickets to a Steelers game in front of him and he'd be out the door in a flash."

Still a bit puzzled about what I'd seen at the campground, I found myself ignoring my friend's chatter. I was also puzzled about the change in the cast. "Nita, you see Warren Hendricks frequently. Do you know if he replaced any of the actors during rehearsals?"

"Not that he mentioned. Knowing Warren, if he had, he would have been moaning about it at Vocaro's, and everyone would have heard. He thought he might lose one of the actresses, but it didn't happen. Do you want me to ask him next time I see him? You could also ask Cora, since she's in the play."

"No. That's all right. It's not important." I remembered my run-in with Cora and didn't want to repeat the experience.

"By the way, Norman was in the lobby while I was there. He came out for *his* wife's interests. I can't wait to see how Cora performs."

The sound of music from a scratched recording began to play and the lights dimmed, signaling the start of the production. I shrugged and settled back in my seat. I usually enjoyed *Arsenic and Old Lace*, but tonight my mind wasn't fully on the play. I kept thinking of Tyrone and Will Parker.

At intermission, Nita and I walked toward the lobby. Seeing Norman well ahead of us, I motioned to Nita to hurry. "Come on, Nita, let's talk to Norman. I want to see if we can get any information out of him about the proposed development on Winston Lake."

"You go ahead. Ted's at the bar. I'll go ask him if there's anything new with Tyrone's case."

Nita walked away, and I wondered again if I'd been wise involving her in my effort to help Tyrone. She seemed to be enjoying it far too much and I worried she wasn't taking it seriously. I'd always been more serious, so it wasn't surprising. It was Nita, the adventurous and fun-loving one, who kept me from becoming too serious.

I hoped Nita would use a little more finesse with Ted Wojdakowski than she had with Connie Stockdale when we met for tea. Since Ted had told me earlier nothing new had transpired, I doubted Nita could do much damage. Besides, her cousin could handle her.

Walking through the lobby, I'd lost sight of Norman. Not seeing him anywhere, I stepped out into the cool spring night and looked around. A group of smokers was gathered under the streetlight near the corner of the auditorium. Norman was standing among them, lighting a cigarette. Dressed in a navy blazer, gray trousers, and a silk cravat at his neck, he looked like the owner of an English country manor.

Norman saw me approach and held out a pack of Camels. "Hey, Laura. Want to join me for a smoke?"

"Thanks, but no." I shifted from foot to foot in the cool air, trying to think how to ease into my questions about his activities. "Cora is terrific playing Aunt Abby. Isn't the performance great?"

"It's okay. With Cora in the production, I have to put in an appearance. It also doesn't hurt having my constituents see me supporting community programs, if you know what I mean." He winked at me. "I'm up for reelection and hope I can count on your vote."

Remembering Cora's accusation about him and Victoria and his reputation in town, I cringed at his wink, trying not to show it. Mrs. Webster was right. What a sleaze ball.

"Norman, I understand you were trying to develop a piece of land on Winston Lake." I hesitated. I was better at dealing with misplaced furniture and awful décor than I was controlling my nerves when questioning a possible murder suspect.

If he was surprised at my question, he didn't show it. "Why yes, I was. It's being held up for a bit while we work out plans to run a road through the property. That shouldn't be a problem. Serving in the legislature now might even help." He winked again. "Why do you ask? Want to invest in it? We still have a few shares available." He looked me up and down slowly. "I might be able to help you get in before this opportunity closes."

Again, I tried hard not to roll my eyes. I was getting as bad as Tyrone with that. "I heard Victoria recommended the investment to Phillip Hamilton. It sounds like it's going to be a great place once completed." I was stretching the truth a lot, wondering whether he would acknowledge Victoria's involvement or deny it.

"You heard about Phil's investment?" He seemed surprised.

"Yes, but I understand he may have gotten in a little over his head."

"Only the person doing the investing can judge his own financial situation." He looked uncomfortable.

"Do you think he was sufficiently recovered from his stroke to make that kind of financial investment? Did his son, Doug, know about it?"

"Why, there's Cora." He pointed to the actors standing at the side entrance.

I turned and saw Cora staring coldly at us.

Norman must have recognized her look as an unspoken warning and turned to leave, glad to escape my questioning. "Let me know if you want to talk about investing. It's a good long-term investment."

Without a backward glance, he walked briskly over to Cora and escorted her back inside the building. He couldn't risk having Cora think I was his latest love interest. He also had escaped without answering my questions.

During the second act, my thoughts were fully on the mystery of Victoria's death and not on the bodies hidden in the window seat on stage. Victoria *had* been the link between Norman and Mr. Hamilton. Norman hadn't denied it. Could Mr. Hamilton or Doug have wanted revenge on Victoria for leading a man who wasn't himself following a stroke into making a questionable investment—one that nearly bankrupted him? If so, could one of them have wanted revenge enough to murder Victoria? If so, why Victoria and not Norman?

My thoughts strayed back to Norman. Mrs. Webster's description of him had been accurate. He had always given me the creeps, but now even more so. Had Victoria known more about his dealings than he wanted revealed, especially now that he was in public office? I recalled overhearing Victoria's phone conversation in the library when she threatened to go public with something. Could she have been threatening to expose Norman's investment scam, if it had been a scam? More than likely, he had known there was no access road into the property and hadn't revealed that to potential investors. If Victoria had threatened to expose his scam, could he have committed murder to keep her quiet?

Applause at the end of the performance brought me back to the present. The audience reception was enthusiastic, and Nita and I found ourselves sitting through three curtain calls before we could make our way out.

I watched Doug and Monica leave. They looked as though they were having far too good an evening. Remembering my suspicions about her and Derrick, I could almost feel sorry for Doug if he got involved with her.

"Terrific play." Nita fanned her face with her program. The auditorium had become uncomfortably warm and getting outside again was a relief. "Who would have thought Cora could act so well? She has a real flair for comedy."

What about Cora? I still wondered whether Cora could have been angry enough about their partnership debacle to murder Victoria. Or even more far-fetched, could Cora have wanted to protect Norman from Victoria disclosing his business scam? As the wife of a politician, Cora knew what a scandal could do to his career and to their standing in the community.

Cora had said she needed the money from Victoria to leave him, but what if she was too comfortable in her situation to actually do so? She had been putting up with his affairs for years. Why the urge to leave now? Her business loss and Norman's recent affair with Victoria may have pushed her beyond reason. I shuddered, remembering that any of the individuals I'd questioned could have murdered Victoria. If the killer suspected I was getting too close with my questioning, could I be next?

Chapter 26

Dog nose and paw prints on a glass front door will not make a good first impression. Keep spray window cleaner handy for a quick cleanup.

"You're being awfully quiet." Nita tossed her handbag into the backseat of her VW and got into the driver's seat. "Didn't you enjoy the play?"

I slid into the passenger seat. "Sorry. I've been thinking about Tyrone's scholarship application. The committee will be making a selection any day now, and I haven't discovered anything to help free Tyrone. If he isn't cleared of Victoria's murder soon, he'll never get the scholarship. Worse, he could be found guilty and sent to prison. It's so frustrating." Snapping on my seatbelt, I slumped back in my seat. "And I still haven't gotten an update on Will Parker. Only that he's in ICU."

"Guido's cousin works at St. John's Hospital. Maybe she can investigate and get back to us."

"Your family is amazing. You have relatives in every corner of town."

"That's the joy of big Italian-American families—also one of the woes. As a teenager, every time I did something stupid, someone in the family always witnessed it and called my parents."

Nita studied me. "Seriously, there's something more on your mind. I can tell."

Nita knew me all too well. "I keep thinking about the man I saw coming out of Josh's place. I'm fairly certain he's one of Carlos' helpers—one of the men we saw at the campground today."

"What about him?"

"Josh said the man sold him an antique wooden chalice or vessel of some type. He's pretty certain it's a fake, but the price was right and it's a nice-looking piece, so he bought it.

"What's that got to do with anything?"

"I've always wondered whether Victoria caught someone stealing from the house the night she was killed. It's hard to prove since no one can say if anything is missing. Skip hasn't lived in the house for a few years and wouldn't know what Victoria accumulated or gave away after he left."

"But how does Carlos' helper come into this?"

"He's living in a small, rickety trailer at the campground. It made me wonder how he came by a piece like that to sell to Josh."

The traffic light turned red, and Nita slammed on her brakes, stopping in the middle of the intersection. At the best of times, Nita's driving made me cringe, and tonight was no exception.

Nita shifted into reverse and backed out of the intersection. "You think he could have stolen it from Victoria? Aren't you being a snob? Who's to know what he owns or buys with his salary, even if he lives in an old trailer?"

I decided not to remind her of her suspicions about the motorcyclists. "Seriously, you should have seen the piece. It looks like it should have been in a museum. It just doesn't fit."

"And what do you know of museum quality pieces?"

"You're right. I don't know anything, but it still makes me wonder. I'm so lacking in clues I'm willing to consider anything."

"Okay. Let's go check it out. We can go there on the way home."

"What? Tonight? It's already after ten."

"Didn't you say earlier at the campground one of Carlos' helpers recognized you? Maybe seeing you there made him think you were checking on them. Have you thought about that? They could be clearing out of there right now."

"I should call Detective Spangler and let him handle it."

"And tell him what? Someone who *might* have been one of Carlos' helpers sold Josh a wooden chalice that may or may not have belonged to Victoria and, therefore, he's Victoria's murderer?"

As much as I hated to admit it, Nita was right. "Okay. We'll have a quick look around the campground, but that's all." I rested my head on the seat back, feeling weary.

When the light changed, Nita accelerated but we found ourselves going in reverse. Thankfully, no one was behind us. She put the gear in drive, and we started down the road again. Fortunately for her children, Guido had been the one to teach them to drive.

Nita pulled into a parking space in front of Mason's Pharmacy and grabbed her handbag from the backseat.

"What do you need so urgently right now?"

"Hair spray." Nita pushed open the door and hopped out, pulling her cell phone from her bag. "I also need to tell Guido I'll be a little late."

I opened my car window and called after her. "You're worried about your hair at a time like this?"

"No. It's for self-defense. Cheaper than mace and it's legal. You never know what characters you'll run into creeping around in the woods.

"In that case, get two."

When Nita returned to the car, I was studying the map spread out in front of me. "At this time of night, campers may need some kind of card to activate the gate to get back into the campground. If we drive up and don't have a card, we'll draw attention to ourselves.

Mrs. Dexter already thinks we're crazy." I refolded the map and returned it to the seat pocket. "If we park on Orchard Road, we can walk across the field that's next to the campground and get in from the back. No one will see us."

"I believe you're really getting into this."

"Not on your life."

Nita drove to the campground in record time and parked under low-hanging tree branches along the road. I breathed a sigh of relief we'd arrived there alive. When the car lights went out, the area was dark, but, after a while, my eyes adjusted. The full moon peeking in and out from behind thick clouds brightened the area enough to help us see.

We stepped out of the VW onto a gravel shoulder. I stumbled when my boot slipped on a rock and caught myself before falling. "I'm not exactly dressed for trekking across fields."

Nita handed me a can of hair spray and the flashlight she had taken from the glove compartment of the car.

"Duck." Nita pulled me down. "A car's coming."

I crouched beside her. "Aren't you being a bit dramatic?"

"If they see us, they might think we're stranded and offer help. Or they might call 911."

"The car didn't even slow down."

"Well, you never know." Nita stood, surveyed the area, and pointed toward the tree line. "The campground is that way. You have the flashlight, so lead the way."

"We can't use a flashlight. A moving light can be spotted from miles away." Again, I was thankful for the full moon, which gave us some light. I patted my jacket for a pocket to hold the flashlight and slipped it in. We might need it later.

When we reached the field, I gingerly climbed over a split rail fence that marked the boundary of the field, trying to hold onto the hair spray can as I grasped the railing. Stepping down on the other side, my foot sank into something soft and slippery. "Nita, what do they use this field for?"

"Grazing. Brown's dairy farm is around the bend. Why do you ask?"

"Just wondering." My boot made a sucking sound as I lifted it free. Yuck. I wiped my boot on the grass, trying to remove whatever it was I'd stepped in, thankful I wasn't wearing open toe shoes.

"Isn't this fun? We haven't done something like this since the night we slipped out of our cabin at Girl Scout camp."

"Fun. We ended up with two weeks of kitchen duty."

"Ouch." Nita moaned.

"What's wrong?"

"Something with thorns attacked me." She pulled a vine away from her pant leg. "I should have heeded today's horoscope. It warned me to stay in bed with the covers over my head."

Avoiding yet another hole, I wished fervently I'd stayed in bed.

The growth covering the field was getting thicker, slowing our journey. To make matters worse, heavy clouds occasionally blocked the moonlight, pitching us into darkness. The light from a lone campfire acted as a guiding beacon, but we needed the moonlight to avoid any more squishy patches.

Nita shivered and wrapped her jacket closely around her. "I'm freezing. Do you think we can go over and warm ourselves next to that fire on the campground?" She danced from foot to foot, trying to warm herself. "Maybe this wasn't such a good idea after all."

"Now you decide that." I blew on my hands to warm them.

Something flapped its wings and flew at us. Nita shrieked and waved her hands wildly around her head, trying to ward off whatever it was. In the process, she dropped her can of hair spray and scrambled to the ground, trying to find it like a cowboy who'd dropped his gun during a shoot out.

"Got it." Nita jumped up triumphantly, holding the can in front of her like a weapon.

"Come on, Tex. Let's find the trailer and get out of here."

"How are we going to find it?"

"Look for the most rundown trailer we can find with a beat-up truck parked next to it."

When we reached the edge of the field, we faced another split rail fence, this one separating the field from the campground. I climbed to the other side and reached back to help Nita, who was struggling to get over it.

"You make it look easy." Nita grasped my hand and pulled herself up.

"Longer legs and yoga sessions help."

Nita landed on the other side of the fence with a thump. Straightening her five-foot frame, she brushed herself off. "I'm tired of being vertically challenged."

We found a road that wound its way through the campground and followed it, I hoped in the right direction. When a trailer door slammed, we stood frozen, waiting to see if anyone approached. Hearing no further noise or footsteps, we continued. Fortunately, lamps within the campground now made it easier for us to find our way.

A dog barked loudly in the distance. The memory of being chased by a Boxer made my leg muscles tighten, and I was ready to run. Relieved when no dog approached us, we continued, passing by luxurious recreational vehicles, some with lights on, but most of them dark.

Finally, I saw a dilapidated trailer and pointed to it. "That's the one." The pickup truck parked next to it was equally dilapidated. Over the trailer door an awning sagged at one end, and the paint on the trailer had faded to a point where it would be impossible to determine its original color. Aluminum folding chairs, missing much of their strapping, were scattered around the front door. The glass window in the storm door was smeared and dirty. It was one sad place.

"Get ready." Nita popped the lid from her hair spray can as

though she were cocking a pistol.

Nita was being silly, but I did likewise.

"What do we do next?" Nita asked. "Maybe we can pretend to sell something and then peek inside when someone opens the door."

I tried not to roll my eyes. "Can you imagine what they'd think we were selling this time of night?" I rubbed my hand over my forehead and paced back and forth, trying to come up with a plan. What would Janet Evanovich's Stephanie Plum do? Investigate or run like the devil? I'd never viewed Stephanie as a role model, but I knew she wouldn't turn tail and run, especially with Grandma Mazur's prodding. Imagining Mrs. Webster prodding me, I straightened my shoulders, resolving not to give up now. I motioned to Nita to follow me. "Let's go around back. There may be a window on the other side we can peek through."

Nita nodded and followed me. Music blared from the trailer, the beat so strong the structure nearly shook from the sound. It helped cover any noise we made, but it would also prevent us from hearing each other well. When we reached the back of the trailer, I viewed the window with relief. It was above our heads, but I spotted the fence railing close to the trailer and motioned to it. The top railing would be the right height for one of us to sit on and peer through the window. Nita shook her head vehemently. I took that as a signal I would have to be the one. I stepped on the lower rung and swung my other foot over the top railing, reaching out to the side of the trailer for balance.

At the sight of the thick curtains in the window, I groaned. Fortunately, the curtains weren't long enough to completely cover the opening, and a narrow band of light appeared along the bottom. Relief flooded through me when I discovered if I stooped down a little, I could see through the narrow opening.

As I peered into the trailer, the bright light temporarily blinded me, and, for a few seconds, I couldn't see anything.

Eventually, my eyes adjusted to the light. Someone stood directly in front of the window, only inches from me. All he had to do was turn around to see my eyes visible below the curtain. *Oh, gosh. I've turned into a peeping Tom.*

I inched along the railing, attempting to see around the man blocking my view. My neck began to ache, and when I reached up to massage my tight neck muscles, I started sliding off the railing. Trying to regain my balance, I knocked the can of hair spray against the side of the trailer and froze at the loud sound. I was convinced someone fifty feet away could have heard the noise and waited for someone to come investigate. With the din of salsa music, no one in the trailer seemed to take notice. For once I was thankful for music too loud to be comfortable.

The man with his back to me was talking animatedly to someone in the room. I couldn't hear his words but could see him gesturing wildly. When he moved away, I caught a glimpse of his face and this time recognized him as one of Carlos' helpers. He definitely was the man I'd seen at Josh's place.

Since he no longer blocked my view, I could see into the room. Dishes piled high in the sink looked like they could topple easily, and the remains of a recent meal covered the table. Even though the windows were closed, I could smell fragrant spices from whatever they had cooked recently. My empty stomach growled so loudly it was a surprise the people in the trailer hadn't heard it. How could I be hungry at a time like this?

I shifted on the railing to get a better look at the far end of the room and gaped. A row of wooden chalices, identical to the one Josh had purchased, stood on the countertop. Each of them looked like a fine piece of woodcarving. Well, so much for my knowledge of museum quality pieces.

I watched as one of the men polished an unfinished chalice with a stained cloth, while another man used a device like a dental pick to create crevices in another. They had an assembly line going, producing fake pre-Columbian wooden chalices.

If the men were making the pieces, they hadn't stolen one from Victoria and, more than likely, hadn't been responsible for her death. I hadn't wanted to think one of Carlos' helpers had murdered Victoria. That they passed off a fake antique chalice to Josh Sheridan was another thing.

"What do you think you're doing?"

Startled at the male voice, I turned and let loose a jet of hair spray—directly into the face of Detective Spangler.

Nita and I huddled in the backseat of the police cruiser, trying to get warm, thankful for the hot air coming from the car heater. Through the closed window, I watched Detective Spangler pour water from a plastic bottle over his eyes and then wipe them with his sleeve. He squeezed his eyes closed and blinked several times. Remorse filled me, and I wondered whether I'd blinded him.

When he looked up, he glared at us, his expression leaving little doubt as to how angry he was. He paced back and forth alongside the cruiser, as though trying to gain control of his temper before interrogating us. Several times he started to approach the car and then abruptly veered away again.

Eventually, he opened the front car door, slid into the passenger seat, and turned toward us. I sank farther into the seat, ready for the full blast of his fury. It didn't take long.

"What were you two twits trying to do?" he asked between clenched teeth.

"We were—"

"Do you know I could charge you with obstructing a police investigation and assaulting a police officer?

"A police investigation? You were watching Carlos' helpers after all?" My hopes soared. He *was* looking at suspects other than Tyrone.

"No, we weren't! We were on stakeout watching an RV we suspected housed drug dealers. You two nearly derailed our investigation." He rubbed his eyes again and glared at us. "Lucky for you they didn't come back tonight. You and your antics would have given us away. Anyone seeing you creeping around here peering into windows was bound to call the police, and we would have had to send an officer out to investigate. It could have put our suspects on alert."

He looked at us as though we were truant teenagers. "Instead, we spotted you two. What were you doing? Surely you weren't chasing some good-looking guys like high school girls?"

My temper flared. "We were doing what you should have been doing—investigating possible murder suspects."

Detective Spangler did the worst possible thing. He laughed.

"Go ahead and laugh," I sputtered. "They could have been the ones who broke into Victoria's house and murdered her."

"And why do you think that?"

"One of them sold a quality antique to Josh Sheridan that could have been stolen from Victoria." Yep, it sounded just as stupid as Nita said it would. "Forget it. It wasn't an antique, and they were making them in the trailer."

"Am I going to have to call my husband to come bail us out?" Nita looked more subdued than I'd ever seen her. If Guido had to get her out of jail, the whole family would learn of it, and Nita would never live it down.

"I should take you down to the station and book you." Spangler looked directly at me. "It might teach you to stay out of things not concerning you. This time I'll let you off with a warning."

For a second, I thought he'd winked at me. More likely the effects of the hair spray.

"If I catch you doing something like this again, I won't be so lenient. Now, get out of here before I change my mind."

Nita and I scrambled out of the police cruiser, mumbling

apologies, and dashed toward her VW parked nearby.

"Ladies, smart move carrying the hair spray," he called after us. "But use wasp spray if you really want to hit a target—ah, wasps. It propels up to twenty feet."

I looked back at Detective Spangler, who stood next to the police car. He might have been letting us off easy, but I still needed to prove him wrong about Tyrone.

Chapter 27

If a desirable feature isn't obvious in your home, draw attention to it by posting a note nearby pointing to it.

Dawn came all too early for my comfort, and I found it difficult getting out of bed. Exhaustion and embarrassment overcame me, remembering our adventures of the previous night. Of all the stupid things to do, and to be caught by Detective Spangler.

After showering, I fed Inky and gave him a little loving. I didn't want him being upset with me as well.

After attending church, I decided to escape to the Denton house, hoping to make a little headway for a few hours. On the way, I paused along Battlement Drive, where Will had been hit and wondered how he was doing.

After parking my car in the Denton driveway, I went around to the front door. As I rummaged through my tote bag for the key, I looked up to see a sheet of paper attached to the door with tape. In large block letters written with what could have been Magic Marker, the note read:

DO YOU WANT TO END UP LIKE WILL PARKER?

I stared at the paper, questions racing through my mind. Who was the message for? Skip didn't live here and rarely came by, so I didn't think it was meant for him. I was the only one coming to the

Denton house on a regular basis.

What could it mean? Who put it there? Regardless of how naive I was, and hard as it was to accept, I knew I could hardly view it as anything other than a threat. Will was in a coma and near death, and someone was threatening me with the same fate.

My experience on that rainy night when a driver attempted to run me off the road now made sense. The driver hadn't randomly selected me to harass. He had been giving me a warning not to raise issues he didn't want raised.

That also answered my question about Will's mysterious accident. Putting everything together, it was hard for me now to believe Will had been injured unintentionally. Could someone have wanted Will silenced? If I could discover who it was, I might also know who murdered Victoria—the same person who wanted to silence me. The thought unnerved me, and I sank into one of the wicker chairs I'd recently added to the porch to make it more inviting.

Taking deep breaths, I managed to calm myself and entered the house, locking the door behind me. I rushed to the kitchen and grabbed the receiver of the old-fashioned wall phone. Again, I regretted my failing cell phone and the poor connectivity on the hill. I had to find a cell phone I could use anywhere, if that were possible. With trembling fingers, I dialed the number Detective Spangler had given me. When he answered, I blurted out, "You need to get here right away." I didn't care if it was Sunday.

Detective Spangler hadn't given much credence to my argument Tyrone couldn't have murdered Victoria. He described it as wishful thinking on my part. With the threatening note, Will's accident, and the driver who had terrorized me, he would have to rethink the charges against Tyrone.

I stared at the note. An avid reader of mystery novels, I knew not to touch it and left it hanging on the front door. Whoever had placed it there might have been smart enough not to leave fingerprints, but I was still hopeful the culprit hadn't read many mysteries and slipped up.

I paced up and down the hall, annoyed with Detective Spangler for taking forever to get there. When I became bored with the pacing, I walked into the living room, where I moved a paperweight from one table to another, then moved it back again. If the detective didn't arrive soon, I would explode. I knew this was going to result in Tyrone being set free.

Through the window, I finally saw the tall, muscular frame of Detective Spangler walk onto the porch. I flinched seeing his red eyes, from the hair spray I'd aimed at him the previous night. When I opened the door, he studied the note and shrugged dismissively.

"I don't know what to make of it. It could be a practical joke by someone with a sick sense of humor. Or someone wanting to make sure no one else on this road gets run over. Have you been walking there?"

"I stopped on the road once to talk to Will Parker, but other than that, I've only driven along it." I pointed to the note. "Look, Detective, someone is threatening me."

"That's assuming the note is for you, which we don't know since it was posted on the door of the Denton house." His dark eyes challenged me. "And, like I said, it may not necessarily be a threat."

"You may view me as being imaginative, but when I think of the night a driver tried to run me off the road, Will Parker's hit and run, and now this note, it's all pointing to me and the questions I've been asking to help Tyrone."

"Someone tried to run you off the road and you didn't think to report it to us? And what about Will Parker?" Using a pair of plastic gloves, he removed the note from the door and inserted it into a plastic evidence bag.

I described the car incident. "I admit I should have reported it. But since I couldn't identify anything about the car or driver, what could be gained? Besides, at the time, I didn't think it had anything to do with Victoria's death. As for Will, he called me the night before his accident and left a message on my home phone. He said something had been nagging at him about the night of Victoria's murder, and he wanted to tell me about it. Someone stopped him before he could talk to me. That someone doesn't want me asking questions."

He sighed. "You've been under a lot of stress since the murder, so it's understandable you'd think these things are connected. However, there's nothing to prove these events are anything other than coincidence. They could be totally unrelated."

"Maybe so, but I truly believe Will wasn't hit accidentally. Since he's unconscious, he may never be able to identify the driver who ran him down. What if the person thinks Will might recover? Wouldn't he want to make sure Will couldn't identify him?" *Or her?* "Will needs to be protected."

"Maybe in a TV drama." Spangler studied me for several long seconds and then smiled. "I'll see what we can do."

"Do you promise?"

Spangler crossed his heart as though humoring a young child. "I promise."

"Thank you." I was sure relief showed on my face. "There's another thing. When you first interviewed me, I forgot to tell you that before Victoria's death, Cora Ridley and Victoria got into a heated argument at the house. I don't like to—"

"We've already talked to Mrs. Ridley."

"And?" I asked with a hopeful note in my voice.

"Their disagreement is nothing new. They have been arguing over their business loss for a long time. We have nothing to link her to the murder."

My shoulders slumped. My hopes of seeing Tyrone released soon drained away.

"Stop playing Miss Marple."

I wanted to smack him. "Meaning what?" I resented being

compared to the elderly amateur sleuth and not the youthful Nancy Drew.

"Meaning that if a killer were still on the loose and you kept asking questions, you'd be endangering yourself. Fortunately for you, we have the right person locked up, even though you don't want to accept that." Spangler pulled keys from his pocket and strode to his unmarked police car. Being Sunday, it might have been his own car.

I dashed after him, calling from the porch. "What about Cora's husband's affair with Victoria? Couldn't she have wanted revenge against Victoria for that?"

Spangler opened the car door and stood in the opening, looking at me wearily. "Just to let you know we are doing our jobs, so you don't have to run your own investigation, we questioned Mrs. Ridley. At the time of the murder, she was with others who confirmed her presence."

He got in the car, turned on the ignition, and rolled down his window. "By the way, how's your aunt Mariah? I heard about you and Mrs. Webster showing up at the jail." Grinning, he drove away.

He found out.

Detective Spangler's car disappeared down the long drive and I collapsed into one of the wicker armchairs on the porch. My body was limp, as though all the stuffing had been pulled from me. Even the beauty of the nearby Allegheny Mountains didn't give me pleasure.

Sitting there pondering how I would tell Mrs. Webster the pool of suspects was drying up, I watched elderly Mrs. Jankowitz and her grown son walk across the lawn toward me. Their home sat close by. Mrs. Jankowitz looked worried. Her mentally challenged son, Roy, wore a bright smile. Whatever was worrying Mrs. Jankowitz wasn't affecting Roy, who always radiated sunshine.

Mrs. Jankowitz and her son had been among the first to arrive at Victoria's funeral service. She was of the generation that believed if you knew the deceased you went to the funeral—whether you liked the person or not. As a result, she and her son were present at most of the funerals in town.

During the short reception after the funeral, I'd enjoyed hearing about Mrs. Jankowitz's travels with her husband, a former State Department official. I'd been fascinated with her stories about living in exotic places like India and Singapore. She said it had been a little harder traveling after Roy had arrived later in their lives, but they had managed.

"Is everything okay, Laura?" Mrs. Jankowitz clasped her entwined hands tightly against her chest. "With Detective Spangler out here again, I got worried, especially after what happened to Victoria and to the poor man hurt on our road. You know Roy and I are here on our own."

Looking at her drawn face, I decided not to add to her worries. "Everything is fine. Detective Spangler stopped by to make sure everyone here on the hill is okay. His men drive by periodically checking on us, so don't worry."

"Are you sure that's all it was? I was concerned they came because of Roy."

"Roy? Why would the police be asking about Roy?" I looked at her quizzically.

"Because of this." Mrs. Jankowitz took a bright yellow canvas bag from Roy and handed it to me.

I looked into the bag. Inside were the coasters and several other small items I couldn't find earlier. "These were on the patio. How did you get them?"

Mrs. Jankowitz looked worried. "I found them in Roy's room. He didn't steal them, honestly. It was a game he used to play with Victoria. She would hide things in the garden and let Roy search for them. It evolved from the Easter eggs hunts she used to have for him. He had such fun with her. He saw these colorful items on the patio and thought Victoria left them for him to find. He doesn't understand she's gone."

She took Roy's hand. "When I found the items, I was worried you'd missed them and called the police and that they might try to connect Roy with the murder. You won't tell the police about this, will you?" She looked frightened. The solution to the missing items was as simple as that.

I was stunned to hear about a side of Victoria few people knew about. I smiled at Mrs. Jankowitz and hugged her. "I'm sure Victoria would have been pleased Roy found these. Don't you worry about this."

As they turned to walk away, I called after them. "Mrs. Jankowitz, please wait a minute. I know the police questioned you the night of the murder. Since then, have you recalled seeing anything that night, or later?" I didn't want to say I was trying to find the real killer. Mrs. Jankowitz would only worry more.

"I wish I could help you, dear, but I don't think I can. I've seen so many people coming and going up here. All my days are similar, and I've been so worried." Mrs. Jankowitz took Roy's hand to lead him away and then stopped. "One night someone walked down Victoria's drive, but I can't remember when it was. It could have been before she was murdered, or it could have been after. These days my memory isn't as clear as it used to be. I'll think about it. Something may occur to me."

I watched from the porch until mother and son made their way back to their home. *A man walking around Victoria's property after dark.* It could have been the night Victoria was murdered and the person had been the one in the house. I hadn't wanted to put more pressure on Mrs. Jankowitz. The poor lady already had more than she could handle. I decided to talk to her in a day or so. She might have a clearer mind then and be able to pinpoint which night she had seen the lone figure.

After Victoria's funeral, Mrs. Jankowitz had invited me to come view the items she and her husband had collected during their travels. She might be lonely, so I decided to visit her, sooner rather than later. Just like Will Parker, she might remember more than she realized. I needed to caution her not to tell anyone what she saw. It could put her and Roy in danger.

Chapter 28

Fireplaces are highly sought after by buyers. Clear away furnishings that might block them and clean and repaint the firebox. Stack fresh logs in a wood-burning fireplace.

Late in the afternoon, I visited Mrs. Webster to give her an update on what had been happening. I decided there was no sense keeping things from her. She was too intelligent to be fooled and would dig everything out of me eventually.

"Laura, dear, please be careful. When I asked you to help Tyrone, I never thought it could put you in danger."

I was moved by the worry and fatigue showing on Mrs. Webster's wan face. With Tyrone away, she didn't have anyone to fuss over. Instead, she spent most of her days alone, giving her far too much time to worry about her only grandchild. Tyrone had come to live with her when he was five, following the death of his parents, and there was a special bond between them. I knew Mrs. Webster missed Tyrone terribly and wondered whether more redecorating projects or time out of the house would help.

"Come, let's go for a drive. If you're interested, I'll take you up to the Denton house so you can see what Tyrone and I have done there." Realizing what I'd suggested, I added, "That is, if you'd feel comfortable being there."

"My Tyrone didn't have anything to do with Victoria's murder, and I've been in houses where people have died before. It won't bother me, and it would please me to see Tyrone's work. Besides, after the way Victoria Denton treated Tyrone, if her ghost shows up, I'll happily give her a piece of my mind."

It was dusk when we arrived at the house. I began switching on lights, which added a warm glow to the rooms. As we entered the living room, I pointed to the wainscoting and described how dark the room had been before Tyrone's suggestion to paint it white. It made a world of difference.

I watched Mrs. Webster wander around the room and then stare at the high, coffered ceilings.

"All of this space for one person." Mrs. Webster sniffed. "It's like a museum, but you've done a good job making it feel comfortable."

"Thank you." I marveled to myself how far we'd come in transforming the room. In the dining room, I described a few touches I planned to make before completing the room.

"Tyrone picked out the prints you see hanging here," I said as we walked down the long hall toward the kitchen. They featured early twentieth-century British and American racing yachts, and the muted colors in the prints complemented the decor. "Believe it or not, he framed pages from an old calendar."

Just then, a loud thump sounded from above us.

We stopped talking and listened. I stood frozen, curious, and at the same time wanting to grab Mrs. Webster's hand and run. The memory of the last time I'd heard a noise from above was all too fresh in my memory.

"Come on, girl," Mrs. Webster grabbed my arm. "Let's go confront Victoria's ghost."

I knew ghostly activity hadn't caused the sound, but I didn't want to stay around to discover what had. Mrs. Webster, made of sterner stuff, strode over to the staircase, intent on investigating.

Watching her climb the steps, I admired her courage and wondered why the older woman hadn't conducted her own investigation. She had been an excellent nurse, but she might have been an even better detective. When we reached the landing and started down the hall, I tried to push Mrs. Webster behind me to protect her, if needed. Mrs. Webster would have none of it and gave me a look, requiring no interpretation. She wasn't someone who wanted to be protected.

I put a finger to my lips to signal silence, and, side by side, we walked along the corridor toward the library, peeking into each open doorway. When we reached the library, I stared at the closed door. There was something about the library, following Victoria's death, that always bothered me, but whatever it was lay buried deep in my subconscious and had never surfaced.

Growing impatient, Mrs. Webster turned the carved brass doorknob and pushed open the library door.

There, behind the desk and holding the purple-covered Louiston High School yearbook in his hands, stood Warren Hendricks.

"Warren," I gasped. "What are you doing here?"

Looking up wide-eyed, Warren dropped the yearbook and walked toward us, flapping his hands. From the books scattered on the floor, it was obvious he had knocked them over, causing the noise we'd heard.

"Stay right where you are, young man," Mrs. Webster said sternly. "Laura here knows karate, and she's not afraid to use it."

I sighed and positioned myself in what I assumed might be a karate stance.

"Please, Laura, I'm sorry. I don't intend to harm anyone. Let me explain," Warren pleaded.

"Sit down." Mrs. Webster pointed to a brown leather sofa. "Laura, get one of those fireplace instruments over there." She turned to Warren. "If you move, Laura will bop you a good one."

Warren, all six feet of him, plopped onto the sofa, with tiny Mrs. Webster looming over him. His Adam's apple bobbed, and he kept clearing his throat.

"Okay, now fess up," Mrs. Webster demanded.

I didn't know whether to laugh or scream. Between Nita and Mrs. Webster, who needed me? "Warren, what are you doing here?" I asked again, this time a bit calmer.

Warren stroked his graying beard nervously with both hands. "Believe me, Laura. I mean no harm. I only came to get something."

"How did you get in?" I'd carefully locked up when I left the house earlier.

"I climbed in through a small window in the pantry. The window's ancient and wasn't hard to wiggle open. Though, getting through it was a bit hard." Warren picked at a small tear on his jacket sleeve and grimaced. "I may have ruined my jacket." A smart dresser, he looked like he regretted that more than being caught red-handed going through the Denton library.

"What were you searching for?" Mrs. Webster voice was steely cold. She wasn't feeling any sympathy for him or his jacket.

I wondered what it had been like for Tyrone being interrogated by her when he'd gotten into trouble. No wonder he'd turned out so well. Doubtless he'd been too afraid to do otherwise.

"You better explain, or I'm calling the police." The fireplace poker was still in my hand. Remembering Detective Spangler's technique, I started slapping it into my left palm, hoping to intimidate him. All it did was hurt my hand and make me feel silly.

"Okay, I'll tell you everything." Warren held up both hands as though we were pointing a gun at him.

I rested the poker down next to my leg and stared at Warren. What a wimp. Had he always been like this?

"But before I start, I want you to know I had nothing to do with Victoria's murder, though there were times I wanted to strangle her." Warren gulped, his face turning red and his eyes bulging. "Maybe I shouldn't have said that."

"How are we to know you didn't kill her? My grandson is accused of the murder, when all along it could have been you."

"I couldn't have. The evening she was murdered, I conducted rehearsals of a scene with Cora and some other actors. You know, Laura, the scene where Mortimer realizes his aunts have been poisoning lonely old men. Cora can tell you I was there. Most of the cast had the night off."

There went my theory about Warren and about Cora. He couldn't have murdered Victoria either, unless he was lying. Warren must have been the one who gave Cora the alibi Spangler talked about.

"Okay, go on." I tried my best to control my tone and make my words sound like a friendly prompt. If he relaxed a bit, he might be more willing to confess the truth.

"I came to get the list you said you found in the yearbook." He leaned over and picked up a piece of paper from the floor and held it between thumb and forefinger, a guilty look on his face.

"The list of loans you made to her? But why would you need that? She can't repay you now."

"It wasn't a list of loans." He looked sheepish and let out a slow but steady breath. "They were payments I made to keep her quiet."

My forehead creased in surprise. Maybe slapping the poker against my hand had worked if he was so willing to spill his guts. I shook my head, trying to think sensibly and less like a noir film character.

"She was blackmailing you?" Mrs. Webster stared at him, looking as perplexed as I felt. "Why?"

"I had a young man working for me awhile back, and Victoria somehow found out he had been taking jewelry and other valuables from people's caskets before we took them out for burial. I fired him, but she threatened to expose the funeral home, and I couldn't risk that."

"But if it wasn't you, why didn't you let her expose who it was?" I asked.

"Because no one in town would trust us after hearing about the thefts. It didn't matter who did it. My grandfather and father built up the business, and I didn't want to be the one running the place when it failed."

"How did Victoria discover the thefts?" Mrs. Webster eyed him suspiciously. "After a casket is closed, the family members wouldn't know. The person in the casket couldn't have reported the crimes."

"What can I say? He was stupid. He bragged about it to his buddies, and Victoria got wind of it. She wasn't above upping her income by putting pressure on me."

"But, Warren, there wasn't anything on the list but dollar amounts and dates. Why did you think it was important to get it?" I couldn't hide the skepticism in my voice.

"I didn't know what else she had here related to it. If I could find the list, I might discover other things she had. Please believe me. I'm sorry I frightened you ladies. My only goal was to get the paper and get out."

I recalled his offers of help. "No wonder you were so anxious to come out here to help me. You wanted to search for the papers."

"I'm sorry. I needed to protect the family business."

"Can't trust any man," Mrs. Webster said bitterly.

"What do you think, Mrs. Webster? Should we let him go? He has an alibi we can easily check."

"Let him go." Mrs. Webster's disappointment we hadn't caught Victoria's killer was evident, and she glared at Warren. "But we'll be checking your story."

I replaced the poker. "Okay, Warren, you're off the hook for now. Please don't do anything so stupid again."

"Believe me, Laura, you have my promise on that." Seconds later, he was gone. It was only then I wondered whether Mrs.

Jankowitz had seen Warren walking outside the Denton house. Could I have been too hasty in my decision to strike Warren off my list of suspects?

Chapter 29

Buyers will look into all corners of your house. Make sure your closets and cabinets are clean and orderly. Don't leave out hampers overflowing with dirty laundry.

I dropped Mrs. Webster at her place and then drove home. It had been a long day. Still feeling unnerved from our run-in with Warren, I opted to park in the driveway rather than in my garage. The shadows cast by low-hanging tree branches across the path from my detached garage to the house were more than I wanted to deal with tonight.

I prepared for bed and lay there thinking about that evening. I couldn't get over Warren's actions and debated whether I should report them to Detective Spangler. After what seemed like hours, I eventually dozed off.

When the phone rang, it was as though the sound came from a great distance away. It took me a while to wake up enough to answer it, and even then, I dropped the phone twice before I could speak. I don't know who was more disturbed at being awoken in the middle of the night, Inky or me.

"Hello." I pushed aside the covers and struggled to wake up.

"Don't end up like Will Parker," a muffled voice said.

With that, I was fully awake and jumped out of bed.

"What did you say?" I still wasn't sure I'd heard the caller correctly. There was no response. I switched off my phone and then plopped down on my bed before my trembling knees gave out. I hadn't recognized the voice and couldn't even tell whether the caller had been a man or woman. One thing I did know for certain, the message mirrored the note on the door. Now I had no doubt the note had been intended for me.

Whom had I talked to or what questions had I asked that had triggered this threat?

The clock showed it was after midnight. Pulling on my robe, I raced to each door and window to ensure they were locked. Inky meowed and followed behind me. I'd locked up before crawling in bed, but now I needed to assure myself no one could get in. It was at times like this I wondered whether I should get a dog as well—a really big dog.

When I was calmer, I dialed the number that had come up on my caller ID. It rang and rang. Finally, a gruff voice answered. "Harry's."

Harry's? "Can you tell me who this number belongs to?"

"Man, I don't know. Probably Harry. He's the owner. This is a pay phone outside Harry's."

"Owner?"

"The owner of Harry's Bar and Grill. Look, are you trying to reach someone in the bar? If not, I need to make a call."

Muffled voices and music came from the background.

"Did you see anyone just make a call from this phone? Please, it's important."

"I didn't, but the phone's outside. I'm the only one out here now. You trying to reach your old man?"

"Uh, no. Thank you," I hung up. If the phone was outside, anyone could have used it. And that meant the call couldn't be traced back to the caller.

I debated whether to call Detective Spangler. He would say the call had been a prank, and, with my being half asleep, I'd only imagined what the caller said. I'd consider calling him in the morning. When I went back to bed, I eventually fell into a troubled sleep, dreaming about a car chasing me as I ran through town.

The next morning, I awoke with a start, suddenly remembering the telephone call I had received the night before. The memory of it sent shock waves through my body, and I felt disoriented. For a moment, I couldn't remember what day it was. Should I be getting ready for work or dressed for church? After checking the date on my phone, I realized it was a workday, and I needed to get to the Denton house. The sound of Inky's purring next to me on the bed helped to calm me.

After taking a quick shower, which didn't do much to make me feel more alert, I rummaged through my crowded closet, searching for an outfit to wear. Long days spent at the Denton house hadn't left me with much time to do laundry, and finding clean clothes was becoming a challenge. I pushed aside heavy winter clothes until I located a pair of jeans I hadn't been able to fit into for a while. I was pleasantly surprised when the zipper pulled up easily. Long days of hard work and missed meals had provided one benefit.

Once I was ready, I went into the kitchen, opened a can of cat food for Inky, and fixed myself a cup of tea and a bowl of Cheerios. They wouldn't stay with me for long, but I couldn't face eating more than that. The idea of stopping at Vocaro's for strong coffee sounded appealing, but I needed to arrive at the Denton house early to let Angelo and his crew in so they could finish painting the bathrooms.

Grabbing my canvas tote bag, I walked across my front porch to the driveway, wishing I could put my car on autopilot for my trip to the Denton house. I was no longer comfortable driving anywhere and had gotten into the habit of continually checking my rearview mirror to see if anyone was following me. I'd always viewed Louiston as a safe place, but not so much now.

As I approached the car, something about it seemed off. It looked strangely short. Then it struck me. All four tires were flat. Walking around the car, I saw gash marks in each tire. Who could have done this?

I regretted not putting the car in the garage the previous night. I would have to call Detective Spangler now. If nothing else, I would need to report the vandalism to the police to substantiate an insurance claim. I hoped my insurance would cover the cost of new tires. I let myself back into the house to call Detective Spangler. Sighing, I discovered my cell phone needed to be recharged again and went over to my home phone.

When he arrived, I showed him the car and described the phone call I'd received the previous night.

"Obviously, you've riled someone." He walked around my car, inspecting the damage.

"Obviously." I was growing tired of his offhand manner. My first instinct had been to respond "Duh," but that would have sounded juvenile.

"And you didn't hear anything outside?"

"Don't you think if I'd heard noise outside or seen a person slashing my tires, I would have done something, maybe even have called the police?" Seeing his surprised expression at my sarcasm, I added, "Sorry. I didn't sleep well last night after the threatening call, and now this."

"Are you sure what you heard was a threat?"

"Detective Spangler, at this point, I'm not sure of anything. Right now, all I want to do is report the vandalism to my car for insurance purposes and get moving." I realized then I couldn't move anywhere without my car.

"Car vandalism happens all the time. I can't say this isn't connected to the string of things happening around you, but neither can I prove it. Regardless, I would advise you to be careful. I'll send someone over to Harry's to find out if anyone saw somebody make a call from the phone there last night.

"I've already called there, but the man who answered hadn't seen anyone."

"These places have regulars, and the regulars there might have noticed a stranger. If the caller wasn't a stranger, that might be harder. I'll also have a patrol car drive by here periodically."

"What are you doing to protect Will? You are doing something, aren't you?"

"We've taken steps, and that's all I'm going to say. Now, stop questioning people. I don't want to add your name to a list of victims."

For a second, Detective Spangler appeared a little friendlier. What would it take to get a smile or a glimmer of personality from him? When he wasn't frowning at me, he appeared human and even attractive. Where had that thought come from?

After phoning my insurance company, I called Angelo and asked him for a ride to the Denton house. If necessary, I would sit on the tarps or paint cans in the back of his panel truck, but I needed to get there today. I could ill afford any more delays.

During the planning stages for the Denton house project, Tyrone and I had selected a palette of colors for the four bathrooms in the house—colors appropriate for a historic home. Angelo would be painting those today. I'd also purchased a new set of crisp white towels and shower curtains for each of the bathrooms to create a hotel spa feel. A few well-placed accessories would add the finishing touches. The tile and fixtures were in good condition and wouldn't need to be repaired or replaced. That would have taken a big bite out of my budget.

I was pleased with how the house was shaping up and believed I would be ready for the real estate agents walk-through prior to the open house. The agents would be judging my efforts, and they could be harsh critics. It was important I make a good impression since they would be my primary source for future staging work.

Waiting for Angelo and his painters, I contemplated everything that had happened over the last few days. I was getting close to whoever had killed Victoria, and that person was trying to scare me. Whoever it was had been successful.

This was far more than I'd signed on for when I promised to help Mrs. Webster. My home had been my haven from all the stress following Victoria's murder, Tyrone's arrest, and everything related to both events. Now, whoever was attempting to frighten me knew where I lived and had followed me home. It was no longer the safe haven it had been.

Chapter 30

Stage outside areas by adding furniture and accessories to patios and decks to show additional living spaces.

Basking in the warm spring sunshine, I stood on the Denton patio and admired my handiwork. The last few days of work had been busy, but the house was shaping up beautifully. With the landscaping Carlos had completed and the new wicker furniture and market umbrella I'd added, the resulting outdoor living area looked good enough for *House Beautiful*. Taking one last look, I made a mental note to ask Nita over to take more photos.

"Hello, anyone here?" a voice called, startling me.

Adrenaline coursed to my toes and back again. I hadn't realized how on edge I'd become and jumped at the sound of the voice. I was relieved to see Doug Hamilton emerge from the house through the patio doors.

"I knocked on the front door, but when no one answered, I let myself in. Sorry if I startled you."

I was alarmed I'd left the front door unlocked and was determined not to do it again. After Warren's late evening visit, I didn't want any more surprises. Then I realized Victoria must have given Doug a key. Representing Hamilton Real Estate, he would have needed one. Thinking about a key to the house, I remembered

Detective Spangler's question about who had a key. I planned to call and tell him Doug had one, but he might already know that. A lockbox hadn't been placed on the door yet for real estate agents to use, so I could discount anyone getting into the house using a key from a lockbox.

Doug looked around and whistled. "Wow, this is terrific. What a difference all this makes."

I pressed my lips together to prevent looking smug at his reaction. "Do you think it's up to Monica Heller's standards?"

"Ouch. I guess you heard me advise Victoria to contact Monica?" His embarrassed expression gave him an almost boyish look.

I nodded, savoring this moment.

"Sorry, but you were an unknown entity, and someone had recommended Monica. With so much riding on this sale, I thought she might be the better bet." Doug looked around again, as though trying to take it all in. "I see I was mistaken. My apologies."

"Well, at least you're honest. Want to see what I've done so far?"

Doug nodded and followed me into the house.

As we walked from room to room, I pointed out the fresh paint colors, especially the white wood wainscoting and trim on the ground floor, the bright and cozy kitchen, decorated in shades of yellow and cobalt blue, and the tranquil bedrooms that would be a quiet sanctuary for anyone fortunate enough to occupy one of them.

"I'm impressed," Doug admitted as we completed our tour. "It's amazing how you blended everything and made it all look so comfortable." He shook his head. "I can hardly believe this is the same place."

I beamed with pleasure. "Tyrone helped a lot earlier, and I have to give Skip some credit. He increased the staging budget and gave me a free hand, which I didn't have with Victoria. He hasn't lived in the house for years and isn't as emotionally attached to it as Victoria was. I doubt Victoria ever saw a knickknack she didn't like. Removing them and a lot of excess furniture helped create a sense of spaciousness."

"Skip is definitely going to get more money for the house now, thanks to you and Tyrone. I'll have to see if he's interested in listing it with furnishings. It would take a lot of furniture to fill this house, and someone might be interested in taking the whole package."

"I still have more to do, but I'm close to being finished. It was a relief when you delayed the open house."

"It made sense. We don't need the people who would come through only to gawk at the scene of a murder."

Doug's mention of the murder made me think about Tyrone sitting in jail unable to do anything to help his situation. Trying to balance my desire to help him with my need to meet the deadline for the open house had raised my stress levels considerably.

When we arrived back on the ground floor, Doug paused as if in thought. "Listen, I'm afraid we got off on the wrong foot—my fault. How would you like to have dinner tonight at my place?"

I looked at him in surprise and stepped back a bit wary. "I'll be cooking for my dad," Doug added quickly. "If you could join us, I know he'd enjoy the company. He doesn't get out much these days. It would also give us a chance to start over."

Spending time with Doug and his father would give me the opportunity to question them. It didn't seem honorable using dinner with his father as a means of conducting a murder investigation, but the urgency to free Tyrone called for ruthless measures.

"I'd enjoy that. I had problems with my car today, so Nita's husband, Guido, is going to pick me up. Once I get home—"

"Why don't I give you a ride home after dinner? Then Guido won't have to come out here for you."

"Thank you. That would work. Give me a second to call him

and then lock up."

On the short drive to the Hamilton home, I didn't say much, the memory of seeing Doug and Monica together still fresh in my mind. I knew I was being ridiculous and wondered why seeing them together should bother me, but it did. If he had been with anyone other than Monica, I wouldn't have thought twice about it.

When we arrived at the Hamilton home, Doug opened the door and ushered me into the living room, telling me to make myself comfortable while he went to find his father. The house was a lovely, old colonial with high ceilings and lots of crown molding and wood trim. A blend of antique and reproduction eighteenth-century furniture filled the living room.

I looked around me in awe. "This is lovely and so true to the period. Thomas Jefferson would have been right at home here," I told Doug when he returned.

"It's my mother's doing. Dad always said the trip they took to Colonial Williamsburg in Virginia was one of the most expensive vacations they ever took. She fell in love with the colonial style and came home and totally redecorated the house."

"She did an excellent job. Coming from someone in home decorating, that's high praise."

"I wish she could have lived a few more years to enjoy it. That's a portrait of her." Doug pointed to a painting with ornate wood framing over the fireplace. "She had a wicked sense of humor and had it painted and framed to give the impression it was done in the eighteenth-century."

"It's perfect in this room. A modern painting wouldn't have fit in as well."

"She was delighted when people asked her if it was a portrait of one of her ancestors."

Taking my arm, Doug led me through the house. "Let's go into the family room. Dad's in there. We can join him for a glass of wine before dinner. It won't take me long to throw a few things together."

After Doug made the introductions, I settled into a comfortable chair next to the fireplace. I was able to study both Doug and Mr. Hamilton at the same time. Doug had slightly graying blond hair, still cut in a military style, and a body that hadn't started to soften yet to civilian life. Mr. Hamilton was an older version of Doug, still handsome in his golden years. It was easy to imagine Doug at his father's age.

"I hope you don't find the fire too warm." Phillip Hamilton pointed to the blazing fireplace. "Since my stroke, I get chilled easily, and the temperature on these spring evenings can still dip fairly low." He stroked the longhaired cat in his lap. "Ginger here helps keep me warm. Do you have any pets?"

"She's beautiful. I live with a cat, Inky. He makes it clear that I don't own him. He only allows me to care for him."

The heat from the fireplace eased the chill I had been feeling, and I began to relax.

"Can I offer you a glass of wine?" Doug held up a bottle with a colorful label. "It's an Australian Shiraz, which I highly recommend."

"Yes, please." I accepted the glass of ruby wine he handed me and settled back.

As much as I enjoyed the wine, I decided to go easy on it. After a sleepless night, I was already becoming drowsy, and, although I wasn't trying to attract Doug, I didn't want to come across as dopey. Mr. Hamilton had dozed off in his chair, and I envied his nap.

"He takes frequent catnaps." Doug removed the glass from his father's hand. "The doctor said he'd need them less as he recovers. Why don't you bring your wine into the kitchen and keep me company while I cook?"

I watched him place salmon in the oven, sauté broccoli, and toss a salad. When I recalled his former career, I was surprised at how comfortable he seemed in the kitchen. I half expected he would throw well-marbled steaks onto the grill instead of the healthy salmon he prepared.

Placing dinner on the table, he went to call his father. I was impressed with how solicitous he was of him. Mr. Hamilton was still showing the effects of his stroke, and I couldn't bring myself to ask him anything pointed about his investments or his relationship with Victoria. He still looked a little feeble, and I didn't want to be guilty of pushing him over the edge.

If I were going to find the murderer, I was going to have to become hardened. I'd often cringed hearing reporters ask pointed questions, and now that I was in the position of having to do the same, I found myself reluctant to be a tough interrogator. As a result, we talked about everything except Victoria's murder. It was as though we were all ignoring the elephant in the room. I also thought of Detective Spangler's warning not to get involved. That wasn't an option. I was committed to helping Tyrone.

After dinner, Mr. Hamilton excused himself, explaining he needed his beauty sleep. Seeing his condition, I couldn't imagine Mr. Hamilton climbing the stairs at the Denton house or lifting Victoria into the laundry chute. My list of suspects continued to dwindle.

Doug and I went into the family room with our coffee. "It's not what you'd get at Vocaro's, but it's better than some I drank in the Navy."

I offered to help with the dishes, but Doug said he would take care of them later. After the day I'd had, I didn't insist.

"What got you into home staging?" Doug added wood to the fire and took a chair across from me.

I burrowed into the comfortable upholstered chair, noticing the beige brushed denim slipcovers, which went well with the indigo blue walls. "Staging always appealed to me, and, according to the friends I've helped, I'm pretty good at it. After my husband's death and then my mother's death, I decided on a new career, got some training, and became a certified home stager. At some point, I would like to expand into home renovations or restorations, but staging is a good start. The Denton house is my first paid staging work."

"If what I saw there today was an indication of the work you can do, I don't think it will be your last."

"Thank you. I can only hope." I put my cup on the coffee table. "I've given myself a year to make a go of it. If I'm real frugal, I can manage financially until I make a profit. Otherwise, it's back to an IT job, which paid well but bored me to death." I shifted in my chair. "Why did you leave the Navy?"

"Vision problems. Nothing serious, but enough to prevent me from flying, especially off aircraft carriers. So, when Dad had his stroke, I decided to retire and come home to help him get back on his feet. I'm not a licensed agent, so all I do is help out at the agency, do some leg work, and let them do all the contract work. If the truth be known, the agents in the office could run the business fine without me."

"You knew enough to advise Victoria to have her home staged."

"Truth be known, one of the agents suggested that. I'm still learning."

"Do you think real estate is something you will continue with? I'd think with your experience you'd get a job in the aerospace field or another job like that. You won't find those types of jobs here, except maybe crop-dusting."

Doug laughed. "That's always an option. Right now I need to be here. Besides, after living all over the world and being at sea for so many years, it feels good being back here and able to spend time with Dad."

Doug was starting to appear human, and I didn't want to find myself warming to him. I gritted my teeth, and, before I could stop myself, I said, "I understand your father invested heavily in the Winston Lake development put together by Norman Ridley. Is that so?" I was appalled at my gall, but, for Tyrone's sake, I was willing to sound nosy.

Doug looked thrown by my question. "I don't know how Norman convinced Dad to invest in that venture. If he had been more like himself, he would have investigated the access rights to the property and seen the lack of road was a problem."

"If I'm not being too personal, how is he dealing with that?" I couldn't very well come right out and ask him if his father had been upset enough to want Victoria murdered in revenge.

"Now that he's recovering, he's a bit embarrassed at having made such a large investment without doing more research. But, he's also philosophical about it. He views it as karmic balancing for the good investments he made."

"But didn't the investment nearly bankrupt him?"

Doug looked surprised. "Where did you hear that?"

"Most people believe his financial situation is the reason you came home, to rescue him financially."

"I returned home to look after him and to help out at the agency, but only until he gets better. Actually, that's only an excuse. His stroke, although a slight one, shook me up. I've spent so many years away and realized if I didn't spend time with him now, I might never have the chance. With my mother gone, it's especially important to me now."

I was impressed with how natural he was and how comfortable I'd become being with him, especially in his home. It was unusual, given the way I reacted to most men. I leaned over and placed my empty cup on the table in front of me.

"Can I get you more coffee?" Doug asked.

"No thank you. It's time I left for home."

On our drive, Doug glanced over at me. "You're awfully quiet."

"Sorry. I was thinking of Tyrone. I'm worried about him."

"I can understand that. When sailors under my command got into serious trouble, I found it frustrating. You wish you could help them or set them on the right path, but sometimes you can't do anything."

I rested my head against the headrest, forcing thoughts of Tyrone, Victoria, and murder from my mind. Before I realized it, we were parked in front of my house and Doug was gently shaking my arm.

"Sorry, I must have dozed off. It's been a long day."

"Again, I apologize for the way things started out between us. I'm much better at flying than I am at helping my dad sell real estate. With any luck, I won't step on too many toes and lose all of Dad's clients."

"I'm starting out as well. We'll have to learn as we go. Thank you again for dinner and the ride home."

"It was my pleasure. I enjoyed the evening very much."

For a second, he looked like he might lean over and kiss me. I quickly reached for my bag, ready to get out. I couldn't be kissing the suspects.

"Do you need a ride tomorrow?"

"I should be okay. Nita's husband took care of my tires today. Thanks anyway."

"Good night, then." He reached into the backseat and grabbed a small paper bag he handed me. "A little leftover salmon for your cat."

Surprise made me momentarily speechless. "Why...thank you. Inky will appreciate that." I was discovering aspects of Doug I couldn't believe were there.

Doug waited until I let myself into the house before he drove away. I was relieved he hadn't walked me to the door or said anything about seeing me again.

For once, his looks hadn't affected me. My instincts told me I might have to take him off my list of suspects. But not quite yet.

Chapter 31

Depersonalize your home by removing family photos and diplomas. You want buyers focusing on your rooms, not on your family mementos. Buyers need to imagine themselves in the setting.

At Vocaro's the next morning, I sat slumped in my chair, feeling very much like someone who had worked an all-night shift. I'd found it hard to sleep and spent much of the night staring at the ceiling. Dark smudges appeared under my eyes, and my hair looked as though I had come through a hurricane. Stifling a yawn, I brought Nita up to date on all that had been happening. I didn't mention my dinner with the Hamiltons. Nita would hear about our casual get-together and move directly into wedding-planning mode.

"This is becoming dangerous." Nita patted both her cheeks nervously. "I admit investigating a murder sounded exciting and adventurous at first, but now, with it putting you in danger, I don't think it's such a good idea. Maybe you should tell Detective Spangler what you've learned so far and leave the rest to him."

"That's the problem. I really don't know much, and he doesn't take me seriously. Besides, he's still convinced Tyrone did it. Unless I have concrete evidence pointing to someone else, he's not going to pay attention to what I say.

"Do you have anything pointing to someone in particular?" Nita pushed aside her untouched muffin.

My friend was more concerned about me than I'd have thought. Usually nothing dulled Nita's appetite. "No, but I must be getting close. Why else would somebody be threatening me?"

"Look at what happened to Will Parker. He may have known something, and now he's in the hospital. I think you should give up on this. Mrs. Webster wouldn't want you to continue if she knew everything that was happening. Aren't you frightened something could happen to you, too?" The worried look on Nita's face caused deep lines to form between her eyes, and she nibbled at her thumbnail. She did that only when she was nervous.

"Of course I'm frightened. Thinking about it, though, I realized if I give up because of fear and Tyrone is convicted, I'd be haunted for the rest of my life by what I might have been able to do. Besides, now I'm angry. Someone in this town is letting Tyrone take the fall for him and is now threatening me. I don't want to live like this. I'm not giving up. If I did, I could never look Mrs. Webster in the face again."

"So, what's next?"

"I don't know. What I'd like to do is hide out on a beach in Florida until this blows over." I shook my head several times, trying to shake the image of sandy beaches from my thoughts. "Instead, I'm going to go see Will's daughter this morning. She may know why he called me. I don't know which house she lives in, but I'm going to go up and down Battlement Drive until I find the right house. There aren't many houses along there. After I talk to her, I'll go back to work at the Denton house."

"Considering all that's happened, will you feel safe there on your own? We don't have many patients scheduled this week. I could come up there and check on you once in a while."

"Don't tempt me. I have plenty to do to keep me busy, and

people will be coming and going with last-minute deliveries and supplies. I won't always be alone."

"If you get nervous, give me a call and I'll come over, not that I could provide much protection. Be careful and don't talk to anyone." Nita pointed to the *Louiston Mirror*. "Your horoscope today says Capricorns should duck out or call in sick."

Later, I stopped at several houses along Battlement Drive inquiring where Will Parker lived. Most places no one answered, but I eventually found one lady at home who directed me to the end of the road. Just before the road opened up to fields, one house remained sitting under a canopy of flowering dogwood trees, their spring growth almost obscuring the house from view. I surmised I'd found the right place when I heard the squeal of children playing in the backyard. Will had said he had a number of grandchildren.

I knocked on the heavy oak door, which needed refinishing, and waited. The door flew open with a bang, and in the opening stood a giggling child who couldn't have been more than two. Behind her stood Will's dog, Pinto, panting and wagging his tail. From his friendly manner, he either recognized me or he wasn't much of a watchdog. I was relieved the police had been able to return him to Will's family.

"Abby, what have I told you about opening the door." A woman with a halo of burnished red hair rushed over and swooped up the tiny girl and shooed Pinto away. "Sorry about that."

"I'm the one who should be sorry. I didn't mean to come without calling, but I didn't have a number for you, and I had to guess what house was yours." I extended my hand. "I'm Laura Bishop. I've been working up at the Denton house, getting it ready for sale."

"I'm Claire Halston, but you already know who I am since you came here looking for me." She chuckled. She had the same glint in her eye Will had. She shook my hand, causing me to wince. She also had the same forceful handshake.

"I wanted to talk to you about your dad and find out how he's doing."

Her face fell. "Please come in." She led me down a long hall with Pinto following close at our heels.

As I followed her, I studied the picture gallery along the hall. Framed photographs of children of varying ages covered one wall. Another wall prominently featured photos of a much younger Will Parker astride bucking horses and fierce-looking bulls, waving his hat high over his head. One frame contained a magazine with Will's photo on the cover. He must have been good if he appeared in magazines.

"That's my father. Those pictures are from when he was on the rodeo circuit. He was pretty well known out west."

She led the way into a large living room covered wall to wall with toys of all shapes and sizes. "Abby, sit here and play." She put the child on the floor and motioned to the pile of toys. "She wants to be outside with my other children, but she's too small to play in the yard without me watching over her."

"I met your father briefly on the road not long ago. I was so sorry to hear about his accident."

"Thank you. It was tragic someone left him lying there." Claire Halston looked as though she was going to cry. "I don't think the kids will ever get over it. The younger ones don't understand much about how it happened. I don't understand what happened myself."

"If you don't mind my asking, how's he doing?"

"He's still in a coma and in ICU but stable. I only get to see him for a few hours each day. Please sit down." Claire pointed to a sofa covered with toys and a longhaired cat she shooed away. I gingerly took a seat, trying not to make much contact with the cat hair. It would be clinging to my black pants when I got up. I didn't want Inky sensing another cat on me and showing his displeasure. Pinto ambled over and sat next to my feet.

Claire sat on a large ottoman, taking a small toy out of Abby's mouth and putting it in her pocket. "I'm pleased you know my father. How'd you meet?"

"He was walking along Battlement Drive, and I stopped to talk to him. I wanted to find out if he had seen anything unusual along the road the day Victoria Denton was killed. I've been attempting to gather information for the grandmother of the young man who was accused of the murder. We know he didn't do it, and we're trying to discover anything that might point to whoever did."

"Did my father say he'd seen anything?"

"That's the problem. I don't know. He left a message on my answering machine at home saying something had been nagging at him about the night of Victoria's murder, but he wasn't sure if it could be connected in any way. He asked me to stop and see him along Battlement Drive the next day. Unfortunately, I got up there far later than I expected and saw the emergency vehicles. Had he said anything to you?"

"Sorry. He didn't. I knew he was preoccupied because he was unusually quiet. It was like he was mulling over something. He kept muttering something about the shrubbery. Dad particularly cared about keeping the road well tended, so I wondered if a car had driven into some of the shrubs or some homeowners needed to trim theirs. I wish I could tell you more, but I've been in such a fog since the accident and can't think straight. As soon as my husband gets home, I'm going back over to the hospital."

"I'm sorry I intruded on you. I wouldn't have if it hadn't been so important."

Claire shrugged, flashing a wan smile. "You're not intruding. In fact, with so many children here, it's good to see another adult. I wish I could tell you more."

"Would you mind if I asked you to call me if anything occurs to you?" I dug around in the bottom of my canvas tote bag, pushing aside a pair of pliers, overdue library books, and a number of dead batteries, trying to find one of my business cards. The cards had spilled out of the box they had been so neatly packed in. Finding one, I blew at the fuzz clinging to it, and handed it to Claire. "Your father is a special man. Not everyone is civic-minded enough to keep such a long road clean."

"He is special. Between you and me, I think he does it to escape us."

I thanked Claire, carefully patted Pinto on the head, and left without mentioning my suspicion someone had tried to kill Will Parker.

Chapter 32

Make sure your home is spotless. Dirty carpets and floors, walls, and especially bathrooms will turn off potential buyers fast. They will wonder what else has been neglected.

After I left Claire Halston, I drove directly to the Denton house, mulling over what Claire had told me. Will had been concerned about the shrubbery. What could it mean, if anything? Will usually walked the length of Battlement Drive and passed numerous homes on his trek. The shrubbery on any of those properties could have bothered him.

Realizing time was running out before the open house, I hurried my pace, parked quickly, and jogged along the drive to the front of the house. I wanted to complete my work in the bedrooms, which were close to being finished. With so many bedrooms, I'd been able to be creative and come up with a variety of styles to fit any mood—contemplative, romantic, whimsical—while still keeping them within the character of the house. The attic had provided me with a wonderful selection of vintage items to work with. I particularly liked the way the vintage luggage I stacked and used as a bedside table in a bedroom turned out. In another bedroom, I used an old steamer trunk covered in travel labels from places like Nice, Rome, and Vienna. Someone who'd lived in this house had traveled extensively. I thought of my cancelled trip to Europe because of my late husband. Marry Derrick or take a trip to Europe? I had chosen Derrick, and what a mistake that had been, especially since he had turned out to be a less than desirable husband. Feeling a bit more charitable toward him these days, I hoped his rest was peaceful. When I had a moment to breath again, I planned to update my bucket list with travel plans that wouldn't be determined by my love life, or current lack of.

As I bounded up the steps to the front porch, I was surprised to find the door wide open. I was certain I'd locked up when I left the day before. Could Skip, or even Doug, have come by to check on my progress? I stared at the open door, not knowing whether to enter or not.

Deciding I'd had enough of feeling afraid, I boldly walked in, calling out.

"Hello. Anyone here? Skip?"

Hearing no response, I walked down the hall, peering first into the living room and then the dining room. No one was there and nothing was amiss. When I reached the kitchen, I stared at the scene before me. A white powdery substance covered every surface of the room. I didn't know what to make of it. The ceiling was intact, so falling plaster hadn't caused the mess.

I tiptoed into the room and then stopped in my tracks. The floor was not only white but also tacky. My shoes were sticking to the floor.

What was covering everything? Stooping down, I reached out my hand and ran my forefinger over the floor. It felt powdery and sticky at the same time. Tentatively, I raised my finger to my nose, sniffed the substance, and then carefully touched my finger with the tip of my tongue. After moving my tongue around my mouth, trying to figure out what the taste was, I sighed with relief. It was honey and what could be white flour.

Then I realized what a stupid thing I'd done. Even Sara

Paretsky's detective V. I. Warshawski wouldn't have done something like that. The substance could have been lethal.

Seeing the mess, I wanted to scream. Who could have done this? Someone had actually vandalized the house, spreading flour and honey all over the kitchen. Why? Then it struck me. Again, someone was trying to unnerve me so I would go away. Whoever it was must be trailing behind me and knew where I was working and what I was doing. Was it a message for me to stop asking questions? But how had that person gotten in? I knew I had locked the house the last time I was here. If someone could get in when I was gone, what would prevent that person from getting in when I was there, even if I locked the doors?

Drained of energy, I looked at the mess and wondered what I should do. Clean it up, of course. First, I should call the police to report it. This had to be connected to Victoria's death and my investigation, but again, I couldn't prove it.

"My, my—you are creative," drawled a familiar voice from behind me.

My heart thumping, I whirled around. Monica and Doug stood in the doorway.

"Is this a new approach on how to brighten a room?" Monica's mocking tone grated on me, making the situation worse.

"What happened?" Doug looked bewildered.

"What are you doing here?" I squeaked, wishing a hole would open in the kitchen floor and swallow me, even if it took me to the basement—anything to be somewhere else. I still couldn't take in everything that was happening, but having Doug and Monica witness it made things far worse.

"Monica knows somebody who may be interested in the house and wanted to check it out." Doug pointed to the mess in front of us. "But before we get into all that, how about explaining this?

"I can't explain it. I only arrived here myself, found the door open, and came in to investigate."

"The door was open?" Monica asked. "Didn't you lock up the last time you were here?"

"Of course I did." Heat climbed up my neck and across my face, and I knew my skin would soon look blotchy. "After all that's happened, I'm careful about making sure the house is secure. This has to be connected to Victoria's death."

"How could you possibly come to that conclusion?" Monica looked and sounded as imperious as ever. "You left the door unlocked and kids got in and had a good time. You're fortunate they didn't spread it throughout the house." She paused. "They didn't, did they?"

"I didn't see any problem in the other rooms on this floor, but I haven't been upstairs yet."

Doug started for the stairs. "Both of you stay here while I check the rest of the house."

Within minutes, he returned. "Everything is okay upstairs and in the basement. We were lucky. Whoever did this acted fast and then fled quickly to avoid being caught."

"If Laura hadn't been so careless..." Monica trailed off when she saw the look on my face, which was far from friendly.

"All right, let's not argue about whose fault it was. It happened, and we need to report it to the police. I'll call them." Doug pulled out his cell phone and left the room. I wondered if he'd get any better reception here than I'd been getting with my phone.

"Yoo-hoo." A voice called from the doorway. I'd recognize that Hungarian accent anywhere. Madam Zolta.

"Sorry to bother you, darling, but I sensed something was wrong here and started to worry. I just popped in to check on you."

I cringed. I started to ask whether she had come by car or broomstick but didn't want to be unkind. Monica and Madam Zolta. Could it get any worse?

Peering over Monica's shoulder, Madam Zolta clucked her tongue when she saw the white powder covering the kitchen. "I knew I should have burned some sage when I was here before." She pulled a stone bowl out of the capacious bag she carried. "I'll burn some now."

Surely, she didn't think this was the work of someone in the spirit world. "That really isn't necessary," I sputtered, but gave it up as a lost cause and followed Madam Zolta as she went through the house, leaving a trail of ashes from the burned sage as she went. Great. More for me to clean up.

Pausing in the library, Madam Zolta shuddered and then went on. I studied the room mystified. What was it about the library that bothered me?

I left Madam Zolta talking to Doug and Monica and walked into the dining room. Dazed and depressed, I stared out the window. The spectacular view of the valley below didn't even register with me.

"Are you okay, Laura?" Doug came into the room and placed a glass of water on the table near me. Studying me, he smiled, and taking a clean white handkerchief from his pocket, he gently wiped the tip of my nose. "Flour on your nose." He looked slightly embarrassed by what he had done.

I was surprised at the feel of the soft cloth. I didn't think many people used a cloth handkerchief these days. The more I came in contact with Doug, the more I realized he was in a class of his own.

Doug refolded the handkerchief and returned it to his pocket. "Finding this mess must have been a shock for you, especially after—"

"Thanks, Doug." I didn't want to be reminded of the other incidents. I reached for the glass. "You don't know the half of it."

"I thanked Madam Zolta for her concern and saw her back to her car, so you can relax."

"That was kind of you. Thank you."

"She said to tell you there would be no charge for the visit. I didn't know psychics made house calls."

I laughed. "Until recently, I didn't either. With Madame Zolta, it's a public service."

Monica came into the room and continued to harangue me about forgetting to lock up and anything else she could think of to annoy me. Thankfully, soon after that, Doug took Monica back to her office, and I waited for the police. What was taking them so long?

When Detective Spangler finally arrived, he looked around and made a few entries in his ever-present notepad. "I don't know what to make of this. More than likely kids."

I threw my hands into the air. "Can't you see it's another warning? All these things are tied to Victoria's murder."

"I'm beginning to wonder about that." Spangler looked as frustrated as I felt. He sat down next to me and fiddled with his ballpoint pen for a while, clicking it opened and closed. "If Doug hadn't called me, I planned to come see you anyway. You were right about keeping Will Parker's room under surveillance. Someone got into his room last night."

I sucked in my breath. "Is he dead?"

"No. He's still unconscious, since they have him pretty doped up. But, other than that, he's okay. I had arranged for an officer to watch the room. He stepped away for a few minutes, and when he returned, he saw someone in white standing over Will. When the officer questioned him, the man went for the officer with a syringe. They struggled, but the man still got away."

"Did he see who it was?"

"No. The man wore a hospital cap, gown, and mask and looked like any other hospital staff member."

"How did he find Will? I could never get his room number."

"We have no way of knowing, but we're stepping up security and will keep someone there around the clock."

My shoulders sagged, and I felt as though I'd aged over night.

"Look," Spangler said gently. "Even if he regains

consciousness, Will may never be able to identify who hit him. And, even if he did, we have little to link his accident to Victoria's murder."

"With all this happening, can't you see it couldn't have been Tyrone who murdered Victoria?"

"I wish I could. All of those things are strange, but they still aren't enough for us to clear Tyrone. Besides, if someone else were responsible for her death, my releasing Tyrone would put the person on guard. Right now, that person, if there is someone else, is feeling secure he or she isn't under suspicion. Please don't rock the boat."

"Just so long as Tyrone doesn't go down with that boat."

Chapter 33

Kitchens and baths sell houses. Wow buyers with either, and you'll
have a better chance at a sale.

After work the next day, the front door of the Webster house swung
open before I could even knock, revealing Mariah Webster standing
in the doorway with her hands on her hips.

"Girl, where have you been? I never thought you'd get here."
Mrs. Webster's face looked pale and drawn. "I've been pacing the
floor waiting for you."

"I came as soon as I got your message." I'd discovered Mrs.
Webster's message on my home phone when I arrived, dirty and
tired from working at the Denton house. Much to my surprise,
Doug had helped me clean up the sticky mess after he took Monica
back to her office. Of course, there had been no offer of help from
her.

Hearing Mrs. Webster's request to come right away, I'd
ignored my fatigue and made the trip to the Webster house in
record time. "What's wrong? Is Tyrone okay?" I knew Mrs. Webster
had planned to see him that afternoon.

"He's fine. I needed to tell you something important, but I
didn't want to do it over the phone—you never know who's
listening."

I almost laughed and then realized Mrs. Webster's fear was rooted in her memory of sharing a telephone party line with others in town. Or maybe she had watched one too many movies about wiretapping.

I was relieved Tyrone was okay. "What's happened?"

"When I visited him today, he told me Danny Liles had been arrested last night—for driving under the influence—and ended up in Tyrone's cell. Tyrone didn't tell me under the influence of what, but I suspect liquor. Anyway, Tyrone caddied for him a few times at the golf club one summer, so they got to talkin' there at the jail. It's what he told Tyrone you might find important. You know, for our investigation."

I smiled. Now it was our investigation. What a team we made. At least she was no longer viewing it as only my investigation. "I don't understand. Danny Liles isn't one of our suspects. How does he fit into all of this? Did he even know Victoria?"

"Be patient and let me finish." Mrs. Webster led the way into the kitchen. "I don't know if he knew Victoria, but he's buddies with Skip Denton. They play poker together. Tyrone said Danny was full of himself, saying how much money he had won off Skip the previous night." Mrs. Webster leaned over and whispered, "Skip has a real problem with gambling."

"What significance did Tyrone put on that?" I wondered where this was leading.

"Because Danny said it was unusual. Skip hadn't been playing much lately because he's been tight for cash. Last night Skip had been flush with cash. He told them he'd come into a lot of money recently. When Danny pushed him for more details—drink will make you do things like that—he said he'd borrowed heavily on a life insurance payout he would get soon."

Follow the money. I didn't get any satisfaction in learning my suspicions might have been right on target. The news saddened me. Could Skip have killed Victoria for her life insurance? I liked Skip and didn't want to think of him as a murderer. Maybe Victoria's death had been an accident and he'd tried to cover it up.

"It sounds like Skip Denton could be our man. What are you going to do about it?" Mrs. Webster demanded.

"Well, I can't make a citizen's arrest." Seeing her face, I regretted my blunt response. I couldn't blame Mrs. Webster for her desire to get Tyrone out of jail, but I also wasn't prepared to say how I would proceed. I had no idea.

That evening, in the large Martino kitchen with Nita and Guido, I recounted my discovery in the Denton kitchen and then my conversation with Mrs. Webster, leaving out the bit about Mrs. Webster's concern about being overheard on the phone.

Guido poured me a glass of wine. "Hate to say it, Laura, but it was pure vandalism, nothing more."

"After all," Nita pointed out. "Nobody left a message written in the flour for you to find."

"There is that." If there had been, I would return to the Denton house again only with an armed guard.

"That story from Danny Liles sounds pretty damning." Guido was serving up bowls of polenta with tomato sauce and pepperoni, one of my favorite meals. Guido, who loved being in the kitchen, did most of the cooking, which was fine with Nita. As the only daughter in a large family of men, she had been assigned more than her fair share of kitchen duties while her brothers had gotten off relatively easy. Nita didn't buy her mother's explanation that that was the way of the world. When her own children came along, Nita divided the household chores between her daughter and her son, and she was pleased by how self-sufficient they both had become.

I held up my plate and, like Oliver, requested more, please. "It may only mean Skip is the beneficiary of a life insurance policy on Victoria. It's not proof he killed her to collect on it. The policy was one they may have taken out years before their divorce. People frequently forget to change their designation of beneficiary when they get divorced or remarried. That once happened to a friend of mine. Her ex-husband died, and she received notice her name was still on his policy."

"Wow. What did she do?" Nita poured each of us another glass of red wine.

"She waived her rights to it in favor of the second wife. She said she and her ex-husband had married and divorced young, amicably at her request, and she knew he'd intended to take care of his second wife of many years. She said it was the right thing to do."

"What a remarkable woman," Guido said.

"She is." I took a sip of wine and then dipped a piece of crusty bread into the bowl of fruity olive oil. Nita swore the olive oil accounted for her healthy, young-looking skin. With my hectic schedule, I could use her beauty remedy.

After we finished eating, Guido gathered the dirty dishes and took them to the sink. "If collecting on a policy were grounds for arrest in suspicious cases, there would be a lot of spouses in jail. The policy alone isn't enough proof Skip murdered Victoria.

I looked over at Nita, who hadn't said much all evening, highly unusual for my loquacious friend. "You don't have a theory on this?"

"Sorry. My mind is on work. Mercury must be in retrograde. My computer was acting up, and you know how I am with technology. Dr. M had problems with his truck and arrived late. Then our hygienist gave notice, and I have to advertise for a new one. It almost makes me wish I could work for you. Since I don't know chartreuse from magenta, all I could do would be to lift and tote."

"Sometimes in staging, that's just as important."

Guido looked around the kitchen with its avocado-colored appliances. "If you take her on, Laura, you better be careful. Nita's tastes in decorating are stuck firmly in the 1980s."

Nita threw a damp dishtowel at him. "Hey, buddy. New

kitchens can cost over thirty grand. Still think I should redecorate?"

The wine and their good humor helped me relax. It was hard to be tense around Nita and Guido, with their upbeat attitude about life.

"By the way, Guido, thank you again for taking care of my tires the other day. That was a godsend. I don't know what I'd do without you two."

"It was the least I could do after all the help you've given us over the years. Besides, you're family." Guido brought out a large tray of tiramisu. "How about dessert?"

With everyone feeding me recently, buttoning my khakis was becoming difficult. I thought wistfully of the skinny jeans I'd recently managed to fit into again. Not for long.

Later, as I got up to leave, Nita said, "Don't forget. You're invited to dinner on Sunday at Mom and Pop's. They're looking forward to you coming. The whole family will be there."

At this rate, I could definitely forget the skinny jeans. Mrs. Romano never served anything short of a small feast.

I dug deep in my bag for my keys. "Nita, do you think you could wiggle information out of Neil about Skip's whereabouts on the night of Victoria's death? If Neil is still working with Detective Spangler, he may be able to tell us. And, if Skip's alibi isn't great, he could be our man." I paused, a thought occurring to me. "But then, he could also have hired someone to kill Victoria."

I hadn't thought about that before. Any of the people with concrete alibis could have hired someone. Back to square one.

Chapter 34

*An oversized table will make a dining room look small. Replace it
with a smaller table and fewer chairs to make the room look more
spacious. If necessary, remove buffets and china cabinets.*

On Sunday, I walked toward the Martino car in front of my house,
where Nita and Guido sat waiting to drive me to Nita's parents'
home for dinner.

"Hi, you two." I crawled into the backseat. From their grim
expressions, I knew something was wrong and my throat tightened.
"What happened?"

"I'm sorry, Laura," Nita said. "Word at Vocaro's is Will died
during the night."

"Oh, no. Poor Will." I put my head back against the seat and
thought of his daughter and grandchildren and then selfishly of
myself. Now he would never be able to identify who hit him. All
hopes of seeing Tyrone freed were fading away.

Will had been a bit of a character, but I was deeply saddened
to hear of his tragic death. His efforts to keep the roadside clean,
even if he had done it to escape the noise of several grandchildren,
showed genuine concern for the community and said a lot about
the kind of man he was. How would Battlement Drive look in the
future with him gone?

"Would you rather not go to Mom and Pop's for dinner?" Nita asked. "I'm sure they'd understand if you decided to stay home."

"No, I'll be fine. Being around the family will help." I wanted this occasion to visit with the family but also to question the Romano brothers about Ernie Phillips, who had been at the Denton house washing windows the day Victoria was murdered. They knew him well.

After we arrived at the Romano house, I stood at the back door with Nita, looking into the kitchen at a familiar scene—Mrs. Romano in front of a steaming stove, with her jovial husband towering over her, trying to taste whatever was in the huge pot she was stirring. The Romano brothers, now men with families, were cheering some sporting event in the adjoining family room, with the Romano grandchildren galloping about, being pursued by their mothers.

"Laura's here," Nita announced as we entered the house.

Shouts of greetings came from the family room. Mrs. Romano, who looked like an older version of Nita, ignored my offers of help and shooed me out of the kitchen. I was hugged and greeted by everyone, the men with an eye still on the game.

Taking me aside, Nita whispered, "You're going to be besieged with questions about the murder and our investigation."

My heart sank. Again, I wished I'd kept quiet about the investigation. Nita's outgoing nature made it almost impossible for her to keep anything to herself, and anything she knew, the family knew.

"Everything's ready," Mrs. Romano called from the dining room.

I looked fondly around the table at the boisterous Romano family—all of them kind and hardworking. They had been a godsend to me in so many ways.

After everyone joined in saying a quick blessing, Mrs. Romano passed dishes filled with Romano favorites around the long table, and the chatter grew louder. I loved this family that had made me one of their own. I especially enjoyed their Sunday gatherings. With my mother, meals had been almost perfunctory, but in the Romano household, eating was an activity to be celebrated, and the food was worth celebrating.

On one occasion, my mother had joined us. She said later she couldn't understand the appeal of spending time with a big, noisy family. I never tried to explain it to her. She wouldn't have understood.

"Laura, tell us about your investigation." Carmen, the youngest Romano brother, grinned at me, mischievous as usual. In school, he had developed a crush on me, but when a sudden growth spurt sent me towering over him, he transferred his affections to a much shorter girl. "We hear you're the Jessica Fletcher of Louiston."

"Yes, tell us the latest," Angelo echoed.

"I expect to apprehend the killer shortly."

All chatter at the table stopped.

"Aw, come on, Laura. Don't take offense. We're curious. Maybe there's something we can do to help," said Nicco, the oldest brother. "Tell us what you've been able to discover so far. Maybe we can come up with ideas."

I smiled. These big husky guys really cared about me, so I could put up with a little ribbing. I gave them a summary of what I knew or suspected, withholding some of the names of the people involved. I was conscious I could be casting suspicion on people who might turn out to be innocent.

"I'd like to get my hands on the jerk who rammed into the back of your car." After years of working in construction, Dominic's huge hands would have made short work of any felon.

"Have you discovered anything more about who it could have been?" Sal asked.

I shook my head. "No, and I don't think I ever will."

Sal reached across his brother for more bread. "Go to the

mattresses, Laura—like in *The Godfather*."

"What's with you guys and *The Godfather*?"

"Anytime you feel threatened or uncomfortable, you call any of us right away, you understand," said Guido."

I knew all of them would willingly help or protect me. "Thanks, Guido. I don't know if I can help Tyrone, but I'm trying." A sense of helplessness overwhelmed me.

"You're not alone in this." Nita said. "Is she, guys?"

"We're here for you, Laura," Nicco said. "While you're looking, follow the money."

I swirled the Chianti in my glass and studied it, my thoughts miles away. Follow the money; look for someone desperate; look for a man who could dump a hundred-pound woman down a laundry chute; and worse, go to the mattresses—guidelines and clues that hadn't helped me so far.

Dominic punched Nicco in the arm. "You've been watching too many movies."

I looked at them fondly, thinking they were still like the young boys I'd first met.

"That's good advice, guys," I said. "But, Angelo, let me ask you something you might be able to help me with."

"Old Angelo can help you, Laura. He's watched so many episodes of *NCIS* he could solve the murder himself." Nicco helped himself to the platter of roast lamb and potatoes being passed around the table.

"Yeah, sure," Angelo said, not appreciating Nicco's humor.

I never attended a Romano gathering where there wasn't good-natured teasing or competition; I had to interrupt them to ask my question.

"I wanted to ask you about Ernie Phillips. Since he was at the house the day Victoria was murdered, I should consider him a suspect as well as the others." That got their attention. "Would I be crazy trying to connect him to Victoria's death?"

"It's smart to consider everyone. Have you thought about Angelo here?" Sal laughed and pointed to his brother. "He was there the day Victoria was murdered."

"Give me a break." Angelo threw a bread crust at him.

"Stop it, you boys." Mrs. Romano glared at them. "This is serious business. Laura is seeking your help."

"You're right," Sal said. "Sorry, Laura."

"Ernie left before I did." Angelo accepted the platter circulating again. "Like lots of others, I know he's been feeling the pinch with the way the economy has been. People having a hard time paying their bills can do without clean windows."

"You can take Ernie off your list of suspects." Nicco finished his glass of wine.

"How do you know?" Sal interrupted. "He could have slipped back there—"

"Because, you dummy, I'm the one who can give him an alibi." Nicco sat back and poured himself another glass of Chianti.

The dining room became quiet and everyone stared at Nicco.

"What?" Nicco shrugged. "If I'd known you suspected Ernie, I would've said something earlier. He dropped his son off at the church hall that evening for a Scout meeting. We were down one leader, so I twisted his arm to hang around. His son is one active kid. Ernie stayed until we finished. Believe me, it was one long night. Besides, the police already know he was there."

I sat there, looking stupid. "I'm glad to hear it." Again, I was relieved the people I knew and liked couldn't be guilty of harming Victoria. Fine investigator I was. I wasn't the least bit impartial or unbiased.

Dominic held up his plate. "Now that we've solved the problem, what's for dessert?"

Chapter 35

Spruce up the front of your house with new street numbers, outdoor lights, a mailbox, and a new cover for your doorbell. Add a new doormat as the finishing touch.

Later in the evening, wrapped in a thick terrycloth robe, I sat on my bed sipping chamomile tea. Inky lay curled up at the end of the bed by my feet, helping to warm me. The temperature had dipped low, and the hot tea helped warm my hands. It tasted awful but was supposed to aid relaxation. I hoped it would work since my active mind was keeping me awake. The pull of work, when I wanted to focus on Tyrone's situation, was taking its toll on me. How successful would Agatha Christie's Miss Marple have been unraveling a mystery if she'd faced work deadlines?

Taking out my notepad, I reviewed my list of suspects. If an alibi wasn't sufficient grounds for clearing the suspects of murder, at least in my mind, I needed to go back to analyzing motives and benefit to be gained from Victoria's death. Who could have wanted Victoria dead enough to hire someone to do it?

I started to cross Carlos' name off the list, thinking it unlikely the gardener would've had sufficient funds to pay someone to kill Victoria. Then I stopped. How much money would be enough to convince a person to commit murder? Could Carlos have hired one of his cousins? Were they desperate enough to prevent Victoria from reporting them to the immigration officials that they would murder her for a few dollars? I liked Carlos. Since I'd discovered his helpers were at the campground, I wasn't so sure I could discount any of them. No wonder I was no good at this. I wanted to mark off the list the ones I liked and leave on all the others.

If I disregarded their alibis, I still suspected Warren and Cora had motives for wanting Victoria out of the picture. Warren because Victoria had been blackmailing him, and Cora because of the money she believed Victoria owed her and because of Victoria's affair with her husband, Norman. They both had money to pay someone. If Cora took revenge against all the women who had been involved with Norman, a good portion of the town's female population would now be dead. Maybe the money Victoria owed her was more important to her and she wanted revenge for that.

I wondered where in this town a professional assassin or hit man could be found. Or should that be a hit *person*? It wasn't a job one could advertise for in the *Louiston Mirror* or on Craigslist. In my world, assassins didn't exist.

Norman was still a candidate. If he had wanted to silence Victoria because of her knowledge of his questionable business practices, her death would have been convenient. Besides, his investment property, and its lack of access roads, was public knowledge since Norman had had to apply for a waiver of some sort. If he had spurned her because of their affair, Victoria was vindictive and wouldn't have hesitated to destroy his political career. I didn't know what Norman's alibi had been for the night of the murder and decided to have Nita ask Neil about him. Norman had lots of connections—some unsavory enough to commit murder. He was also in a position to grant favors to those willing to do his bidding. I was beginning to think, like Angelo, I had watched one too many episodes of *NCIS*.

Victoria had already been out of Skip's life because of the

divorce, but the financial benefits from her death couldn't be ignored. I wondered whether Detective Spangler had been alerted to Skip's insurance windfall. If Skip was stupid enough to tell his poker buddies about it, it might not take long for word about the money to spread.

Then there were Doug and his father. Doug had been charming and helpful the last time I'd seen him and gave rational reasons why his father might not have wanted revenge, but even cold-blooded killers could be charming. The thought depressed me.

I still couldn't ignore the fact it might have been a random killing. Someone could have gotten into the house during the day when the doors were unlocked and stayed hidden until later when they thought the house was empty. When confronted by Victoria, they could have panicked, hit her on the head, and then dumped her body down the laundry chute so they could get away. If so, the police might never be able to identify the real killer, and Tyrone would suffer the consequences of a random act. It had happened to all too many people before.

Regardless of what Detective Spangler believed, I was still convinced the vandalism, the threats I'd received, and Will's hit and run all pointed to the fact Victoria's murderer was still at large.

I threw down my notepad and pen. No matter how I looked at it, I was running in circles. I kept hoping something new would occur to me. Earlier on the day of the murder, the Denton house had been full of people. Ernie had been washing windows, Angelo and his crew had been there painting, and Carlos and his crew had been working outside. Previously, Nita's brother Nicco had been there working on some plumbing. Doug had come through the house while the crew was still there.

Nothing from any of it sounded an alarm in my mind. Other than Doug, I'd known the others all my life and couldn't imagine any of them coming back to rob or harm Victoria. Again, I was glad Ernie had an alibi.

An enraged neighbor? I laughed thinking of Dr. M or elderly Mrs. Jankowitz committing murder because Victoria's groundskeepers had cut the grass on the wrong side of the property line.

It occurred to me again I'd been the only other person in the house when someone murdered Victoria. Goose bumps raised on my arms and shivers slithered down my spine no amount of hot tea could calm. For this I needed chocolate and dug out the container of English Toffee I reserved for emergencies. The first bite began to soothe my jangled nerves. It might pack on more pounds than the sherry, but at least I'd have a clear head in the morning.

Feeling calmer, I forced myself to go over the events on the day of the murder, one by one. I couldn't think of anything more than what I'd already told the police, which hadn't been much. Even now, recounting the day, nothing occurred to me that had been unusual.

After Angelo had left, I remembered hearing a ground-level door opening and closing, something I thought I'd told the police. At the time, I believed it had been Victoria coming or going from the house, which she tended to do a lot while the crew and I were working. Now, on reflection, I didn't think it had been Victoria opening or closing a door, unless she had come in and someone had come with her. The bell hadn't rung announcing a visitor, so I didn't believe Victoria had let anyone in, unless she had planned to meet someone at the door before he or she could ring the bell. I looked around confused. I'd locked the doors earlier in the evening, so who could have gotten in? Could someone have slipped into the house during the day when all of the doors had been open? There were plenty of places a person could have hidden until later.

Whoever had come in wouldn't have been aware I was still in the house unless they'd seen my car out back. If someone had known I was there, could he suspect I'd seen or heard something and forgotten and was now waiting for me to remember? Could that be the reason I was being threatened—to scare me enough to stop asking questions that might trigger a memory?

I hadn't seen anyone, but the killer didn't know that.

I tried to remember the times Victoria and I had actually talked, not just the times we merely passed in the hall. I recalled Victoria's outburst at Carlos and her argument with Cora—and, of course, her tirade against Tyrone on the day of the murder. Other than that, Victoria had stayed in the library or her bedroom.

Then I remembered the day I walked into the library and found Victoria on the phone being her usual nasty self with the person on the other end. Something about the conversation bothered me, but I couldn't put my finger on what. I wished now I'd paid more attention, but anytime something important happened, people wished they had been more attentive.

Exhaustion finally got the better of me, and I decided to put all thoughts of murder aside until morning. Feeling drowsy, I reached over and turned off my bedside light then switched it back on again.

Chapter 36

Set the atmosphere for your open house by fully opening drapes and shades and turning on overhead lights and lamps in every room.

The day arrived for real estate agents to preview the Denton place before the scheduled open house. I nervously plumped already plumped pillows and straightened already straight picture frames. My attention to detail was becoming excessive and I forced myself to stop. Skip had asked me to stay for the preview, wanting a report of how it went. I suspected his concern about the sale was greater than he was letting on.

I walked through the foyer, once again admiring the effect of the mirrors. Nita might not recognize chartreuse, but she possessed a knack for solving problem areas with her ideas and sense of style. The whole project had been a team effort. I fervently hoped my other team member would soon be freed from jail.

I paused in the doorway of a small bedroom, soaking in the warm feelings it exuded. The colorful rugs I'd found in the attic and had cleaned looked perfect on the oak floors that now glowed, and the antique lamps I'd rewired myself added a nice touch. I switched the lamps on in each room to set the mood.

It was frustrating Tyrone couldn't be there to see the jewel the house had become. I was also frustrated at my inability to find something to help free him. It was causing me to lose sleep and drop weight again, which wasn't a bad thing after my huge meal at the Romano's. As much as I would hate leaving this house when my work was done, I was relieved I could now focus my time entirely on helping Tyrone.

I sat down at the kitchen table to rest and scanned the room again for anything I might have missed.

An hour before the open house, Doug Hamilton strolled in through the front door, carrying two paper coffee cups with a Vocaro's logo. "Thought you could use this." He handed me one.

Surprised, I accepted the cup gratefully. "Thanks, Doug. You're right."

"Late night?"

"So late, I should've brought a change of clothes." Which might have been a practical solution, but the thought of spending a night there caused me to shudder.

The previous day, knowing I would be there until late, I'd parked in the front drive and had carefully locked all the doors inside before I began work. I'd never considered installing an alarm system in my home, but I'd quickly come around to seeing the value of one now, especially after all that had happened. The new owners would be smart to install one or hang up a few besoms. I had hung the one Madam Zolta left with me in the kitchen. It looked good.

The sticky mess in the kitchen remained a mystery. Fortunately, there had been no other instances of vandalism.

"The house looks fantastic." Doug looked around him as though he couldn't believe it was the same place. "Who would've thought this old place could turn out so good? I may not be a real estate expert *yet*, but this place may cause a bidding war."

I enjoyed his flattering comments about my efforts and felt vindicated. I wondered whether Monica Heller would come through the house again. Thinking of the trivial motives for killing

Victoria I'd attributed to her made me laugh. Maybe I should revisit those.

"It's a terrific house." I adjusted a stack of books on an end table. "I hope whoever gets it appreciates it. Would you like a tour?"

As Doug and I walked from room to room, I turned on more lights to make the house look bright and inviting. In the living room, I imagined it during different seasons of the year—with a roaring fire and brightly lit tree at Christmas or crowds spilling out through the French doors onto the patio for a summer cocktail party. I really liked the dove gray walls with burgundy accents. Many times an idea sounded good in theory but didn't work well in practice. This time it had been right on target, especially with the white trim—thanks to Tyrone.

The cobalt blue and yellow suited the kitchen and brought out the colors in the soapstone countertops. I'd been able to retain the original décor of the kitchen while adding modern touches. Much to my relief, none of the owners since the house was first built had gutted the kitchen for a modern makeover. Nothing would have suited this grand house as well as the style of the original kitchen, with the exception of the modern appliances added.

The house was ready.

"We have a few early birds." Doug stood when we heard cars pulling up and went out to greet the first agents to arrive.

Soon the place would be teeming with people. It occurred to me my stint of working on Victoria's house was coming to an end and I'd soon have no reason to be there.

The evening before, I kept thinking of the day I walked into the library and found Victoria there. Images of her sitting at the desk swirled in my head without coalescing into anything tangible. Whatever it was lay buried deep in my memory and wouldn't budge. I'd sensed this before, but nothing would come to mind. Now, free from the stress of getting the house staged on time, I believed I might be able to focus on what was nagging at my subconscious. Going back into the library, it might come to me. If I were going to do some investigating there, it would have to be now. As more agents arrived for the preview, I would have a hard time having the room to myself.

Looking up and down the hall, I slipped into the library and closed the heavy door behind me. I mustn't be seen searching the room by the agents previewing the house. Going through someone's desk didn't fall into the category of home staging. If an agent saw me, I wouldn't get another staging job in this town.

I quickly scanned the room. Light shone through the recently cleaned windows. Since the area had been cleaned and the clutter removed, it beckoned as a place to curl up with a good book. Sniffing, I realized the setting still wasn't perfect. I wanted it to smell fresh and clean, and instead, it smelled of dusty, old books, and the dust was tickling my nose.

I stared at the massive and ornate Victorian walnut desk standing in the center of the room. Walking behind it, I sat down in a green leather armchair and gazed around me. Victoria had been sitting at this desk the day I'd rushed into the library for the fax.

As I reached for the middle drawer knob, the telephone on the desk rang, startling me. My heart pounded and my hand shook as I reached for the receiver, wondering if I should answer it. Abruptly, it stopped. Detective Spangler was right. I wasn't cut out to be Nancy Drew. With nerves like mine, I couldn't sit comfortably through a scary movie, much less play detective in real life.

Victoria had been on the phone the day I barged in. I couldn't recall exactly what Victoria had said, but I recognized her words and tone had been threatening. Something else nagged at me, and it drove me crazy not being able to figure out what.

Working quickly, I opened and closed each drawer, finding a bottle of Canadian Club in one but nothing of interest in the others.

Turning, I perused the extensive book collection on the shelves and wondered whether the books had belonged to Skip's family or if Victoria had bought them by the yard. I chided myself for being snide. Nevertheless, Victoria hadn't struck me as the type to have an extensive library or even to read a book, for that matter.

Books—that was it. Victoria had been holding papers in her hand when I opened the library door. She quickly inserted them into a book as though trying to hide what she had. The book hadn't been the yearbook with its distinctive purple cover. I was embarrassed about barging in on her and hadn't noticed what Victoria did with the book. I needed to find it and the papers to judge whether they held a clue to her death. I was grabbing at something to give me hope, but, at this point, I was willing to try anything. Which book? There were so many.

Stop and think. I replayed the scene from that day in my head. Victoria hadn't moved far from the desk before she stomped from the room, so she must have stored the book within arm's reach of the desk. Otherwise, I would have noticed.

I studied the bookcases, wondering how long it would take me to go through each of the books closest to the desk. As I turned, I glanced down at a small cabinet to the right of the desk. Stooping, I opened the top drawer and found only blank stationery scattered inside. Opening the bottom door, I found more bottles of alcohol. No wonder Victoria disappeared into the library so often.

Still not wanting to miss anything, I stretched out my arm and reached behind the bottles to see if a book could have been wedged in back of them. My search resulted in nothing more than a fist covered in cobwebs. It was all I could do not to shriek. I hated cobwebs.

I stood, rubbing my hands together trying to remove the sticky webs. As I turned to walk away, my foot lightly struck something near the cabinet bottom. I'd barely noticed it. Getting down on my hands and knees, I reached under the cabinet and was surprised when my fingers felt the shape of a book resting on the carpet. I didn't think much of the carpet cleaners I'd hired since they hadn't moved the desk or cleaned under it. I imagined Victoria, not wanting me to see where she had placed it, let the book gently slide to the carpet and then used her foot to push it under the cabinet. Clever woman.

Sitting down in the chair again, I placed the book on the desktop and opened it. Inside were four sheets of letter-sized paper folded in half. Unfolding them, I placed them on the desktop. I was puzzled at what I saw: a fax cover sheet, a photo, one page with a typed message, and one page covered with handwriting. The typed note read:

N. Nickleby. Your payment is overdue. Just a reminder of the consequences if I don't hear from you. Think about what you have to lose.

The next sheet was a photo of the stone edifice of a grand building and under that a sheet showing a portion of a handwritten document too blurred to read.

Who was N. Nickleby, and why did Victoria have this? I scanned the document and read it over a second time. The automatically generated date at the bottom of the fax was two years earlier. Still perplexed, I couldn't imagine what significance it might hold. It could be nothing, but it seemed strange. Who was demanding payment from N. Nickleby and for what? Even in my innocent world, it sounded threatening. Could it have been a blackmail note?

I froze, having a hard time taking in what I was seeing and its implications. Victoria had hidden the document to keep it a secret. Had someone murdered her to ensure it remained a secret?

Chapter 37

Look at your home as though looking through the eyes of a buyer
to see what needs to be improved. Taking photos will help you
notice things you might not see just standing there.

I refolded the papers and stuffed them into the waistband of my skirt. I was breaking every guideline for properly handling what might be evidence as prescribed in the detective's official handbook, if such a thing existed, but I didn't care. My fingerprints were already all over the papers. If I went searching for a plastic bag and gloves for proper evidence collection, I couldn't trust the report would still be there when I got back.

Maybe the papers had absolutely nothing to do with Victoria's murder, but my instincts told me otherwise. Whoever killed Victoria might come looking for them. Until I had the papers locked away someplace safe, I didn't plan to let them out of my sight. Now, with my work finished in the house, it would be empty except for occasional visits by real estate agents and potential buyers. It would be a perfect time for someone to conduct a thorough search for the papers.

I remembered the evening Mrs. Webster and I had discovered Warren searching the Denton library. Had we been gullible believing his story? That was what came from being such amateurs.

I liked Warren and hadn't wanted to believe he was capable of murdering Victoria, so I'd willingly accepted his story. I wondered again about my ability to judge people.

All of it was becoming too much for me to take in. I needed to talk this over with someone with a cool head. That left out Nita, who was excitable and could unwittingly leak the information to others. It also left out Mrs. Webster, who was too emotionally involved. Besides, she would want me to take immediate action, and I didn't know what that action would be.

Feeling lightheaded, I got up, opened the door, and walked out of the library. I barely avoided running into a group of agents heading toward the library. I attempted to look calm, even though I was sure my face looked flushed, which happened to me when I became stressed. My day, which had started on such a high note, was ending on a sour one.

"Here's our fantastic stager now." Doug Hamilton stepped out from the center of the crowd.

As he neared, he stared at me with a puzzled expression. Had he noticed my flushed face?

Doug turned to the group of agents. "Ladies and gentlemen, if you would like to step into the library, you'll find features showing what a gem this house is."

"Are you okay?" Doug leaned toward me as the group of smiling agents shuffled past us. His voice was filled with concern, and I was touched.

"The smell of fresh paint is getting to me. I'll go outside for a little fresh air. Let me know if anyone has any questions I can answer."

Stepping outside, I took advantage of one of the comfortable chairs I'd placed on the patio and sat down, putting my feet on a cushioned ottoman. The sun was warm, so I was thankful for the cool breeze and the cover of the large market-style umbrella.

I pressed my hands to my hot cheeks. Only a few short weeks

ago, I'd been bored with my life and ready for new challenges. Now I wasn't sure I could handle all the excitement.

A little later, Doug joined me under the umbrella and dropped into a chair. "I'll certainly be glad when my father is well enough to get back into the business. I'm not cut out for this. It was like herding a gaggle of geese trying to keep the group together. In the Navy, I barked orders and everyone jumped."

I sleepily rubbed my eyes, wanting to curl up and take a nap. "They usually wander around on their own." My hands shook, so I put them behind my back. I didn't want my jumpiness showing.

"Maybe that was the problem. Someday I may get the hang of this. In any event, the agents loved the way the house shows and were full of compliments. None of them had seen the house before, so they don't have a clue how much work you put into it."

"Thanks, Doug. That means a lot. I have to confess, though, I'm glad it's over."

"And to think Victoria thought the house was ready to sell the way it was." Doug shook his head.

"It's hard. Most people can't step back and view their homes objectively. They work hard getting it the way they want it, then someone like me comes in and wants to change it to appeal to other people. I'm not sure I'd want anyone walking through my place making changes."

"Nor I." Doug turned his face to the sun, soaking in its warmth. "Over the years, I've moved a number of times, and every time, it was hard. If I'd known someone like you could've helped me, it would have made selling a place and moving a lot easier."

I tried to focus on Doug and less on the papers I'd found. "So, you know how hard it is seeing the things you've worked on being stripped away." I thought of the home Derrick and I had shared. I worked hard to make our home a reflection of us both, but Derrick had shown little interest in it. As long as he had a television and a comfortable chair to watch golf tournaments, he was happy. The rest of the time, he was either at work or on the golf course and later out with other women. Thinking back over our years together, I realized we hadn't shared much.

Doug rested his head against the seat back. "This is such a peaceful place."

Only the chirping of a bird flitting from tree to tree and the distant whirling of a helicopter heading to St. John's Hospital broke the silence. I wished I could remain there all day, pushing aside thoughts of murder, motives, and mayhem. Sadly, I knew the respite would end soon.

I studied Doug for a long moment, observing the poise and inner strength he exuded. Did he come by it naturally or had it been drilled into him during his years in the Navy? Whatever it was, I wished I could tell him about my suspicions and trust him. Before, given my feelings about him based on my first impression and his good looks, that would have been impossible. Now I was tempted to confide in him. The motives for killing Victoria I'd attributed to him and his father had been a real stretch. If they weren't guilty, I hoped I'd soon find out.

The purring sound of a Lexus pulling into the drive jarred me out of my reverie.

Doug jumped up. "I'm on stage again. Can I get you anything before I start?"

"No, I'm fine. I'll be in shortly." I was glad I hadn't said anything to him about my investigation or the report I'd found and decided to wait. I wanted to mull over what I'd learned before saying anything to anybody. I was dealing with people's good names and reputations, and I needed to tread lightly—but not so lightly I continued to endanger myself.

I watched Doug walk away and shifted uncomfortably, feeling the papers at my waistband digging into my abdomen. Noticing no one in the area, and under the cover of the umbrella, which blocked anyone inside seeing me, I pulled the papers from my waistband and transferred them to my large canvas bag. A few hours more and I could leave for home. Then I would decide what to do with the papers someone might have killed for.

Chapter 38

Before showing your house, lock up valuables, collectibles, and prescription drugs—anything that can easily be slipped into a pocket or purse.

After arriving home just before dark, I quickly locked the door behind me, dropped my bags, and closed all the drapes. Feeling a bit more secure, I pulled the papers from my bag and went directly to my computer, where I set it up and made both a digital and paper copy of the pages. I was being a bit melodramatic, but I wanted a paper copy in case something happened to the original pages. I then sent the digital copy to myself as an email attachment. I wasn't taking any chances of it disappearing.

Planning to work with the copy, I decided to hide the originals somewhere in my house, but where? I walked slowly around my living room, trying to recall all the places I'd heard might be good hiding places. For years, I'd hidden my valuables in my lingerie drawer, only to hear burglars searched there first.

I disregarded the freezer since I wanted to make sure the papers didn't get damaged. Under the mattress was too obvious, and I didn't have any loose bricks in my fireplace. My eyes lit on the little red wagon from my childhood, which I now used as a plant stand. I put the papers in an envelope and taped it to the underside of the wagon. Someone might lift the plants to check under them, but they might not think to feel the underside of the wagon. At least I hoped not.

I stood there and laughed, realizing I was being ridiculous. Nita, more than anyone, knew me to be the quintessential Capricorn—cautious to a fault. Today I was taking caution to new heights. Either that or I'd read way too many mystery novels.

With a copy of the papers safely tucked away, I relaxed a little. My rumbling stomach reminded me I hadn't eaten since breakfast. I quickly made a sandwich of tuna on pumpernickel with dill pickles and poured cranberry juice into a Waterford crystal goblet. My mother had saved the goblets for special occasions, and since those had been few, the goblets had rarely been used until recently. I enjoyed the luxury of using them any time I wanted, despite knowing my mother would disapprove.

After gobbling down the sandwich and gulping my drink, I was now able to focus on the papers and not hunger. The food had been very basic, but since my sugar levels had felt as though I hadn't eaten in days, it tasted like pure ambrosia.

I pulled out the copies of the papers, laid them on my dining room table, and studied them again. Nothing new occurred to me. A note addressed to N. Nickleby, a photo of the entrance to a building, and a copy of a paper with handwriting.

Picking up the fax cover sheet, I studied it again. The cover showed the name of the person it was being sent to, *N. Nickleby*, and another block for the person's fax number.

The number seemed familiar, so maybe it was Victoria's fax number. However, looking at it more closely, I realized the number wasn't right. The last digit was a five. Victoria's fax number ended in six. Whoever sent it had written the number on the form correctly but had made a mistake when keying the number and sent it to Victoria's fax.

I recalled when I gave Nita the number for Victoria's fax, she'd commented how familiar the number was. So many people in town had similar numbers.

When my phone rang, I jolted and relaxed when Doug Hamilton's name appeared on the phone display.

"Laura, this is Doug. You didn't look as though you were feeling well when you left today. Are you okay?"

In a flash, I decided to trust him with my discovery, even if I came across as an idiot. I needed to talk to someone whose thoughts hadn't become muddled up with investigating a murder.

"Doug, I know this is an unusual request, but could you come over to my place right away, or could we meet? I have something urgent I need to discuss with someone."

"Give me a few minutes, and I'll be right there." He had said it without hesitation, which impressed me. Fifteen minutes later, he was pulling into my driveway.

To his credit, Doug didn't laugh when I told him about my ongoing investigation and discovery of the papers. But the grim look on his face showed he was taking what I said seriously, and I expected him to lecture me on how dangerous my activities had been.

"N. Nickleby," he mused. "The only Nickleby I've heard of is Nicholas Nickleby, the hero of Charles Dickens' novel."

"*Nicholas Nickleby*. When I was sitting in the library at the Denton house, I came across a copy of Victoria's high school yearbook. In it was a photo of her with Warren Hendricks, Jack Malcolm, Tony Rowe, and others when they performed in *Nicholas Nickleby* during their senior year. I don't see how it could relate to this fax, but I'll take another look at Victoria's yearbook to see if it identifies who played Nicholas Nickleby. That might tell us something."

I wondered again about Warren and his appearance at the Denton house the night Mrs. Webster and I had found him there. Was that the link? Had he been trying to find those papers?

What if he had used the name N. Nickleby and the faxed papers had mistakenly gone to Victoria? Maybe she connected the name with Warren and had been blackmailing him about the thefts from the funeral home? Or could she have been blackmailing him because of something else?

"It may have nothing to do with it, or everything to do with it." Doug tapped the paper with his finger. "There must be a reason Victoria had this. Could she have been the one being blackmailed?"

"No. They were faxed to her number, but the number on the fax cover sheet is one digit off. It must have been sent to her by mistake. I checked the phone book and online, and there is no one in town with the name N. Nickleby. At least none I could find."

"But why N. Nickleby?" Doug asked.

"That's the puzzle."

I sat there silently and thought. As an actor and director, Warren would think himself awfully clever coming up with the name of a character from a play he had performed in. Could I tell Doug this? The words wouldn't form on my lips. Despite it all, I didn't want to believe my old friend Warren was a murderer.

I recalled again the day I'd barged into the library while Victoria was on the phone holding the papers in her hand. *Think, think.* What had she said that day? I tried to remember the sequence of events to prod my memory.

"When I went into the library, Victoria was on the phone. She said something about going public. Could that be it? Could she have been threatening someone she would go public with information if the person didn't pay up?"

As the memory became clearer in my mind, I looked toward Doug and decided I had to tell him. "It might have been Warren. He could have been the one following me the night after rehearsals. I'd asked him questions about Victoria, and he could have been worried his information might get out. He may have been trying to frighten me away from asking questions." Tears welled up in my eyes. Had I betrayed Warren, or had it been the other way around?

"That is a pretty strong accusation if you aren't sure," Doug said. "What about the night of the murder? Did he give the police an explanation of where he had been?"

"That's the problem. He had an alibi, a good one. He was conducting rehearsals and had witnesses. That wouldn't have prevented him from hiring someone to kill Victoria." I sounded doleful. I liked Warren and didn't want him being guilty of killing anyone, even if the person had been blackmailing him.

"That's possible, but not likely." Doug didn't sound convinced. "Most murders result from sudden anger or passion. He may have come to confront Victoria and, in a fit of anger, hit her, but he wouldn't have hired someone. He would only have left himself open to a different blackmailer."

Doug's words reassured me, but a tiny voice inside me warned it still might not be wise to trust anyone.

"Maybe the rehearsal didn't go on as late as he'd told the police. Or they started later than he indicated."

"Franklin Auditorium isn't far from the Denton house. If they took a long break, he might have been able to get over to the house and back again before anyone noticed."

"Poor Warren." I wiped away the tear rolling down my cheek with my sleeve. "And even more so, poor Victoria. If she stumbled on a blackmail scheme or had been blackmailing someone herself, it caused her death. They both lost out in this tragedy."

"We should talk to Detective Spangler about this." Doug frowned as though he didn't like his own suggestion.

"Linking the murder to a note that could simply be a demand for repayment of a personal loan to an N. Nickleby? He'd laugh me out of the station and then lecture me about wasting police time. I've already gone to him about the threats and the damage to my car, even about the vandalism at the house." I then told Doug about the note and calls I'd received and my flattened tires. He knew about the kitchen but was surprised by the other incidents.

"I wish you had said something earlier, especially following the kitchen mess. It has to be connected."

"I wasn't sure whom I could trust." I sighed, my voice half its usual volume.

"Well, you can trust me. We shouldn't delay on this. Given those threats and the episode with the car, you're still in danger."

"I'll be careful and try my best to avoid contact with Warren." I rubbed my forehead and yawned. Fatigue was overcoming me, and I could no longer think clearly.

"Why don't you sleep on it, and we'll talk about it again tomorrow. How about if I meet you at Vocaro's in the morning? And if you decide to go to the police station, I'll go with you. That is, if you want me to."

Again, I was touched by Doug's concern for me. It had been a long time since any man had shown me concern, other than the men in the Romano family, and they were like my brothers. But, lately, given my poor judgment of people, I needed to remain cautious.

"Okay. How about around eight? I'm meeting Nita there before she heads to the dental clinic."

Doug reached out and took my hands, squeezing them gently. "Try not to worry. We'll take care of this tomorrow. Get some sleep."

When Doug left, I carefully bolted the door and went to bed—again with my light on.

Chapter 39

Set your thermostat at a comfortable temperature for the open house. A place too warm or too cold could chase away buyers.

"What's been happening?" Nita asked the next morning. "You've been awfully close-mouthed about the investigation recently."

Nita and I were wedged into a corner table at Vocaro's, lucky to have found seats. The early morning crowd was heavier than usual, with the regular customers being pushed out by families in town for activities at nearby Fischer College.

"I know, Nita. I'm really sorry. Everything has gotten so complicated. I've come to realize people's reputations are at stake and it wouldn't be fair of me to cast suspicion on them without actual proof. Some things have come to light—so ridiculous as to be unbelievable, or else I'm close to *cracking* the case." Even to my own ears the words sounded corny.

"How can you not tell me?" Nita looked offended. "You know I'll die of curiosity wondering what's going on. Besides, I'm your partner in this whole thing."

I began to tell her but froze when Warren Hendricks walked through the doorway, followed a few seconds later by Dr. M. I could barely see them in the crowd of people milling around the counter waiting to order or find tables. I'd never seen Vocaro's so crowded.

The room was also becoming increasingly warmer.

I needed to avoid Warren. I had little or no acting talent and found keeping a passive face almost impossible. He'd be able to read me like a play script.

I turned my chair slightly away from where Warren stood in line and hoped he wouldn't see me. Fortunately, Nita and I sat at a small table for two with no empty chairs around us, so he couldn't join us, even if we were forced to invite him. I fervently hoped he wouldn't stop by to say hello. I wouldn't have been able to act naturally.

Dr. M, coffee in hand, elbowed his way through the crowd toward the door. Warren, a short distance behind him, yelled, "Nick, wait up."

Nick? As in Nicholas? I became lightheaded.

"Nita," I said unsteadily, "Warren just called Dr. M 'Nick.' What was that all about?"

"He's called him Nick for years. It came from the time they were in high school together. Dr. M played Nicholas Nickleby in a play, and the name stuck. A few people call him Nick."

I swayed slightly in my seat.

"What's wrong?" Nita reached over and grabbed my arm.

I ignored Nita's concern. I needed to process all this. The name on the note, the high school play photo in the yearbook, Dr. M's nickname. I now recalled the night at rehearsals when Warren had given stage direction to someone named Nick. Since I hadn't recognized a few of the actors on stage, I'd assumed Warren had been speaking to one of them. Now I understood why the name Nick hadn't appeared in the program. There was no one else on the program with the name Nick—except Dr. M.

Dr. M had to have been the one the demand note was intended for, except it had gone to the wrong fax number. Victoria's fax and not his. Earlier, Nita had mentioned how familiar Victoria's fax number was. Whoever sent it had used an old nickname, either out of habit or to keep the dealings anonymous. When Victoria received the fax by mistake, she linked the name and the fax number on the coversheet and connected them to Jack Malcolm, her old friend and costar from high school.

Could Victoria, desperate for money to save her home, have made the connection between the note and Dr. M and been blackmailing him?

Suddenly, it all made perfect sense. Warren hadn't murdered Victoria—Dr. Jack Malcolm, aka Nicholas Nickleby, had.

I jumped up, my heart thumping wildly. "Nita, I'm supposed to meet Doug Hamilton here this morning. When he arrives, would you please tell him I had to leave? I need to go up to the Denton house right away."

Before I told Detective Spangler what I'd discovered, I needed proof that my theories weren't crazy. And I had a strong hunch that proof was near the Denton house.

"You, meeting Doug?" Nita couldn't have looked more surprised than if I'd just confessed to an affair with Norman Ridley. "When did all this happen? There's a lot you're not telling me, Laura."

"Sorry, I'll explain later. Also, please tell Doug it wasn't Warren."

"Wait, Laura," Nita called after me. "Be careful. Your horoscope today says you should be cautious in your dealings with medical professionals."

"You don't know how close to the mark that hits." With that, I dashed for the door.

Chapter 40

Stage your garage. Remove excess items to make it look more spacious and replace old garbage cans and recycling receptacles.

I drove quickly to the Denton house, parked in the driveway, and paced alongside the house, contemplating my next steps. I had nothing to connect Dr. M to Victoria's murder, other than a nickname—and trying to bring a case against him using it would be laughable.

I strongly suspected Dr. M was also responsible for Will Parker's death. To prove any of it, I would have to draw a connection between the note, Victoria's murder, and the hit-and-run accident that had killed the older man.

Will Parker's daughter Claire had said he had been muttering something about shrubbery the night before he was struck down. Dr. M's house was on the other side of the hedge from the Denton house. Skip once said that Dr. M would squeeze through the hedge to visit him and Victoria for an occasional happy hour. Could Will Parker have seen Dr. M using the shortcut the evening Victoria was murdered? If he had, it was only after I asked him if he'd seen anything unusual that he began to wonder about Dr. M's stroll.

Nita said Dr. M had been driving his truck to work. At the time, I'd assumed his Mercedes was being serviced. If it was, as I suspected, the Mercedes had sustained damage when Dr. M struck Will. If so, he couldn't have it repaired because the police were still searching for the vehicle involved in the incident. The car had to be hidden in his garage, and I needed to see it to confirm my suspicions. Maybe then Detective Spangler would take me seriously.

I stopped in my tracks. On the day I'd picked up Nita at the dental clinic, I told her, in front of Dr. M and Doug, that Will Parker wanted to talk to me about the day Victoria had been murdered. Doug had been the last patient of the day, so Dr. M could have left and gotten to Battlement Drive long before I arrived there. He couldn't take the chance Will might tell me something that could cast suspicion on him.

If I hadn't told Nita about him in front of Dr. M, Will might still be alive. I was horrified I might inadvertently have been responsible for his death. If that were true, it was something I'd always have to live with. I tried to console myself that if I could prove my theories, Tyrone might not end up spending the rest of his life in prison. Right now, though, it didn't make me feel better.

I needed to see the front of Dr. M's car.

Through the hedge dividing the Denton and Malcolm properties, I could see the Malcolm garage. Like many of the homes in Louiston, the garage was a freestanding building set well away from the house. It had old-fashioned bi-fold doors and small windows at the door tops. Even jumpy with stress, I noticed the place lacked curb appeal.

I looked around to see if anyone could observe me. I walked along the hedge until I was parallel with the garage then squeezed between a break in the branches. Once on the other side, I crouched down, hoping no one could see me. I would have been less conspicuous if I simply walked erect directly to the garage.

When I finally inched my way to the garage, I tried the bi-fold doors, only to discover they were locked.

"Drat." After rattling the doors unsuccessfully, I swung my hip at them, trying to force them open. All I got for my efforts was shooting pain radiating from my hip to my knee. This time, I used much stronger language.

Slowly, I walked around the perimeter of the garage, thankful the landscaping around Dr. M's property hadn't been well maintained. The overgrowth provided me with more cover. As I turned the corner, I glimpsed a window at the back of the garage. Even at my height, I wasn't tall enough to peer into it.

I surveyed the area for something to climb onto and spotted an old metal garbage can with a flat rusty lid. The smell from it overwhelmed me, and I almost gagged as I picked it up. Knowing Dr. M, I surmised it hadn't been emptied it in some time. Holding my breath, I positioned it below the window. I was thankful my years of high school and college gymnastics, and later yoga, had made me fairly agile and able to climb up onto the can. I didn't trust it would hold me for long.

A thick layer of grime coated the window glass, making it difficult to see inside. Grabbing the frame, I shook it and discovered it was so rickety I had no problem dislodging the ancient peg keeping it closed. Finally, something was going my way.

I stuck my head inside the opening. Cobwebs hanging over the window opening stuck to my face, sending shivers down my spine. Fortunately, they didn't prevent me from seeing the front of Dr. M's black Mercedes. Staring at me was a broken headlight. I could also see stains on the bumper—Will's blood? Dr. M had always had a reputation for being sloppy, and, in this instance, I was thankful he'd been too lazy to wash the car before hiding it in the garage. He believed he was above suspicion and the car wouldn't be discovered. Or he could claim he hit a deer. Blood tests would reveal the truth.

I was so focused on the car, I wasn't immediately aware of the sound of a vehicle turning into Dr. M's driveway, heading toward the garage. Once I heard the vehicle, I peered through the small windows at the top of the garage doors and was shocked to see Dr. M's small pickup truck approaching.

Jumping back, I banged my head on the window and nearly saw stars. My hand flew to the back of my head, and when I pulled it away, found my fingers smeared with blood. I stared at it for several seconds, trying to comprehend what had happened.

At the sound of the truck door slamming, I jolted out of my trance, wondering whether I should jump down or stay in place.

When the garage door remained closed, I realized Dr. M planned to leave the truck in the driveway and not pull into the garage to park next to the Mercedes. My relief was short-lived when the garbage can I stood on abruptly gave way, sending me tumbling to the ground. I landed with a thump, tearing the knees of my Dockers, and sending me skidding on my hands and knees into the decaying contents of the can. My hands came to rest in a pile of crushed eggshells, coffee grounds, a very rotten potato, and a number of things too gross to identify. *Ick*. I was barely able to stifle a scream.

I scrambled to my feet and bolted around to the other side of the garage, away from the driveway. My heart pounded madly. If Dr. M found me, I wouldn't be able to explain why I was crouching behind his garage, covered in rotting garbage and smelling like the county dump.

I heard his footsteps on the gravel and knew he was coming to investigate the cause of the noise. Fear and the revolting smell of garbage caused me to hold my breath. I didn't dare bolt for the hedge, certain Dr. M would see me. If he came around to the other side of the garage, I would be trapped.

The sound of the footsteps got closer then abruptly stopped.

"Darn animals," he muttered. "What a mess."

My relief at hearing him walk away nearly buckled my knees. I wasn't out of danger or garbage, yet. I still needed to walk across the lawn to get away. Since he had been the one threatening me, he already knew I suspected someone. Finding me at the garage, he would realize he was my number one suspect. Dr. M had already killed twice. I didn't want to become victim number three.

I stood behind the garage until I heard the door to Dr. M's house close. I didn't think he was going for a broom and pan to clean up the garbage, but, just in case, I ran for all I was worth.

Chapter 41

A few well-placed accessories can complete a room and add just the right touch.

I needed help right away—someone to witness the condition of the Mercedes. I realized too late I could have taken photos of the car with my cell phone. Hindsight was wonderful but didn't help now. Besides, I had left my phone in my carry bag locked in my car.

Racing toward my Corolla, I realized by the time I found a witness or went back to take photos, Dr. M could drive his car away and, with it, the evidence I desperately needed to help free Tyrone. I needed to call someone, if not Detective Spangler, then Doug or anyone else I could get in touch with. I unlocked my car and grabbed my bag and cell phone, praying that I could get reception. Despair swept over me when I saw that my aging phone was dead.

I could go down the road to get Claire Halston, but with all her children at the house, I couldn't drag her into this. Besides, I didn't want Claire to see the car that had killed her father. I needed someone in town to come out to the house fast.

Deciding to use the phone inside the Denton house, I grabbed my overfilled bag and fumbled in the bottom for the house key, upbraiding myself for carrying too much stuff. My fingers found the sought-after key, and I unlocked the front door with trembling hands. Once inside, I carefully locked the door behind me, wishing it had a slide bolt.

After all the activity during the days of staging, the house was eerily quiet, and my footsteps echoed as I walked toward the kitchen wall phone. I looked around, wondering if I would ever have another house staging as challenging, or as dangerous, as this one.

My hand shook as I picked up the phone receiver and contemplated calling Detective Spangler. He might not be willing to come out on what he would view as another of my fanciful theories, and I didn't have enough time to convince him otherwise. I needed something concrete to show him.

I couldn't drag Nita into this. She had worked for Dr. M for many years and wouldn't believe it of him.

Mrs. Webster was definitely out. She was feisty, but I knew she couldn't run fast enough if the situation warranted a rapid getaway. Then I realized I couldn't call Doug either. I couldn't remember his number.

In desperation, I knew I would have to call Nita after all. She would be a witness when we took photos of Dr. M's car, if he didn't move it in the meantime. As I started to dial the number on the old rotary phone, I heard a voice.

"Put the phone down, Laura."

My hand froze in midair, grasping the receiver. I turned. Dr. M was standing in the kitchen doorway.

"Dr. Malcolm, what are you doing here?" My voice sounded like an imitation of Minnie Mouse, but I managed to act as though his appearance was a pleasant surprise and I should offer him a cup of tea.

"Shouldn't you be asking instead how I got in here?" Dr. M dangled a set of keys from his fingertips. "It was foolish of Victoria to forget she gave my ex-wife these keys in case she ever got locked out. I used them to get into the house that night."

"What night? I don't know what you're talking about." My voice had risen another octave. So much for Madam Zolta's broom to ward off unwanted outside energies. Dr. M was definitely an unwanted energy.

"You really are no actress, Laura. I thought you discovered that years ago when you tried out for the Players."

"Maybe you're right, but you should know I called the police before you came in." I hoped my acting skills had improved over the years. "If you hurry and leave, you'll have a good chance of getting away before they arrive."

"Nice try. However, I was right behind you, and I know you haven't had time to call anyone. You thought I didn't see you near my garage, but I did. After a quick trip into my house to grab something, I tailed you here." He held something in his right hand, but I couldn't see what.

Was he smirking at me? I tried to stay poised and appear calm, but I worried he could hear my heart beating, giving away how frightened I was. "If that's the case, why didn't you stop me while I was there?"

"I wanted to make sure you were away from my place. If anyone saw you, they would have seen you walking away. I can't have you linked to my place, now can I?"

"I saw your car and know you hit Will Parker. The police will see your car and know what you did." I realized I was babbling.

"It was unfortunate Will saw me when I went through the hedge. I didn't think he'd noticed me. However, that was a good tip-off you gave me."

I flinched as though he'd struck me. Again, the pang of guilt for contributing to Will's death came over me.

"What if he saw you going over to Victoria's house? It wouldn't prove you killed her. You could say anything—that you were cutting through, taking a walk."

"I couldn't take that chance."

"Which means you murdered Victoria as well."

"I think you already know that. The witch was blackmailing me, and the payments were bleeding me to death. My practice wasn't as prosperous as it should have been. As a dentist, you'd think I'd have a better income. I couldn't afford to keep paying her to keep quiet, and she threatened to expose me."

Sister Madeleine's words echoed in my memory. "Find the person who became desperate." Had the police interviewed Dr. M? If so, they must have been satisfied with his alibi. A pillar of the community and old friend of the Denton's without a motive to murder Victoria. Had they been fooled!

"You mean the blackmail demands faxed to you?"

His face slackened. "So, you found out about that, too? The news would ruin my practice. How did you discover that? Did Victoria tell you?"

"I found the papers hidden in the library following Victoria's death." My mind was racing, wondering how much to tell him.

"You are a clever girl connecting them to me. What gave me away? Did she write my name on them?"

"I didn't make the connection at first. It was the name the fax was addressed to—N. Nickleby. I'd recently seen a picture in her high school yearbook of you, Victoria, and Warren in the play. Actually, Warren calling you Nick helped me make the connection—that and your fax number."

"Unfortunately, Victoria received the fax and made the same connection." He placed his finger on his lips, as though casually pondering whether to paint a room blue or green. "She went even further and figured out what the photos on the fax meant."

"The photo of a building and some handwriting?"

"Actually it was a photo of my old dental school. A classmate used to sit in for me for some exams. We looked a lot alike, and, with full beards, people had a hard time telling us apart." He began pacing back and forth as though trying to decide how much to tell me.

"He helped me get through dental school, for which I paid him *very* well. He even took the licensing exam for me. Unfortunately, he got greedy and wanted me to continue paying him. He was resourceful enough to get copies of some of the exams with my name on it but with his handwriting. With the slight matter of a malpractice suit hanging over me, you could imagine what the news would have done to my practice."

"But won't he continue blackmailing you? What was to be gained from getting rid of Victoria?"

"The fool became too impatient for my payments and kept sending me more and more threatening notes. On one occasion, he keyed in the wrong number, and one of the notes went to Victoria. We occasionally got each other's fax documents. He sent them by fax because they couldn't be traced back to him. Now he's no longer a problem. Last year he had a tragic accident. The stairs in his building were awfully steep." For someone who had just confessed to two murders, he looked almost gleeful as he boasted about his role in this drama—always playing to the audience, even if only an audience of one. Was that why he was revealing so much?

Thinking of Will Parker, I realized Dr. M had committed three murders. Was I to become number four?

"But getting rid of him didn't rid me of the threat. With the fax going to Victoria by mistake, she picked up where he left off."

"But what could she tell from a building photo and some handwriting?"

"It amazed me she was able to put it all together. The unfortunate use of my nickname." Dr. M grimaced. "I traded one blackmailer for another." He continued to pace. "It really was all my father's fault. If he had allowed me to become an actor like I wanted, instead of forcing me to go to dental school, this wouldn't have happened. I really wasn't cut out to be a dentist."

I studied him, trying to determine how he could commit three murders and blame it on his father. "With Victoria and your classmate both gone, you don't have anything to worry about. I'm certainly not going to blackmail you." I said it with as much sincerity as I could muster. "You can trust me." To coin an old cliché, butter wouldn't have melted in my mouth. I wondered if I could get him to fall for it as I inched toward the door.

"I wish it were that simple." He looked at me sadly as though I were a trying child in need of discipline and he wasn't sure how to do it. "Now, what am I going to do about you? I tried warning you so it wouldn't come to this."

"That's why you sent me those notes and tried to run me off the road."

"I admit I called you and left the note, but it wasn't me in the car." He grinned, delighted to be revealing a secret. "That was Cora."

"What?" Now I was thoroughly confused. "But—"

"Never mind that." He walked toward me, extending a hand holding a hypodermic needle. "Soon, it won't matter."

I stared at the needle. That was what he'd gone into his house for. I frantically looked about me for a way to escape. Mild-mannered, funny Dr. M planned to permanently end my need for future dental work.

"I've always liked you, Laura, even if you did stop coming to me as your dentist. So, I've decided to make this easy for you. A little prick then you'll feel nothing."

Slowly, I backed away and my head started to spin. The sight of needles always made me feel woozy. I shook my head to clear it and looked around for anything I could use to defend myself. I spied my tote bag on the floor near the doorway, but Dr. M was blocking my path to it. If I could get to the bag, maybe I could hit him with it. It was heavy enough to stun him so I could run away. Then I remembered the can of hair spray Nita had given me. If I could spray him in the eyes, he wouldn't be able to chase after me. I needed to maneuver myself closer to the bag.

"You still have time to get away," I said with as much bravado I could muster. I inched my way toward my bag, hoping he wouldn't notice. "I won't call anyone. If you go now, you can get a good head start."

"Sorry, but I can't do that. I'll simply put you in my Mercedes and get rid of you and the incriminating car."

As if reading my mind, he pushed the bag behind him with his foot. A lot of good hair spray was going to do me if I couldn't get to it.

"Now, Laura, this isn't going to hurt." Next he'd tell me it was going to hurt him more than it was going to hurt me.

As he came toward me, I looked around desperately for something to use as a weapon, regretting I'd removed so many items from the kitchen and left little on the countertops. Then I spotted, close at hand, one of Victoria's kitchen accessories I'd used in the staging—a large decorative jar of olive oil.

It was heavy, so I'd have difficulty swinging it at him, plus he might catch it. Instead, I grabbed the jar with both hands, and with all my might, threw it down onto the terracotta floor. It smashed into pieces, splattering oil all over the immaculate tiles.

At first, Dr. M looked amused, but when he came after me and started to slip on the oil, his amusement turned to irritation.

The oil spread into every crack and crevice, making the tile floor every bit as slick as an ice rink. It was as though millions of beads of ice were now beneath Dr. M's feet, and he resembled a beginning skater, arms flailing in the air. He slipped, falling onto one knee before regaining his balance. If my situation had been less dangerous, I might have laughed.

Instead, the scene before me made me feel sick on every level. Now wedged in the corner of the kitchen near the breakfast area, my heart pounded as though a thunderstorm had startled me awake in the middle of the night.

Dr. M was still coming at me, slipping occasionally, his hand reaching out to me. Blood streamed from his left pant leg, where his knee had come into contact with a shard from the broken jar.

He was only inches from me now, his breathing raspy. I stumbled backward, hitting the wall. Something jabbed me painfully in the back. The besom I'd hung there. Grabbing it, I swung it at Dr. M as fiercely as though I were the last batter at the World Series, hitting him squarely on the side of his head. He wavered and then plummeted to the floor, hitting his head soundly on the stone tile. I stood over him in my best batter pose, ready to swing again, but it was clear he was out for the game.

Thank you, Madam Zolta.

Leaning over with my hands resting on my knees to support myself, my breathing became labored, and I could barely stand. With each deep breath, I became all too aware of the smell of garbage still clinging to my clothes.

I also became aware of Nita and Doug standing in the doorway, a look of astonishment plastered on their faces. Detective Spangler stood right behind them.

"Where were you five minutes ago?" I choked out before slipping onto the oily floor.

Chapter 42

A professional home stager can help prepare your home so it sells faster and for more money.

"Have another piece of strawberry pie, Laura." Mrs. Webster stood over me with a pie dish in one hand and a server in the other, poised to scoop out another slice. I inwardly groaned and let my belt out another notch, knowing Mrs. Webster wouldn't take no for an answer. She was delighted to have Tyrone home again and was lavishing food on everyone.

It was a happy band of people gathered in Mrs. Webster's dining room to celebrate Tyrone's release from jail. Nita and Guido sat next to Mrs. Webster, with Doug, Warren, and me at the other end of the table, flanking Tyrone. Kayla, who had continued to believe in Tyrone when lesser young women would have been scared away, sat next to him, under Mrs. Webster's close scrutiny. Madam Zolta sat on her chair as though it were a throne. I especially requested that she be included.

I studied Tyrone, who wore a wide grin and had been animated throughout dinner, anxious to hear everyone's stories about the investigation. I wondered how deeply he had been scarred by his arrest and imprisonment. Time would tell. In the meantime, his other friends and I would be there to help him recover.

"What I can't understand is how Doug and Nita knew to go to

the Denton house in the first place," Tyrone said as he took another piece of pie from his grandmother.

Mrs. Webster beamed at him in approval.

"When Laura jumped up and left me at Vocaro's with a message for Doug, I knew something was up." Nita relished being the center of attention. "I also realized she must have cracked the case when she said it wasn't Warren. To know it wasn't him, she must have discovered who it was."

Warren flinched, but his good nature and manners prevailed. "Hey, Laura, how could you have suspected me? I'll bet it was in revenge for not giving you a part in a production."

"Let Nita finish," Tyrone interrupted. "I want to hear all the details."

Nita flashed Warren an impatient look. "When Doug came in, I gave him the message and told him Laura had rushed off to the Denton house. He asked me what made her leave, since they had planned to meet that morning. When I said she had acted strangely when Warren called Dr. M 'Nick,' Doug nearly jumped out of his chair as well."

"It fell into place almost right away," Doug picked up the tale. "The night before, Laura showed me the faxed papers she'd found. Like Laura, hearing the name Nick in connection with Jack Malcolm helped me put two and two together. I wasn't taking any chances and called Spangler to meet us at the Denton house."

"Doug insisted he was going up there, and I wouldn't let him go without me," Nita said. "Fortunately, Doug had a key, so we let ourselves in."

"I wish you could have gotten there sooner," I said. "Then I wouldn't have had to bash Dr. M in the head."

"How's he doing, anyway?" Mrs. Webster didn't show any real concern for his condition.

"He'll survive." Nita shook her head as though trying to dispel the image of Dr. M in jail. "The gash on his knee was far worse than the bump on his head. He's officially been charged with Victoria's death."

"What I can't understand is why he pushed Victoria down the laundry chute," Tyrone said.

"Detective Spangler explained why." All eyes were on me. "Dr. M confessed he was so upset with her bleeding him financially, he struck her in anger, and when he realized what he had done, he dropped her down the chute—as though disposing of his problems. It was a whim."

"What confuses me was why Dr. M accused Cora of ramming into you." Doug looked at me.

"He said he saw Cora follow me out of the lot. Driving behind us, he saw what she was doing, which was when he got the idea of trying to scare me off."

"Why would he blame Cora?" Mrs. Webster circled the table with a pot of coffee in her hand. "He's already in so much trouble, it won't help him."

"Because it *was* Cora. Detective Spangler said Cora admitted to it. She was convinced I was at the auditorium questioning Warren about her because I'd witnessed her argument with Victoria. She was worried I suspected her of the crime. She knew she wasn't guilty, but she wasn't so sure about her husband, Norman. She thought Norman might have wanted to silence Victoria. When she followed me, she decided to frighten me so I would stop questioning people."

"You risked a lot to help me, Laura." Tyrone beamed at me.

"I'm relieved it's over and you're finally free." I put down my cup in time to feel Mrs. Webster's warm embrace.

"I knew you could do it, girl. The Lord guided me to you, and you didn't let us down."

I choked back my emotions. I hadn't thought I could do it, but now it was over, I was more amazed than anyone that I had, in fact, found the killer. Maybe, as Mrs. Webster had promised, the Lord had given me all the help I needed.

"Gran is right." Tyrone shook his head. "For a while, I believed I was a goner. If it hadn't been for you, I'd be designing sets for the Penitentiary Players. I can't thank you enough, Laura."

"Speaking of thanks, I'd like to thank Madam Zolta not only for sweeping the Denton house of negativity but also for helping to save my life. If it hadn't been for her, I wouldn't have had the besom I used to defend myself."

Madam Zolta sat, grinning from ear to ear. "Thank you, my dear. That's kind of you to say. I'm sorry I didn't realize it was Dr. Malcolm's energies next door I was sensing."

Mrs. Webster rolled her eyes. So that's where Tyrone got it. I smiled at her and whispered, "Remember, 'the Lord sends us helpers to overcome our difficulties.'"

Mrs. Webster nodded in agreement and smiled.

"I've made one decision as a result of all this." All eyes stared at me with curiosity. "I'm not waiting until I can afford it. I'm getting a new cell phone now."

My friends laughed.

"It's about time," Guido said.

"With this check from Skip Denton for the final payment on the staging, you can well afford it." Doug handed me a check. I was astounded at the amount, which was far more than Skip and I had agreed to.

Doug held up his glass. "I'd like to raise a glass and toast Laura Bishop, who helped sell the Denton house. We received an excellent offer on the house, far more than we ever expected. Thanks to Laura, the staging more than paid for itself. Thank you."

The group broke out in cheers and clicked glasses.

"You mean it sold already?" I was astonished and quite pleased. The wicked side of me couldn't wait to hear how Monica would react to the news that my staging had been so successful.

Doug continued. "A couple from Pittsburgh fell in love with it and are buying it, furniture and all. They intend to turn it into a bed and breakfast."

"That's terrific. It would make the perfect B&B." I waved the check and whispered to Tyrone. "We have money."

"That's your money, Laura. I wasn't there to do the job." He spoke so softly only I could hear him. Again, I wondered about those scars.

"Nonsense. You worked hard on the house, and I completed the work based on your designs, so we both benefit. I'm sorry we weren't able to solve the crime before the Quincy Scholarship committee made its decision."

"There's always next year." Tyrone was ever the optimist.

The doorbell rang, and Mrs. Webster disappeared to answer it. I heard voices coming from the front door but was too busy talking to pay much attention to them.

Mrs. Webster stood in the doorway. "Laura, there's someone here to see you."

Curious, I looked up and my jaw dropped. Detective Spangler stood there, supporting a tired-looking, but very much alive, Will Parker.

"What? But they said you were dead."

"You can't hold a good man down." Will sank gratefully into the chair Tyrone brought for him. "Detective Spangler here came up with the idea to say I was dead."

Everyone turned to Spangler. "Laura insisted Will was in danger. When someone attempted to kill him, again, we decided the best way to protect him was to let everyone think he was dead. We got his daughter's permission and then spread the word at Vocaro's, hoping it would get to the right ears. We didn't want to make it too official by putting it in the papers. If it backfired on us, we could say it was a rumor."

"That dang car hit me from behind." Will looked ready to tear someone's head off. "When I finally come to, I wouldn't have been able to identify the driver anyway."

All this time I thought I'd helped cause his death. Seeing Will alive, the guilt lifted from my shoulders. It truly was a happy day.

Everyone started talking at once.

Warren waved his hand to get everyone's attention. "Since I'm no longer a murder suspect, can I say a few words?"

"Of course." I wagged my finger at Warren, still remembering the stunt he pulled in the library.

"We're very pleased to have Will back among the living. On another note, Tyrone, you'll be happy to know the head of the Theater Arts Department at the college was greatly impressed with the sets you created for our production of *Arsenic and Old Lace*. So much so, he wants you to design the sets for their next production."

Tyrone let out a surprised breath before bursting into a broad grin. Mrs. Webster, standing behind him, squeezed his shoulders.

"There's more." Warren said. "And this is the best part. The brother of the department head is a producer. When he comes into town to see the college productions, he brings along a lot of folks from Broadway."

"It seems this cloud has a silver lining." Doug raised his glass in a toast.

"Wow, it certainly does." Tyrone looked as though he was still trying to get used to the idea he was now a free man, and one with a bright future.

"The only unhappy person here today is Nita," said Guido. "With Malcolm now in the clink, she no longer has a job."

"Oh yes, she does," I said. "Staging for You is going to be quite busy now that we have a reputation, and I'm going to need a lot of help. Nita, are you game?"

"Absolutely. But are all the houses we stage going to involve this much drama?"

"That remains to be seen." I rubbed my hands together. "That remains to be seen."